Mission
Impawsible

Center Point
Large Print

Also by Krista Davis and available from Center Point Large Print:

Murder Most Howl

**This Large Print Book carries the
Seal of Approval of N.A.V.H.**

Mission Impawsible

KRISTA DAVIS

CENTER POINT LARGE PRINT
THORNDIKE, MAINE

This Center Point Large Print edition is published in the year 2018 by arrangement with Berkley, an imprint of Penguin Publishing Group, a division of Penguin Random House LLC.

PUBLISHER'S NOTE
The recipes contained in this book have been created for the ingredients and techniques indicated. The Publisher is not responsible for your specific health or allergy needs that may require supervision. Nor is the Publisher responsible for any adverse reactions you may have to the recipes contained in the book, whether you follow them as written or modify them to suit your personal dietary needs or tastes.

The text of this Large Print edition is unabridged. In other aspects, this book may vary from the original edition.
Printed in the United States of America
on permanent paper.
Set in 16-point Times New Roman type.

ISBN: 978-1-68324-961-0

Library of Congress Cataloging-in-Publication Data

Names: Davis, Krista, author.
Title: Mission impawsible / Krista Davis.
Description: Center Point Large Print edition. | Thorndike, Maine : Center Point Large Print, 2018.
Identifiers: LCCN 2018030908 | ISBN 9781683249610 (hardcover : alk. paper)
Subjects: LCSH: Murder—Investigation—Fiction. | Hotelkeepers—Fiction. | Murder—Fiction. | Large type books.
Classification: LCC PS3604.A9717 M57 2018 | DDC 813/.6—dc23
LC record available at https://lccn.loc.gov/2018030908

*Dedicated to
veterinary technicians
and technologists
everywhere*

ACKNOWLEDGMENTS

As always, there are so many people to thank. The members of the Nose for Trouble Facebook group came to the rescue when I was looking for a name for the animal shelter in Wagtail. I believe Bree Herron and Stephanie Evans were the first to suggest the word Guardian. Several others suggested it or variations, as well. Thank you all! It is now officially the Wagtail Animal Guardians or WAG.

But it was the members of Delicious Mysteries who helped me work out the phonetic pronunciation of "Darling, put your puppy down" in a deep Southern accent. We Southerners have a tendency to make two syllables out of one. It was Rae Ann Barnett who nailed the crucial missing link of "put-chore." I can just hear Macon saying it, and I hope my readers will hear him as well.

You may have noticed that Trixie and Twinkletoes grow larger with each cover. I thank my wonderful cover artist, Mary Ann Lasher, for capturing them so beautifully!

I would be remiss if I did not thank Betsy Strickland, Susan Smith, Amy Wheeler, and my family for listening to me drone on endlessly about my stories and for always being so supportive.

Special thanks to Julie Mianecki, who edited

this book, and to Michelle Vega, who saw it to completion.

And finally, my gratitude to my agent, Jessica Faust, for always looking out for me.

The greatest love is the mother's,
then the dog's, and then the sweetheart's.

Polish proverb

RESIDENTS OF WAGTAIL

Holly Miller—co-owner of the Sugar Maple Inn
Liesel Miller (Oma)—Holly's grandmother, co-owner of the Sugar Maple Inn, and mayor of Wagtail
Shelley Dixon—inn employee
Zelda York—inn employee
Mr. Huckle—inn employee
Casey Collins—inn employee
Paige McDonagh—Wagtail Animal Guardians employee
Bob Lane—pharmacist
Aunt Birdie Dupuy—Holly's aunt

GUESTS OF THE INN, VISITORS, AND PARTICIPANTS IN ANIMAL ATTRACTION

Gustav Vogel—inn guest
Macon Stotts—professional matchmaker
Ben Hathaway—Holly's old boyfriend
John Adele
    Cooper, his yellow Lab
Nessie Jamieson
    Celeste, her daughter
    Lulu, her papillon
Sky Stevens
    Maddie, her daughter

Laura Pisani
    Marmalade, her orange tabby
Hank Abernathy—Zelda's ex-husband
Randall Donovan
Axel Turner

ANIMALS

Gingersnap—Oma's golden retriever, canine ambassador of the Sugar Maple Inn
Twinkletoes—Holly's calico cat, feline ambassador of the Sugar Maple Inn
Trixie—Holly's Jack Russell terrier
Huey—white German shepherd mix, available for adoption
Duchess—white and tan mix, available for adoption

Mission
Impawsible

ONE

By six o'clock on Thursday afternoon, one Gustav Vogel had failed to check into his room at the Sugar Maple Inn. Ordinarily, this would not be a matter of concern or great consequence. But it wasn't an ordinary day. It was the first day of the Animal Attraction matchmaking event in Wagtail. All our other guests had arrived and were already participating.

Located on popular Wagtail Mountain in southwest Virginia, the Sugar Maple Inn was always booked in the summer, and this particular week had filled up especially fast. Gustav had a mere three hours to go before he forfeited his reservation and we could give his room to someone else.

It was my turn to take over the Live Love Bark table. I left the mayhem at the reception desk as people poured through the door, hoping we still had rooms available. But Gustav had until nine o'clock to arrive, so we had to turn them away until then. I stepped out onto the front porch that spanned the main building of the Sugar Maple Inn and observed the crowd that had collected on the plaza.

Maybe there truly *was* someone for everyone. People of every possible shape, size, and

15

description milled about, alike only in the fact that a dog or cat accompanied almost every one of them. Yet all these people hadn't found compatible human mates. Why was it so much harder to find the right person than it was to find the right cat or dog?

I was no exception. My dog, Trixie, left my side to scamper down the stairs and join the fun. The little Jack Russell terrier I had rescued at a gas station had blossomed and become my constant companion. White, except for black ears and a black spot on her rump that extended to her tail, which had not been cropped, Trixie had a knack for finding corpses. She had developed a bit of a reputation around town because of her nose for trouble.

My calico cat, Twinkletoes, observed the commotion from the safety of the front porch. Her face was white, with a patch of dark chocolate and one of caramel on her forehead, almost like she had shoved sunglasses up on her head. Her chest and front paws were white too, but her fluffy tail was black. Twinkletoes had chosen me as her person. I would have readily adopted her, but as cats do, she was the one who'd made the decision that we belonged together.

Trixie and Twinkletoes were my nearly perfect darlings. Granted, they did get into trouble now and then, but for the most part they behaved very well. It was my first summer in Wagtail since my childhood, and my first summer in a long time that wasn't spent cooped up in an office. When my grandmother had offered to make me a partner in the Sugar Maple Inn, I had jumped at the opportunity.

Once a resort town where people came for the waters, Wagtail had had to reinvent itself, and it had quite literally gone to the dogs and cats. Not only were they allowed in lodgings and restaurants, but there were special menus and dishes created just for them. The stores in town accommodated them too, selling clothes, collars, leashes, beds, and every conceivable item that any spoiled dog or cat could want.

Trixie and Twinkletoes had learned to play with the guest dogs and cats, though Twinkletoes wasn't always the best feline ambassador of the Sugar Maple Inn. There were times when she insisted on hissing and stalking away. So inhospitable!

Watching the people on the plaza meeting each other and making connections reminded me that my love life was a miserable mess. Nonexistent, really. Maybe I shouldn't have balked at the notion of being matched to a guy this weekend. My grandmother, whom I called Oma—German for *grandma*—hadn't pussyfooted around. She had come right out and told me this was my chance to meet a man. I was a little bit sad that she pushed me because I knew she had hoped I would end up with Holmes Richardson, a childhood friend.

No one else had ever stolen my heart quite like Holmes. I wasn't sure I was ready to give up on him yet. It was complicated, though, because he lived in Chicago and was engaged to be married. It wasn't in my nature to chase a man who was engaged to someone else, so like a fool I waited for his relationship to implode on its own. Sometimes I wondered if it was time for me to abandon that hope.

The daily Yappy Hour parade had ended. I spied Oma at a table on the plaza with Macon Stotts and walked toward them. Wagtail was set up in a long rectangle. In the center, a park, known as *the green,* ran from one end of town to the other. Paths meandered through it, benches were available for resting, and fenced areas allowed dogs to play off leash. Sidewalks ran around the perimeter of the green, where stores and restaurants were located. At the south end, in front of the Sugar Maple Inn, the sidewalks merged into a plaza large enough to accommodate events like Animal Attraction.

Oma and her best friend, Rose, had come up with the Animal Attraction matchmaking idea after hearing about a famous matchmaking week in Ireland. They had hired Macon Stotts, a Southerner who claimed to be matchmaker to the stars, to arrange the various events and help match people up. I assumed he meant Hollywood stars, and wondered if they really needed matchmaking help.

Animal Attraction was a literal name because the people attending were bringing their dogs and cats with them to help with the matchmaking. The benefits, according to Oma and Rose, were that the animals would break the ice, making it easier for their people to meet, and the human participants would know up front that they all shared a love of animals. Their dogs and cats would help them connect.

"Holly!" Oma waved at me. "Still no sign of Gustav?" She hated that she spoke with a German accent in spite of the fact that she had lived in the United States since before my father was born, over fifty years. Most people found her accent charming, but I was so used to it that I didn't notice it much anymore.

"Not yet."

She glanced at her watch. "There is still time. You are here to relieve me?"

"Just tell me what to do."

Oma held up a slip of paper. "Macon has set up a Live Love Bark app and a Live Love Meow app. Here are the addresses and passwords."

I took it and frowned. Wagtail was notorious for its poor Internet connection. Only one cell phone carrier worked at all, and it was iffy at best.

"If they have trouble," said Oma, "these are the forms they can fill out instead. Make sure they know there will be other matchmaking events. This is only one option. When they bring them back, they go into this box. Macon will pick them up and make the matches."

Macon jumped to his feet. "My word! These people are clueless." He swept by me, reminding me of a plump penguin. His straight black hair was combed back and gleamed with some kind of gel. He was short for a man, broad through the middle, and waddled when he walked rapidly. In a slightly nasal Southern accent, he cried out, "Dahlin', put-chore puppy down!"

I couldn't help smiling when he dragged out *down* into two syllables, *day-own*.

The stunning young woman he was addressing, who had skin the rich color of honey, appeared surprised. A fluffy little dog rode in her shoulder bag, his face peering out like a tiny white Wookiee.

"Put him down, sweetheart. He can't do his job matchin' you up if he's confined to a bag."

"On the ground?" Her brow furrowed. "He'll get dirty paws."

"Anybody with a fancy bag like that must surely have booties." Macon held out his hands, palms up.

He'd nailed it. She produced tiny blue dog booties and slid them onto the feet of her dog with Macon's help. Once on the concrete plaza, the dog wasted no time at all mingling with the others.

"They'll bite him!" she said with a desperate look at Macon. "He's so tiny. That big black dog will think he's a snack."

The other dogs seemed very interested in him, but not because of his size. Even my Trixie wanted to know what those funny things were on his feet.

"I have to rescue him. Look what they're doing!"

Macon placed a hand on her arm. "Honey, that's just what polite dogs do. Sniffin' is how they shake hands. Don't you ever let him play with other dogs?"

A group of young men distracted Macon. He raised his hand, pointed at them, and waddled away, shouting, "Young fella, your dog is tryin' to introduce you to the pretty girl with the cat."

The man standing beside me uttered dryly, "Is that Macon Stotts? I thought that old fraud was dead."

TWO

"Fraud?" Oma stood up so fast she nearly toppled the table. "What do you mean *fraud?*"

"Your reaction suggests that you must be the imbecile who was suckered in by him. Don't blame yourself. He's quite skilled. How much are you paying Macon?"

Oma was in her seventies, but she was not one to trifle with. She still looked great, with short, thick hair that gleamed silver in the sun. And my Oma was always impeccably dressed in what she liked to call Wagtail chic. In other words, elegant casual. She drew her head back, clearly appalled by what he was saying.

He didn't appear to care. "Must be good money. Macon doesn't go anywhere unless he's hauling it in."

Oma scowled at him. "Why do you say he is a fraud?"

Fluffy, loose curls the color of coffee with cream framed the man's earnest face. His mustache and beard were carefully trimmed. Brown eyes appraised Oma through rimless glasses. "You appear to be a sensible woman. Surely you don't believe that anyone can make a love match by picking two strangers out of a crowd."

I held out a form to him. "Want to try?"

"Very amusing." He took it in spite of the sarcasm in his tone. "Thank you. This should be entertaining reading. I was wondering if there is a list of attendees."

Oma answered him. "No. People can come any time they want. For one day, for a particular event, or for the entire ten days. There is no roster."

His hand tightened on the form I had given him, crumpling it. He gazed around as though he was looking for someone.

"The idea is that you'll meet people through your dog or cat." I looked around for his animal. All I saw were his pressed trousers and city-slicker leather shoes. "No dog?" I asked.

"Hmm? Oh, spare me. I have no attachment avoidance issues necessitating me to lavish attention on a drooling ankle-biter."

Oh! I glanced at Oma. Her eyes told me what she thought of him. I tried to give him a break. "Are you a cat person?"

"Do I *look* like a neurotic introvert with a need to worship a creature who is completely indifferent to me?"

I was flabbergasted. I had no idea what a neurotic introvert looked like, but I now had a pretty good idea what a stupid jerk looked like. Difficult as it was, I bit my tongue. For all I knew, he might be a guest of the Sugar Maple Inn, and if there was one thing Oma had ingrained in me, it was to always be polite to the guests.

I contemplated telling him he was in the wrong place. Could it be that he didn't know Wagtail was the premier resort for people who wanted to vacation with their pets?

When I didn't respond right away, he continued searching the crowd but asked, "Cats or dogs?"

He didn't appear to be talking to anyone else. "I beg your pardon?"

He enunciated with slow precision, as though I weren't smart enough to comprehend. "Do you like cats or dogs?"

"Both." Trixie returned to my side with a yellow Lab. They sat down contentedly and watched the goings-on. I handed each of them a mini dog biscuit. "Hello," I said to the Lab. "Who are you?" I glanced at the tag on his collar. "Cooper!"

The man finally bothered to look at me. "You do know that he can't understand you, right?"

Oma's face grew red, and I feared she might blow up.

He obviously didn't care. "Sorry, I should have known by the fur on your shirt. My mistake. From the looks on your faces, I can see that I have offended you."

"I don't know who you're looking for," I dared to say, "but Wagtail is all about dogs and cats. And this matchmaking weekend is specifically geared to people who love their furry companions."

"You delude yourself by imagining that the beasts at your feet have any feelings for you whatsoever. What they like is food, and by being the source of said food you have their attention, thus causing you to fancy you have a relationship with these creatures. In truth, you have no more of a relationship with them than I have with the man who served me dinner last night in a restaurant. A man I shall most likely never see again. You have simply projected a loving emotion on your pets because they like to be fed. By anthropomorphizing—I presume you know what that means—you have filled the basic human desire for *human* companionship with an animal who would just as soon eat you. It is, of course, folly. You would do better to find yourself a similarly deluded human counterpart among these masses."

"You have never had a dog or cat, have you?" Oma asked.

"That old retort. I don't need one to know they have brains the size of walnuts. They don't care about you or anything else. They're not capable of that kind of thought or feeling."

He stared at us, obviously sizing us up. "It's people like you who make it possible for frauds like Macon to stay in business. Love is merely an illusion that stems from an irrational dependency disorder." He strode away into the crowd.

Oma sputtered, "What a horrible man! If he does not like animals, then what does he want here in Wagtail?"

I handed two more tiny dog treats to Trixie and Cooper as an apology. "Don't worry. We know he's wrong."

They wagged their tails and gazed at me with loving eyes.

Oma spotted Rose. "You excuse me, yes?" She hurried over to her friend. I took a seat and handed the forms out to ten people. Most of them filled them out on the spot. During a lull, I had a chance to look at the forms.

1. Which of these scents turns you off?
   a. doggy breath
   b. kitty litter box
   c. perfume/cologne
   d. home deodorizer

The answers were an interesting selection and probably pretty telling. Maybe Macon knew what he was doing after all. I glanced at the next two.

2. It's Saturday morning and you don't have to work. You:
   a. leap out of bed to go jogging with your dog
   b. hope the dog and/or cat will sleep in so you can, too
   c. snuggle in bed with your cat(s) or dog(s)
   d. head for the gym

> e. leisurely read the paper over coffee, croissants, and dog or cat treats

3. My cat or dog sleeps:
   a. in the garage
   b. outside the house
   c. in a pet bed
   d. in my bed

I handed out some more forms, skipped the rest of the questions, and read the instructions.

> The more truthful you are, the more likely I can find a good match for you. Return the form before seven p.m. on Thursday. You may pick up your match after eight p.m. in the Dogwood Room at the Sugar Maple Inn.

That was a quick turnaround. My doubts returned. Even if he used a computer to make the matches, wouldn't it take some time to correlate the information?

Paige McDonagh, whom I recognized from the Wagtail Animal Guardians—better known as WAG, the local shelter—walked toward me with a whitish shepherd mix on a leash. Her royal blue T-shirt said *Live Long and Foster* in white lettering.

I grinned at the play on Spock's words from *Star Trek*.

"Hi, Holly! I'm dropping off this sweet guy for the If the Dog Fits program." She handed me the leash.

"Sorry, Paige. There must be some kind of mistake. We don't have anyone participating this week." Visitors to Wagtail enjoyed getting to know dogs through the program. By spending the weekend with a dog, people could determine if they were a good match for adoption. The truth was that it gave them time to bond with the dog. So far the program had a one hundred percent adoption rate. Paige usually dropped off three or four specially selected dogs at the inn for a guest to choose from.

"Hoo-ey," she mumbled, "is for Ben. Very last-minute." Paige ran her hands through shoulder-length blonde hair. I had never seen her when it wasn't tousled. Her eyes slanted downward the slightest bit at the outer corners, and her pug nose was adorable. I knew the animals loved her because she was kind and patient with them, but her friendliness had also endeared her to the human residents of Wagtail.

"Ben Hathaway? My former boyfriend? Ben isn't here, and he doesn't like dogs."

"Really?" she asked. "I can't imagine you dating someone who isn't into dogs."

"Maybe that's why things didn't work out." It was more complicated than that, but it might have helped if he had been an animal lover.

"He must have changed his mind about dogs. You don't mind watching him until Ben arrives." It was a statement, not a question. "See ya!"

"Wait!" I cried. "What's his name again?"

"At WAG we call him Huey." She rushed into the crowd as if she was in a hurry.

Huey had already made friends with Trixie and Cooper. I, meanwhile, was a little bit miffed that Ben thought he could just visit me whenever he liked without so much as a courtesy call. I had two bedrooms in my apartment on the top floor of the inn, but it would serve him right if I told him someone else was staying with me. I wasn't crazy about him popping in without letting me know.

A flurry of participants handed their forms back to me.

Macon emerged from the crowd, dabbing his brow with a handkerchief. "This was a mahvelous idea. I can see bonds forming between couples already. Have you got those questionnaires for me? I'd better get up to my room and make some matches."

I handed them over to him.

"Did you fill one out?" he asked.

"No." I smiled at him, feeling a bit embarrassed.

Macon tsked at me. "Good thing a stubborn girl like you has a cupid for a grandmother."

I was folding up the table when a woman rushed up to me. She shoved a thick strand of lustrous dark hair off her shoulder and fanned herself with her hand. "Are you Holly?"

"Yes." I stopped folding and extended my hand to her. "Holly Miller."

She shook my hand. "Laura Pisani. I'm staying at the inn. I'm sorry to bother you, but my cat, Marmalade, jumped out of my arms. He has a GPS tag on his collar, so as you can see"—she showed me her phone—"he's still in the inn somewhere. Is it okay for him to explore on his own?"

"Sure. In my experience, most cats are frightened when they get away on their own. He's probably hiding in a little nook somewhere waiting for things to calm down."

"That doesn't really sound like Marmalade. He's a very social cat and always wants to be around people."

"Then maybe he's living it up and making new friends. Do you want us to contact you if we see him?"

"That would be great!" Laura showed me a picture of an orange tabby on her phone and wrote down her phone number on the back of a business card. "Just text me, and I'll come running."

I flipped over the card, which belonged to an L. Nicholas Gordon, inventor. I wondered if she knew she had given me someone else's card.

"Oh! Don't worry about that." Her fingers fluttered at the business card. "Just some guy who was flirting with me." She squinched up her face. "So not my type. I'd have thrown his card away anyway."

I smiled at her. "I totally understand. And I'll let the staff know to be on the lookout for Marmalade."

She wandered off, and I carried the table toward the side of the inn. It was a little awkward with Huey on the leash. But he was a good sport and followed Trixie's lead. We made it to the reception lobby, and I stashed the table away.

Zelda, our daytime desk clerk, was touching up her eyeliner. Full-figured and fun, Zelda thought she could communicate with cats and dogs. I had my doubts, but she did seem to have a way with animals. When she wasn't working at the inn, she was building up a business as a pet psychic. Unfortunately, her ex-husband had left her with a stack of his bills to pay off, so she worked long hours to get back on her feet.

"There's an orange-striped tabby running loose in the inn—"

"Marmalade?" Zelda asked.

"How did you know?"

"I checked him in. He was eager to stretch his legs after the trip here."

I still hadn't gotten used to her pronouncements about what animals were thinking. That was probably true, though. "If you see him, text his owner at this number." I wrote it down for her.

Zelda propped the note up on the desk. "Did Trixie match you up with a date?"

I looked at her in surprise for a second. "Trixie?"

31

I looked over at my dog. She sat next to Huey like they were old pals. "You mean Huey?"

I told Zelda about Huey and Ben.

Zelda put away her mascara and fluffed her long blonde hair. "You'd think Ben could have called. But Trixie is thinking about a big yellow dog with ears that flop down."

How could Zelda know about Cooper? Maybe Zelda had taken a break and seen us outside? "That would be Cooper, a yellow Lab."

"And did he have a cute dad?"

"For all I know, he belongs to a woman. Are you ready to take a dinner break? I can cover for you."

"Great! Your grandmother said I can leave as soon as we check Gustav into the last room at nine o'clock. I filled out one of Macon's forms, and I'm eager to meet my date."

"What happened to Felix?" I asked. Felix had been a guest at the inn and had hit it off with Zelda. She was taller than geeky Felix, but they had made a nice couple.

"I wish he didn't live so far away," Zelda said. "I never see him. He's probably dating someone else by now. Too bad. He was such a sweetheart. One of the really good guys."

Then Zelda gasped and her face registered horror. She ducked behind the registration desk.

THREE

"Zelda?" I walked behind the desk and looked down at her. The sliding glass doors opened to admit someone.

Zelda placed a finger over her lips in a signal to be silent.

Trixie yelped at the man who entered. She backed away from him with a growl but never took her eyes off him.

Judging by the stubble on his face, he hadn't bothered to shave in a few days. His unkempt light brown hair was short. If he had done anything to it when he rose in the morning, it wasn't with a comb. He wore a white T-shirt and carried a leather jacket over his shoulder. Altogether he had the type of rugged look that was popular. But something about his eyes made me wary. Not to mention Trixie's reaction to him.

"May I help you?" I asked.

"I hear Zelda York works here."

Zelda's hand clutched my ankle, and I jerked ever so slightly. More deftly than I'd have liked, I lied to him. "She's off today."

He was staring at Trixie, who now peered at him from the far side of the registration desk, which was actually a counter.

Trixie growled softly.

"What's wrong with that dog?" he asked.

She had never reacted that way to anyone before, but it would have been rude to point that out to him. I glanced at Huey, who sat like a perfect gentleman but didn't take his eyes off the man. "The other dog is new. I think his presence upset her."

Another lie. I didn't really like this skill I had developed. I wasn't even sweating or feeling guilty about it.

He nodded and leaned against the desk. "You must be new around here. I don't remember meeting you before."

"Holly Miller. Are you a frequent visitor to Wagtail?"

"Nice to meet you, Holly Miller."

Any polite person would have said the same thing, but there was something about his tone that was slick, like he was trying to flirt.

"I'm Hank Abernathy. Listen"—he reached a hand across the desk—"since Zelda isn't here, how about having some dinner with me?"

The hand on my ankle squeezed like talons.

"I'm sorry. I have to work."

"What time do you get off?"

This guy wasn't giving up. So far I'd told him nothing but lies, which bothered me in principle. But when I looked into his eyes I felt the desire to keep him away from Zelda by getting rid of him. "I'm sorry, but I think my fiancé might object to that."

And at that moment, just like magic, the doors slid open and Ben, my former boyfriend, walked in.

"And there he is now!" I chirped.

Hank's eyes shifted, giving me the willies. "See you around then."

Heavens. I hoped not!

He strolled out the doors. When they closed behind him, I looked down at Zelda. "Who was that?"

"Is he gone?" she whispered.

Ben walked around the corner of the desk. "What's going on?"

"You can stand up now," I assured her.

In spite of that, Zelda raised her head slowly, peeking over the top of the desk at the door before standing fully erect. "*That* was my good-for-nothing ex-husband."

"You're kidding. The one who left you broke and loaded with debt?"

"The very same. It's a shame he's so handsome. He sucks me back in every time I see him."

"Not today," I pointed out.

"Trust me. I have to stay away from that man."

"Was he violent?" I asked.

Zelda snorted and giggled. "Are you kidding? He's too lazy for that. He'd probably like to shack up with me and mooch off of me again. Three square meals a day and a comfy bed at my expense? No, thanks. I'm done with him."

Even though I hadn't looked forward to seeing Ben, he had arrived at a perfect time. Ben wouldn't deter many men, but his mere presence had done the trick of getting rid of Hank.

Bespectacled and studious-looking, he was the ultimate geek. Ben had asked me to marry him by texting me a message of cryptic abbreviations. And then he had followed up that abysmal act with what could only be called a pity proposal. It was more like a business transaction because I had lost my job, and he thought I had no foreseeable source of income. I turned him down and had come to the realization that he wasn't the right man for me. But I didn't mind being friends. My irritation that he hadn't told me he was coming to visit faded. After all, he had gotten rid of Hank by showing up.

I crooked my finger at him and walked over to the beautiful shepherd mix. "This is Huey. Did you really ask for a dog from the If the Dog Fits program?"

Instead of petting Huey, as I would have, Ben studied him. "I thought it would be a small dog, smaller than Trixie. Huey is huge."

"He's a great dog, though. I've had him with me for an hour, and he's been a sweetheart."

Ben nodded reluctantly. "What do I do with him?"

Zelda burst out laughing. "Huey says he would like a long walk and then dinner, preferably beef and a cookie for dessert."

"Ohh-kay," Ben drawled like he wasn't sure. "He's much bigger than I expected," he repeated.

"Are you afraid of him?" I asked.

"No. Well, maybe a little. Has he ever bitten anyone?"

"If he had, I'm sure they wouldn't have assigned him to you." Feeling sorry for Huey, I handed Ben a fistful of tiny dog treats. "Why don't you give him a try?"

Ben brightened up. "You and Trixie could come hang out with us for a bit."

"I can't. I'm working. Why don't you and Huey go get a latte?" Maybe if Ben spent some time with Huey, he would see what a gentle and sweet fellow he was.

Ben pitched his duffel bag into the office and picked up Huey's leash. "Will he just come with me or do I have to say some magic word?"

Zelda elbowed me. It was all I could do to keep a straight face. Ben was clueless. I rushed over with a Sugar Maple Inn GPS collar and fastened it on Huey. "Just in case," I whispered into Huey's ear. He wagged his tail and kissed my nose.

At nine o'clock, a golf cart, better known as a Wagtail taxi since the town had severe restrictions on cars, pulled up outside.

"Here they come," whispered Zelda.

Two women approached the sliding glass doors at the same time.

37

A portly black woman wore her hair up in an elegant twist and toted a small dog in a Louis Vuitton carrier. Her sky blue dress accentuated her curves.

She was flanked by a slender white woman who wore her hair in a grown out pageboy cut that looked like she'd been in a wind tunnel. She wore a white denim jacket and carried a battered leather bag that had seen better days.

The women politely paused as if to allow the other one to enter first. But in the end, they pushed through together and exchanged a frantic look before rushing the desk. They arrived at the same time, and both said, "Do you have a room left?"

A harried man was right behind them. "Me, too!"

Zelda glanced at me. I knew what she was thinking. *What if the guy was Gustav?*

"Your name, sir?" I asked.

The portly woman heaved a sigh. "Do men always receive better treatment in this inn? I believe we were here first."

The slender woman nodded in agreement.

"I'm sorry," I said. "I guess it looked that way. We only have one room available, and it's because a man did not show up. I'm just making sure that the gentleman behind you isn't the one who had a reservation."

The two women gazed at each other briefly then turned their heads toward the man.

Trim and attractive, he didn't appear to be uncomfortable even though he was on the spot. He bowed to the two ladies. "Alas, I did not have the foresight to make a reservation."

The women lost interest in him immediately.

"Please," pleaded the portly woman. "I can pay. Double, quadruple even. Don't you have some kind of fancy suite that no one booked?"

The slender woman tilted her head as if she couldn't believe her ears. "Look, we arrived at exactly the same time. I think we should flip a coin."

"Actually, I think I was here first."

"We came in on the same Wagtail taxi!"

Zelda cleared her throat. "Uh, Holly, Sit has two beds . . ."

"Oh, no." The portly woman cast a critical eye over the slender woman. "I'm sorry, but we're strangers. That"—she coughed—"would not do at all."

Zelda gazed at her. "What's your name?"

"Hmm? Nessie Jamieson." She smiled broadly, clearly believing that she had won the room.

"And you?" asked Zelda, turning to the other woman.

"Sky Stevens."

"Nessie, meet Sky."

The women forced smiles and nodded at each other.

The man behind them lost his patience. "Look,

I'll take the room. At this point, I don't care if it has a sleeping bag in it."

I forced the women's hands a little bit. "I hear the hotel across town is booked."

Sky said, "It's been a long time since I had a roommate. What do you say? I'm pretty tidy, and I don't snore."

Nessie seemed pained. "Are you absolutely certain you don't have another room? Hotels always have some rooms that are out of order. Don't you have one with a clogged sink or something for her?"

Zelda shook her head so hard that her long hair jiggled.

Nessie winced. "Where do we sign in?"

The man behind them strode over to the love seat and turned to his phone.

I asked Nessie if her dog would like a Sugar Maple Inn GPS collar for their stay.

Nessie declined. "Lulu is never more than a few feet away from me."

I showed them to their room. Delicate yellow walls gave it a cheerful feel. A stylish bombé chest separated the two beds. Each double bed featured a white duvet, loads of pillows, and a large yellow-and-white plaid blanket folded at the foot at the bed. Tasseled yellow curtains framed a large window that overlooked the lake and the mountains beyond. Two comfy armchairs in a blue-and-yellow French print flanked a table. A writing desk and another dresser completed the room.

"This is charming." Sky dropped her purse on one of the chairs.

"Do you like dogs?" Nessie opened her fancy dog carrier and a bright-eyed papillon leaped out.

"I love them!" Sky knelt on the floor and Lulu made a beeline for her. Not to be outdone, Trixie raced over and demanded equal time.

Nessie watched them with wary eyes. "I see that you're not wearing a wedding ring, Sky. Are you here to find a man?"

I was surprised by her question, but Sky took it in stride. "I'm widowed."

"Oh! I'm so sorry. That must be difficult. I'm divorced." The corners of Nessie's mouth twitched. "Three times."

Sky looked up from her petting session. "Actually, I'm a little bit embarrassed to admit it, but my daughter, Maddie, is here to meet a boy who likes animals as much as we do."

"Does she know you're here?" asked Nessie.

"No. She didn't tell me her plans until the last minute. That's why I didn't have a reservation. I never expected everything to be booked. There must be a lot of animal lovers looking for their human counterparts."

Nessie let out a guffaw and laughed so hard that she nearly bent double. "My daughter, Celeste, was left at the altar last year. I thought I'd never be rid of the idiot she meant to marry. Nobody ever saw a mama so happy that her baby was hurt like that. I danced the night away." Nessie shook her finger in the air. "That man turned out to have two children he never bothered to mention to Celeste. Can you believe it? Now that girl has come up here to this pet matchmaking thing to meet somebody." She flicked her right hand in the air for me to leave. "Holly, you can go now. We're just a couple of mamas watching out for our babies."

I quickly ran through my spiel. "Information about the inn is on the desk. We serve breakfast, lunch, and afternoon tea. Room service is available on request. You'll see the special dog menu there, too. Just call me if you need anything."

As I took my leave, I heard Nessie saying, "You know, we might be able to help each other spy on our girls. Celeste wouldn't know you, and your Maddie wouldn't recognize me."

FOUR

I closed the door behind me, thinking I was glad neither of them was *my* mother!

When I returned to the desk, Zelda fluffed her hair one more time. "How do I look?"

"Eager and lovely," I said.

She left to get the results of Macon's survey.

The reception lobby was quiet. Twinkletoes sat on the desk, carefully washing her face. Ben hadn't returned with Huey. I wondered where they had gone and hoped all would go well for them.

Ben's apartment wasn't big enough to hold my shoes. It would be a tight fit for Huey. Then it dawned on me that they didn't allow pets in Ben's building. Maybe Ben had finally decided to buy a house? It didn't make sense that he suddenly wanted a dog.

The doors slid open and Cooper the yellow Lab trotted inside. Trixie ran to greet her new friend. Their tails wagged happily at meeting again.

A nice-looking guy in his late thirties followed Cooper.

What if he was Gustav? "Please don't tell me you're Gustav Vogel." I looked at him hopefully.

He tilted his head and little wrinkles etched his forehead. "I don't know Gustav, but it sounds like you'll be happy to know that I'm not him. I'm John Adele."

He said his name like I was supposed to recognize it, but I had no idea who he was. He missed six feet by about an inch. His hair parted on the left and while I gazed at him, he brushed it back a bit with his hand. It didn't hang in his face but was casually mussed—no hair gel for this guy. A round face and mischievous blue eyes gave me the impression that he was fun. But I was confused by his presence. We had filled all our rooms. Surely we hadn't overbooked! "Do you have a reservation?"

"You're Holly, right? It's working already." He motioned toward Trixie and the Labrador. "Cooper loves your dog! That must be Trixie."

Cooper and Trixie clearly liked each other. Both tails waved high as they gave the formal doggy bow that meant *let's play.*

John grinned at me. "So you live in Wagtail? Perfect. What time do you get off? Maybe we could go for a drink? What's your favorite watering hole?"

I stared at him in confusion.

He gazed at the floor and then back up at me, his mouth bunched. "You don't have a clue who I am."

With relief and a great deal of embarrassment, I admitted, "I'm afraid not. Have we met before?"

"We were matched on the Live Love Bark questionnaire for dog people."

That was curious. I didn't fill out a questionnaire. I pondered how to handle the situation. I'd been determined to stay out of the matchmaking scene, but John was cute and seemed like a decent guy.

"I'm sorry, John. I think there's been a mistake."

He blinked at me before withdrawing a sheet of paper from his pocket and studying it. He showed it to me. "There's no error unless there's another Holly Miller who works at the Sugar Maple Inn and has a Jack Russell named Trixie."

And then Twinkletoes had the *nerve* to walk over and head-butt John's chin.

He ran his hand over her head and scratched her cheek. I could hear her purring.

"This has to be Twinkletoes." He tapped the paper with his forefinger. "See? It's all here."

Slightly alarmed by the information he had about me, I scanned the sheet. "I'm sorry. I don't understand how this happened."

"Okay. I get the message." He tucked the paper into his pocket. "Is it me or Cooper that you don't like?"

At the mention of his name, Cooper stopped playing, looked straight at me, tilted his head like he was confused, and pawed the air with his right front foot. He was adorable.

I ventured around the desk to pat Cooper and offer him a Sugar Maple Inn treat. Cooper wriggled from end to end at the attention.

"Cooper is great. It's just that—"

The glass doors slid open, and Ben walked in with Huey.

Trixie barked at him, and Twinkletoes hissed.

"Whoa," said John. "They really don't like that dog."

"It's not the dog," I muttered. "It's Ben they don't like."

John's eyebrows rose in surprise. "I never saw anyone get such a strong reaction. What did you do to them?"

"Nothing. I have no idea why they don't like me." Ben shrugged as though he didn't care.

John shot me a curious look, but said to Ben, "You must be putting out some pretty negative vibes for them to act that way."

"Holly and I get along great. It's just these animals she picked up that don't care for me. When Holly was fired from her job, I asked her to marry me. She would have if it hadn't been for *them*."

"I wasn't fired!"

Ben's eyebrows raised. "Short memory?"

"Okay, I was fired, but it's not like it sounds. There were complicating issues." John didn't need to hear all the details or think poorly of me.

"You two were engaged?" asked John.

Ben said, *"Yes,"* at the exact time that I said, *"No."* I was surprised that I cared what John thought of me and rushed to say, "We dated a long time ago but were never engaged. Ben, don't you need to take your bag upstairs?" I fetched it from the office and handed it to him. Unfortunately, he didn't take the hint.

"People keep asking me what breed Huey is. Do you have any idea?"

As though John knew what I was thinking, he said, "Shepherd. Maybe some husky? Two very intelligent breeds."

Huey studied us with warm brown eyes.

"Would you like another dog?" I asked John. "Huey seems very sweet and well behaved."

John turned to Ben. "You don't want him?"

"It's a long story," Ben said. "I was supposed to be set up with a small dog for the weekend, but they gave me Huey. I called WAG and tried to trade him in for a Chihuahua or some small dog that doesn't have a lot of energy—"

John looked at me, clearly astonished. "Is he for real?"

"He doesn't know much about dogs. Not anything, really."

"Listen, Ben. Bad news, buddy. Little dogs can be hyper. Just because they're small doesn't mean they lie around all day."

"I did not know that," Ben said. "Women carry them in their purses, so I thought they would be less active. It doesn't matter anyway, though. They're out of small dogs at the shelter."

That was actually good news. Not for Huey, of course.

John stroked Huey's back. "I hadn't thought about another dog." He shifted his attention to me. "I was more interested in meeting a girl."

I felt the red blush of embarrassment flooding my face and the tops of my ears. "Maybe you could ask Macon to match you to someone else."

There was no mistaking his disappointment. "Think she'll be as perfect for me as Holly Miller of Wagtail?"

Ben fell into a coughing fit.

FIVE

I made a face at Ben.

John's brow furrowed. "This is all a little confusing. So you have a boyfriend—"

"Had," I corrected him.

"But you still signed up for Live Love Bark, and now you're denying that you ever signed up. Maybe we're not a good match after all."

Ben did not appear to be the least bit contrite.

I was, though. I hadn't wanted to be set up. I hadn't been interested in meeting anyone, yet I wished John didn't think I was an awful person. "I'm sorry. It's not like that. I really didn't sign up."

John nodded, but I could tell he didn't believe me. "Sorry to have bothered you. I'm a pretty simple guy, and I'm not into women who play games. C'mon, Cooper."

When he walked by Ben, he muttered, "Good luck," in a thoroughly sarcastic voice.

I felt awful.

The door closed behind John. It resolved the situation for me, but I didn't like John thinking I was some kind of manipulative worm. Not that it mattered. I probably wouldn't ever see him again. But it still bothered me.

The sad truth was that I had no interest in Ben,

other than as a friend. No matter what *he* thought or expected. And I had been very clear about it.

"What a crabby guy." Ben handed me Huey's leash. "Would you mind watching Huey for a little while?"

"Ben, the point of If the Dog Fits is to spend time with the dog. How will you know if you're good together if you pawn him off on me?"

"Come on, Holly. I just want to take my stuff up and grab a quick shower."

"Then take him with you." I looked at Huey, who watched us intently as if he understood what we were saying. "He's such a sweetheart." I caved when Huey tilted his head like he was pleading with me. "Okay. I need to take Trixie for a walk anyway. Huey can come with us."

Ben was smiling when he collected his bag and headed for the elevator.

He'd barely been gone a minute when Oma appeared on the staircase. It was almost like she had been waiting for him to leave.

Oma took to Huey immediately. She murmured to him in German, and Huey appeared to love it. His long whitish tail wagged happily, but Oma seemed subdued. "I see the Ben has returned."

I hated that she called him *the Ben,* and she knew it. "Oma," I warned, "please don't call him that."

"But Ben is his name, no?"

"*The* Ben. Please don't say that. It sounds weird. Like you're putting him down."

"I do not mean to offend. It is surely my poor English that causes me to make such mistakes."

Poor English, my foot!

"Why does he come here this time? I thought you broke things off with him."

"I did. I guess he wants a dog."

"This one? He is beautiful. If I did not have my Gingersnap, I would love such a dog." Oma tore her attention away from Huey. "Zelda is participating in the matchmaking events. Don't you want to join in, Holly? There will be many men to choose from." I could have sworn I heard her add under her breath, "Far better than the Ben."

"Oma," I groaned.

She squared her shoulders. "I cannot blame you. Love is elusive for me also. But you are young. You should meet with the other young people and have fun."

"Oma, did you fill out a Live Love Bark form in my name?"

"Would I have done such a thing?"

Of course she would have. "Yes."

"I am old. I do not remember."

Hah! Her memory was better than mine. That little sneak!

"Did I hear you say you will walk with the dogs? Perhaps you could take Gingersnap with you? I will close up this entrance and keep an eye on the inn. Yes?"

"Sure." I stuffed my pocket with treats and grabbed a white denim jacket from the office. Although it was summer, mountain nights could be cool. Perfect for sleeping with an open window, but cool enough to want a light jacket on nighttime strolls.

Huey probably wouldn't be happy about being walked on a leash, but I had no choice. I couldn't lose him, and he most likely wouldn't come if I called him. He barely knew me.

Huey wanted to bound along with Trixie through the hallway to the main lobby but was constrained by the leash.

The inn had originally been a mansion. Various owners had built additions over the years, and Oma had expanded it to include a cats-only wing and the registration lobby. The original foyer of the home, where the grand staircase was located, was now the main lobby, where most people came and went. Open to the dining area and the Dogwood Room, our sitting room, it felt expansive and airy.

I stepped outside onto the front porch that spanned the old stone building. Even at the late hour, the rocking chairs were packed with couples getting to know each other. Dogs and cats mingled as well.

Gingersnap, Oma's golden retriever and the canine ambassador of the inn, was busy doing her job.

I called to her. "Gingersnap! Walkies?"

She gave a handsome boxer one last glance before happily introducing herself to Huey. All tails wagging, we set off through the green on a meandering path nicely lighted by Victorian-style lampposts. I was taken aback to see a couple seated on a bench smooching. I wondered if they had just met. Did some people fall for each other that fast?

The delicious nighttime air of summer made me feel carefree, like I was on vacation. No wonder everyone around me seemed to be in an amorous mood.

I headed for one of the fenced dog runs to give Huey a chance to burn off some energy. Safely inside, I unfastened his leash, and he took off springing and playing with Trixie and Gingersnap.

While the dogs romped, I leaned against the fence and considered what Oma had said about love being elusive. Maybe she was right. Maybe I *should* join in the fun. What was the worst that could happen? That I would meet someone really nice? Or that I would have a fun time and not meet anyone interesting? Neither of those options was bad. And if it wasn't any fun at all, I could just walk home at any time.

A surprised cry and the sound of rustling bushes drew my attention. I turned to look, but in the dark, I couldn't see anything awry.

I listened for a minute and heard giggling. "Probably more romance," I muttered to myself.

But in the darkness, I noticed a shadow scuttling by in a hurry, walking like a penguin.

Huey was having a ball. What a shame that the shelter had made such a poor match with Ben. Had Paige made that bad call? She'd seemed surprised that I had dated someone who wasn't into dogs. Maybe she had made an incorrect assumption about Ben. Huey deserved a great home. Ben wasn't the right person for Huey at all. Or for me either.

Ben was a decent guy, no doubt about that. Intelligent, well-read, and he had a level temperament, which I thought very important. He had a great job as a lawyer, even if it was incredibly boring. But Ben was more content in the city, while I loved Wagtail life and my sweet four-legged babies.

A wet nose pressed against my bare knee. I diverted my attention to the happy tail-wagger who wanted petting—Cooper.

"Our paths cross again," said John.

"I'm glad about that. I have to apologize to you. I'm fairly certain that my grandmother filled out that form for me. I didn't know anything about it." I patted Cooper and watched as he joined the other dogs.

John laughed. "She sounds like a hoot."

"I'm glad you think so. She's wonderful, and I love her to death, but it's so like her to try to help me behind my back."

"So what you're saying is that Live Love

Bark may have actually matched me to your grandmother? How old is she?"

I laughed aloud. "In her seventies. Old enough to be *your* grandmother."

"Do I dare hope the apple didn't fall far from the grandmother tree?"

"We're alike in many ways, but I have no idea what she put in that form. Sorry, John. Really, I am. By filling the form out for me, she took away your chance to meet someone who might be the right one for you."

"Or maybe she did me a favor. Is that Huey running with Cooper?" John peered at me in the dim light. "Is Ben here?"

"No. He's settling in."

"Ben left Huey with you? What did you ever see in that guy?"

"Sometimes I wonder that myself. He's really not a bad person. He just didn't grow up with animals and never experienced that special bond. He doesn't get it."

"Meanwhile," said John, "Cooper and your grandmother have been doing their level best to match *us* up."

I knew flirting when I heard it. And the way he said it *was* sort of cute.

"Did you go back to Live Love Bark to be reassigned?" I asked.

"Actually, I did. I was matched to a Maddie Stevens. *She* doesn't have a boyfriend."

Ouch! I guessed I deserved that, though. "You haven't met her yet?"

"Alas, I have. Cooper found her dog boring."

"I'm sure Cooper could deal with a boring dog. What did you think of Maddie?"

"Er, nice kid."

"Too young?"

"I'm afraid Macon Stotts blew it on that match. I much prefer women closer to my age, apparently with the possible exception of your grandmother," he joked. "Maddie was very pretty and seemed nice enough, but other than our dogs, we didn't have much in common. Don't worry, I'm pretty sure the feeling was mutual. After all this running, don't you think the dogs would like a drink?" asked John. "Is there another watering hole in town besides Hair of the Dog or Tequila Mockingbird?"

"The Alley Cat is over in the Shire."

"Like in *The Hobbit*. I've heard about it but haven't been there yet."

"It's across the road, so not technically in the old section of Wagtail," I said. "The architect created amazing little cottages with beams and stone. There are round doors and windows, and some have gardens and lawns on their roofs. Some people call it Hobbitville. It's worth seeing."

"Let's go! Cooper! Trixie! Huey!" He paused and looked around. "Where did the golden come from? There's no one else here."

While we walked along the quiet residential streets of Wagtail toward the Shire, I told him about Gingersnap being Oma's dog and the canine ambassador at the inn.

We paused at the road, which was pitch dark in both directions, before crossing into the Shire, a large subdivision outside of historic Wagtail. There weren't any streetlights in the Shire. At the entrance to the path that meandered through the development, oil lanterns flickered on each end of a long rustic stand of stone and wood about three feet high. It held dozens of lanterns. I slid two out and switched them on.

John took one from me. "These are just here for the taking?"

"It's an honor system. You put them back when you leave."

"People don't steal them?"

"Very few of them disappear. Some people who forget to put them back leave them in their rooms at the inn. I've carted quite a few over here. Most people are pretty decent about it."

We started down the path. Besides our lanterns, the moon and small lanterns hanging on shepherds' hooks at knee height were the only sources of illumination along the paths and bridges. But the houses were at their best. At night, one couldn't make out all the marvelous stonework, but the lights inside glowed through curious windows. Some arched like eyebrows, many were round, and at the peaks of some roofs, tiny half-circle windows beamed.

Cooper and Huey walked on leashes, undoubtedly jealous of Trixie and Gingersnap, who bounded ahead.

"I've never seen anything like this." John was agog.

"I don't think there are many similar places. If the architect and the builder hadn't been Hobbit fans, I don't think it would exist today. They both live here."

"There are no roads?"

"Mostly footpaths, which make it a popular place for walking. A few are wide enough for golf carts. I hear there was quite some discussion about that, but in the end, they had to be practical about residents who might not be able to walk, as well as everyday needs like carrying groceries and trash pickup. It just wasn't practical to do everything by foot."

"It's like we stepped back in time, and we're walking through a medieval village," John said. "I can't believe there aren't streetlights. I had seen some of the houses from Hair of the Dog, but I didn't realize that it was an entire development."

"I didn't live here when it was being built, but they tell me the streetlights were a big issue. In the end, they compromised with the low-hanging lanterns. Wagtail residents put a lot of stock in the moon and the stars."

John paused and looked up. "They're so vivid. It's like I could reach out and touch them. I wish I had known about this. Is it part of Wagtail?"

"Technically."

"I really like Wagtail, but I'd have loved staying here."

"A lot of people would, but there's no hotel and renting of houses isn't permitted. So you would have to know a homeowner to sleep over."

"No renting? That's terrible."

"It's a tightly knit community. They want to know their neighbors and not wake up to new-comers next door every week."

"But we can go to their bar?"

"Sure. People walk over from Wagtail all the time just for the ambiance. It's very popular for romantic dinners, too."

We strolled over an arched bridge. John stopped and lowered his lantern to the ground. "Is this pink stone?"

"Amazing, isn't it? It's completely natural and mined not too far from here. It comes out of the ground that color."

In the distance, a dog barked. "Trixie?" I called.

"Who lives here?" John asked.

"It's like any other place. A mishmash of artists, dog and cat breeders, accountants, veterinarians, people who own or work in Wagtail stores and restaurants."

No sign of Trixie yet. "Trixie? Gingersnap?"

"Are the houses expensive?"

"I've never asked. But they don't come up for sale often." I pointed. "There's Alley Cat up ahead."

"I get it. It's located on a narrow little alley?"

The dog barked again. This time I knew it was Trixie. Unfortunately, I also knew the tone of that bark. My heart sank. "Yeah. Something's wrong with Trixie." I picked up my pace.

"Is that her barking?"

I broke into a full-fledged run. I had heard that bark a few times before. There was a frantic warning edge to it. Completely different from her cheerful bark when she wanted a treat or food was being served.

John and Cooper kept up with Huey and me.

"Trixie?"

Gingersnap ran toward us.

"Where's Trixie?"

Gingersnap turned around and raced along the alley for a bit before plunging off the path into the darkness.

We followed as fast we could. John and I raised our lanterns to see better when we left the alley. We were still on a path, narrower and less trodden, though, with no lights at all. Ankle-high grass lined the sides, showing what the trail would have looked like if dogs and people didn't use it with some regularity. It wound back toward the river, taking us away from the Alley Cat.

I could hear Trixie barking in her agitated pitch, and I feared I knew what that meant. At last my lantern shone on her white and black fur.

And on the man sprawled facedown in the grass.

SIX

I stopped so fast that John ran into me from behind.

"Oof. Sorry! Is Trixie okay?" he asked, moving to my side.

"She's fine, but I don't think *he* is."

I heard John's sharp intake of breath.

Trixie quit barking and nosed around the man on the ground.

He wore a short-sleeved pale blue golf shirt with pressed trousers and city-slicker leather shoes. The short sleeves revealed pale, flaccid arms. This fellow did not work out.

Without a word, John and I fell to our knees and turned him over. All four dogs sniffed him.

"Hey, buddy! Are you okay? Can you hear me?" asked John.

I started to reach for the guy's neck to see if I could get a pulse when John moved his lantern closer to the man's head.

I sucked in a noisy breath of air when I recognized the closely cropped beard and curly hair of the impertinent man who had spoken to Oma and me on the plaza. But there was something different about him. I peered closer.

"Look at that bruise on his face. Somebody slugged him!" John blurted.

There was no doubt about it. He was the man who had ridiculed people who love dogs and cats. His left cheek bore a whopper of a blue and red bruise.

"Do you know him?" asked John.

"Not really. Oma and I were talking to him earlier today."

"Do you think he's dead or unconscious? What's his name?" John pulled out his cell phone and punched in numbers. "I'm calling nine-one-one."

"I have no idea."

I moved the collar of his shirt aside, trying to find a pulse.

"Look at his throat!" John rasped. His hand trembled and the lantern cast a wavering light.

A red welt encircled the man's neck. Shivers shuttled down my arms, and I whispered the obvious. "Looks like he's been strangled."

The light caught on something in the grass. I moved my lantern over to see it better. The man's rimless glasses lay there broken, like they'd been stepped on.

"Why can't I get a signal?"

I handed him my phone. "It's the mountains. We might be in a dead zone."

He took my phone and tried it. "I hope that wasn't meant as a pun."

I wasn't paying attention because I was desperately trying to find a pulse on his neck and wrist. "Do you think we should do CPR?"

"Still no signal. I hope the Alley Cat has a landline. I'll start CPR if you call nine-one-one from the bar," John offered.

"Deal." I took Huey and a lantern and jogged toward the bar. It was farther than I had thought. Even though I could see the lights of the Alley Cat, I stopped to catch my breath and try my cell phone one more time. Still no reception. I resumed my lurching run with Huey.

The warm glow from the arched windows of the Alley Cat was welcoming. Gasping for breath, I burst through the huge double doors. The place was packed. People sang rowdy drinking songs at the bar. A crowd of people, dogs, and cats engulfed us.

Huey and I struggled through them to the bar. "Do you have a landline I can use to call nine-one-one?"

The bartender eyed me. "Nine-one-one? You got a problem?"

"There's a guy outside near the river. It doesn't look good."

"He's probably just drunk. I'll get Sam, the owner."

I jumped up and reached across the bar, grabbing his sleeve.

"Hey! What's wrong with you?" The bartender smacked my hand.

"He's not drunk. Listen to me carefully. He might be dead." I let go of him and nearly fell as I scrambled to find my footing on the floor.

He stared at me for a moment. "Yeah, right. I suppose you just stumbled across him?"

"My dog found him."

"That dog?"

"No. My Jack Russell. Why are you questioning me? This is an emergency."

The bartender's eyes narrowed. "What's your dog's name?"

"Trixie. What does that have to do with anything?"

He brought me a telephone. "You're Holly Miller?"

I dialed 911. "Yes."

"Why didn't you just say so? Everybody knows about Trixie."

Oh, swell.

The dispatcher answered. I gave her a detailed explanation of where the man was and his condition as far as I could ascertain. Then I hustled outside to wait on the footpath.

Sadly, thanks to Trixie's nose for trouble, I knew how it worked. The phone call went to a dispatcher over on Snowball Mountain, who would radio or call Wagtail's own resident cop, Dave Quinlan—affectionately known as Officer Dave—who was undoubtedly maintaining order in Wagtail at the moment.

Dave had been a sailor in the navy. He was sharp and diligent, and living in Wagtail gave him a leg up on investigations because he knew most of the full-time residents. I heard his feet pounding along the path before I saw the beam of his flashlight jerking up and down as he ran.

I showed him the footpath that turned off toward the river, and he raced ahead of me. By the time I caught up, totally winded, Dave was radioing for an ambulance.

"Holly, would you call Trixie and Gingersnap?" he asked.

I whistled to them and stepped back a bit so we wouldn't be in the way.

Dave swapped places with John and continued CPR. His radio squawked.

As usual, I didn't understand a word.

But Dave looked up at me and said, "Can you go to the river and flag them down? They're sending the team that was stationed at the lake."

John went with me, which I thought very courteous of him. The river was only yards away.

"Is this some kind of lover's meeting place?" John asked, looking around.

Under the light of the moon, I had to admit that it was romantic. The calm river reflected the moonlight. An owl hooted nearby. I could make out the bright orange clusters of blooming butterfly weed, and the purple blossoms of horse nettle. A large rock, no doubt worn flat over thousands of years, offered a perfect picnic spot for two.

The rescue squad arrived in no time. We led the way to Dave and the man.

Dave appeared relieved to hand over the job of CPR to them. He was breathing heavily when he asked if I knew the guy.

One of the rescue team members handed Dave a sheet of paper. "I can't find a wallet, but this was tucked in his pocket."

Dave unfolded it with me looking on.

"Oh no," he groaned. "He's a friend of your grandmother's. Do you recognize him?"

"No way. He's *not* a friend of Oma's." I lowered my voice. "He was quite obnoxious to the two of us earlier today."

"So you do know him?"

"No. We had an impromptu conversation on the plaza. He was a stranger. I would be surprised if Oma knew him because she was outraged by what he said to us. If she knew him, I think she would have let him have it."

Dave's eyebrows took a quick dive.

Why had I said that? I certainly didn't want him thinking Oma would have hurt the man. "Verbally, of course. It wasn't a big deal. I didn't mean to imply that. He was just a pill."

Dave held out the letter so I could see it. I raised my lantern. It was written by Oma, all right, to one Gustav Vogel! "I can't believe this. He had a reservation at the inn, but he didn't show up. We were waiting for him, but he never checked in."

Dave groaned. "You're not making sense. You

were expecting him, and you talked to him. So you did know him."

"No, we didn't. I'm sure Oma didn't know who he was. We were expecting a Gustav Vogel because he had a reservation, but we didn't know *this* guy was Gustav Vogel."

I looked at the letter more closely. It was personal, not businesslike. "Aha! Oma didn't know him after all. And this proves it." I pointed at the letter. "It says, 'I look forward to meeting you.'"

"She knew him well enough to invite him to stay at the inn," Dave pointed out.

"But not well enough to know him when she saw him today," I insisted.

"Hey, Dave." One of the rescue squad members approached us. "I've called for the medical examiner."

"Does that mean he's dead?" John asked.

"Only the medical examiner can determine that," said Dave.

That might have been the appropriate official response, but I knew better. "John, they call the medical examiner to declare someone dead. If he were alive, they would be loading him up to take him to the hospital."

"Did you two see anyone out here?" asked Dave.

John shook his head. "Trixie found the guy. We didn't run into anyone. It was silent and peaceful. We didn't even pass anyone on our way into the Shire."

Dave pulled John aside. I could hear him asking John's name, address, and what had brought him to Wagtail.

When he finished, Dave said, "Holly, you and John get the dogs out of here. I'll be in touch."

Gingersnap came immediately when called, but Trixie seemed reluctant to leave. Only the sound of the other dogs munching on treats tore her away.

"Still want that drink?" John asked. "Or would you rather call it a night?"

"If you don't mind, I think I had better break the news to Oma. Dave will probably be paying her a visit as soon as he's done here."

"Of course. I understand entirely."

We headed back somberly.

"Are you all right?" I asked John.

"I'm okay. A little shaken. I've never discovered a dead person before. Even when you don't know the person, it's pretty unnerving. That guy probably came here hoping to find a relationship and never dreamed this would be his last day. He was probably planning for his future." John gazed at me in alarm. "Do you think his dog is lost? What if there's a cat waiting for him somewhere?"

"I don't think we have to worry about that. Given what he said to Oma and me on the plaza this afternoon, he doesn't have a cat or a dog."

John lowered his voice. "And making matters worse, he was murdered. I'll never forget what his throat looked like."

"That was fairly obvious. I didn't see a rope or anything lying around, did you?"

"No. But I was in such a fog that I wasn't concentrating on that. Besides, we might not have noticed it in the dark. It could have been just a few feet away, and we wouldn't have seen it."

"Dave will probably get some guys out there with lights." I looked up at the moon. "I guess they'll rope it off and check it again in daylight, too."

We paused at the road between the Shire and Wagtail to return our lanterns. Crickets chirped in the night. Not a car or golf cart rumbled along the road. We crossed into historic Wagtail.

John sighed. "As cool as the Shire is, I have to say that I'm relieved to be back in the land of streetlights. I never realized how important and comforting they are."

"Where are you staying?"

"I rented a house in Wagtail a few weeks ago because I've been working on a book and this seemed like a nice quiet place to concentrate."

"Fiction or nonfiction?"

"A historical thriller."

"That sounds interesting."

"If only it would pay the bills. I used to be a history professor. These days, I write and edit history textbooks. It's okay but a little boring."

"I don't recall seeing you around," I said.

"I haven't gotten out much. Not knowing anyone has actually been a big plus. I stay home and work most of the time. Sometimes Cooper and I hit the hiking trails for walks. But when I heard about Animal Attraction, I liked the idea of letting Cooper introduce me to someone. Dogs are supposed to be great judges of character."

"I would be flattered by that, but I find a lot of dogs like me because I usually carry treats in my pocket."

"You see? Only a person with a good heart would do that. But my olfactory skills aren't sufficiently advanced to detect dog treats in a person's pocket, so I have to rely on Cooper."

For the first time since we had discovered Gustav's body, I smiled.

"This might be out of line, and I hope you'll say so if it is, but would you mind if I went with you?" asked John.

"To tell Oma?"

"Yeah. It's not very macho of me, but right now I'd rather not be alone."

"No problem. I know exactly how you feel. Sitting alone someplace is the last thing I would want to do at this moment. Come on, there's always plenty of company at the inn."

We walked along the sidewalk that ran the length of the green in the middle of town. Business from the cafés and restaurants spilled onto the sidewalk. Despite the late hour, even some of the bakeries had stayed open. It looked like they were selling coffee and pastries to go.

Oma and Rose's idea appeared to have turned into a business boom for Wagtail.

The porch of the inn buzzed with activity as well. We breezed past the couples getting to know each other, but Nessie saw us enter the inn and made a beeline for me.

"Holly! Holly!" Nessie bustled toward me with Lulu at her heels. "Have you seen Sky? I can't find her anywhere."

SEVEN

I was slightly amused that the woman who hadn't wanted to room with Sky was now looking for her as though they were good friends. I introduced John to Nessie. "I'm sorry, but we haven't seen Sky."

"Honestly! Where did she get off to? My daughter has spent the evening with some guy. He's too good-looking, if you ask me. You know what they say about a book and its cover. I once married a guy pretty enough to be on the cover of a romance novel, but the inside was a horror story."

She eyed me. "Maybe you two could go sit near them and tell me what's going on since Sky isn't available?"

"I wish I could help," I fibbed. I really did *not* want to spy on her daughter. "But I'm busy at the moment. We're looking for Oma. There's something important we have to tell her."

Nessie's eyebrows jumped. "An engagement?" She looked from me to John and back to me. "You sure make a pretty couple, but . . . already? You must have known each other before."

Before I could protest, John winked at me.

"Nope. Cooper introduced us." John pointed at his dog.

"You're kidding me." She gazed down at Lulu. "Can you find Mommy a nice man, sugar?"

Just to be sure she understood, I said, "There's no engagement, but Cooper and Trixie like each other."

Gingersnap and Trixie had sniffed their way to the pet hatch located in the door that led to Oma's private kitchen. I had a sneaking suspicion that I knew where Oma was.

Excusing ourselves, we hustled away.

"Her poor daughter," John whispered. "My mom set me up with a date once, but she never spied on me."

"Did the date work out?"

"We went out for about six months before I had the guts to break up with her."

I swung open the door to the large room that Oma had reserved for family use. "So it wasn't just one dinner. Your mom did pretty well."

He wrinkled his nose. "She was nice enough. But ultimately, I knew she wasn't the right person for me."

I could relate. "Sounds like Ben and me."

Not a soul was in the kitchen. But I spied a corkscrew on the turquoise island. "I bet Oma is outside. It's a beautiful night."

I opened the back door. Oma and Macon sat at a table on the private patio overlooking Dogwood Lake. Lights on boats bobbed in the distance and the sounds of laugher drifted to us. The scents of basil and rosemary wafted from Oma's herb garden. Candles flickered on the table near a wine bottle and two glasses.

I hadn't expected Macon to be with Oma and wondered if I should mention Gustav in front of him. He would hear about it sooner or later, though, so maybe it was just as well that he was present.

I introduced John to Oma and Macon.

"Weren't you two matched up through Live Love Bark?" Macon raised an eyebrow and grinned. "I thought that didn't work out."

"You were matched by Macon? *Ja?*" Oma's voice brimmed with joy.

"Don't get excited. Trixie likes John's dog, Cooper," I said as we joined them at the table.

"Gee, thanks. What about me?" John teased. "All things considered, I think we've been getting along pretty well."

I guessed we had been. Not many people got to know each other by finding a corpse. "Oma, I'm afraid I have bad news. Gustav Vogel has been found."

"Found? What do you mean *found?* Did he have a car accident?" asked Oma.

"He was murdered!" John exclaimed. "It was awful."

"Who is Gustav Vogel?" asked Macon. "A friend of yours?"

I glanced at Oma, who appeared to be stunned

by the news. "He had a reservation but never showed up."

My Oma was a strong woman. She had run the inn by herself for decades. But the news about Gustav clearly shocked her. She sank back in her chair like she had been deflated.

I reached for her hand and clutched it. "I'm sorry."

She shook her head. "No, it cannot be. This is terrible. What happened?"

"Strangled." John uttered the single word and shuddered. "I've never found a dead body before. It's—"

"Unnerving?" Macon suggested.

"*Unnerving* doesn't begin to cover it," John said. "Unnerving times one thousand. I don't know how the police and the paramedics do it. They must have nerves like steel. I didn't even know the guy, but to be honest with you, I'm rattled to my core."

"You *found* him?" asked Macon in a high pitch.

"Trixie did," I said. At the mention of her name, she and Gingersnap came running and sat properly, looking at me expectantly. I fed an itsy-bitsy treat to each of the dogs.

Oma clasped a hand to her cheek. "I am shocked. You called Dave, *ja*?"

"Yes, of course." I excused myself and fetched two wineglasses and another bottle of wine. Back at the table, I said, "Oma, do you remember the man on the plaza today? The one who said dogs can't love people because they have brains the size of walnuts, and that cat owners are neurotic?"

"Ugh. That man. I wish I could forget him."

"Oma, that was Gustav Vogel." I handed John a glass of wine.

She frowned at me. "No. That is impossible."

"I'm afraid so."

Macon sputtered, "Well, no wonder somebody killed him. What kind of idiot goes around sayin' stuff like that? Do they have a suspect yet?"

As Macon spoke, it dawned on me that Gustav had called Macon *an old fraud.* "Did you know him, Macon?"

"I seriously doubt it. I believe I'd have remembered someone with such a distinctive name. Not to mention someone with ridiculous notions about dogs and cats."

If Macon did a lot of matchmaking for large groups, it was certainly possible that the singles who expected to be matched would remember Macon, but he might not remember all of them. Could Macon have made a poor match for Gustav that prompted his remark?

It would be rude to come right out and say *he thought you were a fraud,* so I chose my words carefully. "He seemed to know you."

"Really? How very flatterin'. People all over the world have heard of me."

While I suspected that was a vast exaggeration,

there probably was some truth to what he said.

Oma gripped the edge of the table and rose to her feet. "I hope you will excuse me."

She walked slowly to the door and entered the kitchen with Gingersnap on her heels while Macon said, "Of course, darlin'."

"Excuse me. I'll be right back." I handed Huey's leash to John and followed Oma.

Closing the door behind me, I called out, "Oma?"

She paused and looked back at me.

"There's something else you should know. Maybe you should sit down?"

"Ach. It cannot be any worse." But she perched on the edge of one of the chairs before the fireplace.

"Gustav had a letter from you in his pocket."

She took that news very well. "This is not surprising. It probably contained directions to the inn."

"Oma, did you know Gustav?"

She took a deep breath. "No. I never met him."

"Except today on the plaza, when we spoke to him," I corrected.

"But I did not know that was Gustav at the time."

"Dave will probably be here tonight to ask you if you knew him."

"I will be in my apartment." Oma rose and walked slowly again, as though the bad news had sapped her strength.

Gingersnap sprang to her feet and walked beside her, anxiously looking up at Oma.

It wasn't like Oma at all. I was sorry Gustav had died, too. And it was horrifying that someone had strangled him. But the news had drained Oma's spirit. I watched her go, wondering if she was telling me the truth.

She stopped at the doorway, turned back to me, and said, "Something is not right."

EIGHT

"Do you know something about Gustav's murder?" I asked Oma.

She paused before answering me, which concerned me even more. Was she searching for a plausible response? "I know nothing about it. But this is very, very wrong. I go to my room for a rest now."

Gingersnap accompanied Oma when she left the kitchen.

I had been dismissed. It was late, so not particularly surprising that she would be tired. Still, I was itching to know what she was talking about. Something was very wrong *every* time a person was murdered. I feared Oma knew more and hoped that Dave would be able to coax it out of her.

Reluctantly, I let her be. Oma was very special to me. She had been a source of security for me when my parents divorced. Every summer they had shipped me to Oma in Wagtail. Along with my cousin, and Holmes Richardson, the son of Oma's best friend, I had worked at the inn. None of us realized it then, but we had learned the business from the ground up. Still, Oma always made sure there was plenty of playtime for us, too. We had hiked and played *Star Wars* in the woods, gone swimming and boating, and Oma had carved out special time to spend with each of us.

People kept telling me how much alike we were. That was probably true. In any event, I knew better than to pester her. She would tell me when she was good and ready.

One of the marvelous things about Oma's private kitchen was the refrigerator. Holmes called it magical because it always contained fabulous food and was never empty. A good portion of the inn's daily leftovers landed in that fridge. The rest were delivered to the less fortunate who lived around Wagtail.

I hit the magical fridge now to scrounge up a snack for our guests. Leftovers from the popular cheese and fruit lunch option had already been nicely arranged on a large platter. Grapes, raspberries, local blackberries, and strawberries surrounded a creamy herbed goat cheese from a farm near Wagtail, a smooth orange Gouda, and a pepper-encrusted Brie. I located a crusty loaf of bread and sliced it on a diagonal. It was perfect for the cheese.

The dogs probably needed a little munch, too. The inn's chef cooked specialties daily for dogs and cats. I skipped the full dinners in the fridge because they had already eaten, but found apple barkscotti—twice-baked biscuits that would be good for their teeth.

I loaded everything on the tray and carried it out

to the table, where Macon and John were engaged in conversation.

"Dogs, with their superior olfactory skills, are far better at this than we are." Macon eyed the platter. "Oh, a nosh! Just the ticket."

"Dogs are better at finding bodies?" I asked.

"Um, probably. I imagine they're better at that, too." Macon popped a grape into his mouth and slathered a piece of bread with soft goat cheese.

John leaned over and sniffed me.

I drew back. "I'm not dead yet!"

Macon laughed. "Darlin', we were talkin' about finding a mate."

John inserted a blackberry in his mouth and chewed it. "Macon says we're attracted to people who smell like our parents."

"That's silly!" I shook my head and helped myself to the Brie.

"So if I want to attract Holly, I should find out what kind of cologne her dad wears?"

"That might help." Macon winked at me.

"That's ridiculous. If that were the case, cologne manufacturers would tout it," I joked.

"It's not junk science, sweetheart. Scientists have studied love. It's very mysterious, but there are some things we know about it." Macon held out his glass for more wine. "Romantic attraction, and by that I mean the kind of love one has in a long-lasting marriage, is complex, of course, but, Cinderella stories aside, we know that most people are interested in mates from their same social group and intellectual level. I believe it's because we're more comfortable when we can relate to our mates. Thousands of years ago, we probably had better olfactory skills than we do today. People who smelled like us and our families were favored as mates because they seemed more familiar."

"So that's what happens with the dogs? You mean like Trixie and Cooper?" asked John.

"Well, there's an interesting example. All three of those dogs are getting along very nicely. But do you notice how Trixie and Cooper are lying close together, and Huey is off to the side? He likes them just fine, but he doesn't have a bonding attraction to them."

"Isn't that just pack behavior?" I asked.

"The pack behavior is the gettin' along. But it's clear that Cooper and Trixie like each other more than they like Huey."

"So Trixie's father wore the same cologne as Cooper?" I jested.

Macon guffawed. "You're not too far off. Cooper might smell like Trixie's daddy or a dog that Trixie knew and liked, so she is especially accepting of him."

Hmm. Gustav might have been a jerk, but maybe this was what he meant when he said Macon was a fraud. I could accept that there were subtleties that we might not realize about attraction, but I could also understand why some people would poo-poo the theories.

Macon cut a wedge of Gouda. "Here's another little fact that surprises a lot of my clients. You have four minutes to make a good impression. Maybe not even that long. Most people take ninety seconds to four minutes to determine whether a person is mating material for them."

"No! Really?" John looked at me. "That means it's love at first sight. I thought that was a myth."

Macon grinned. "Yep. It really happens that fast. You wouldn't think so. You'd think people would want to know more about the other person first, but that's how quickly we size up potential mates. You've heard of those speed-dating sessions where everyone moves around and meets potential partners for only a few minutes? They might seem like nonsense, but they work because that's all it takes for us to size somebody up."

"So we base it solely on appearance, then?" I asked.

"Now, don't go mixing up romance with sex," Macon said.

"Don't they go together?" John laughed.

"They do. But sex drive is totally different from romantic love. Sex drive is casual, but romantic love is for keeps. In those first minutes, you don't even realize that all your senses and your brain are judging the person. Appearance is part of it, but there's much more than that. All sorts of interesting things are happenin' in our brains when we meet someone for the first time." Macon drained his wineglass. "I have an early morning with the cat people, so on that note, I bid you a very good night."

Macon waddled into the inn, leaving John and me with the dogs.

"He's an interesting guy." John plucked another blackberry from the platter. "When I got up this morning, I never imagined I'd find a dead body or end the night talking about how people fall in love. What a bizarre day this has been."

"For me, too. Maybe we should call it a night?"

John left for his rental house with Cooper, and I spent a few minutes cleaning up the kitchen and making sure the inn doors were locked.

I took Trixie and Huey outside for their last bathroom break of the night. This was usually a quiet time in Wagtail, but tonight I heard people talking and laughing out on the green. I waited for the dogs in the dark, looking up at the stars.

Trixie let out a little *mmmff.* Not a real bark, more of an alert. I wasn't surprised. In the light of the moon, I could make out quite a few silhouettes of people on their way somewhere.

On our return to the inn, our night clerk, Casey—who always reminded me of a young Harry Potter with his round glasses and dark hair—was at his station by the front door. I said good night and headed up the stairs, wondering, for the first time in hours, what had happened to Ben.

When Oma had renovated the inn recently, she'd carved an apartment out of the attic with me in mind. Except for a huge storage room, nothing else was on the third floor of the inn. My luxurious penthouse spanned the width of the main building. My bedroom overlooked Wagtail, the green, the roofs of houses, and the mountains beyond. On the other side, my living room had a large deck with a view of Dogwood Lake.

When I walked in, the French doors to the deck were open, letting in the balmy night air. One of the curtains twitched a little at the bottom. I called out, "Where could Twinkletoes be?" The curtain wiggled again. I intentionally walked by it, pretending I didn't know she was there. Twinkletoes dodged out, hooked my ankle for a second, and then dashed away. I couldn't help laughing. She jumped on the back of a big easy chair. I scooped her up into my arms. "What's going on? I've hardly seen you today."

She purred a response. I held her for a moment longer than I should have, soaking in the soothing calmness of her purrs. She finally squirmed, and when I released her, she ran to my tiny kitchen. Aha. What had Gustav said? They loved the food we gave them, not us. I didn't believe it for a minute.

I took a second to let Huey off his leash. "You must be tired of being on a leash all day. At least you can run around the apartment without it." I hurried over to the hidden pet door in the dining room and made sure it was closed. I didn't want them all sneaking away while I slept.

But when I returned to the kitchen to feed Twinkletoes, I found her waiting with a companion. A large orange and white tabby gazed up at me. "Who's your friend?"

Twinkletoes rubbed against my ankles. I bent to see the name on the tabby's collar. "Aha. The elusive Marmalade. That's a long name. Do they call you Marma?" He pushed his head against my hand when I stroked him.

I checked the fridge for cat food. "Hmm, chicken. That doesn't seem special enough for a date. How about duck? Very romantic," I assured them.

They must have approved because they wound around my legs so vigorously that I could hardly take a step. I lowered the food to the floor in two bowls and watched them chow down. When they licked their lips and walked away, I snatched up the almost-empty dishes before Trixie and Huey could clean them for me.

Twinkletoes and Marmalade settled on the hearth of the fireplace to wash their faces.

Meanwhile, I sneaked over to the guest room and peeked inside. I didn't knock, just in case Ben was asleep. But he wasn't there. His duffel bag lay on the floor and literature about Animal Attraction was scattered on the bed.

It worried me a bit that he hadn't come back. Socializing with strangers didn't come naturally to him, so it seemed odd to me that he would still be out. Could it be that he had signed up for Live Love Bark, and Macon had accidentally matched him to the right girl? I hoped that could be the case and decided not to phone him. I knew he wasn't right for me, but Ben was a decent guy at heart and deserved someone who would make him happy.

When I returned to the living room, Twinkletoes and Marmalade had curled together for a nap. It was after midnight, too late to call Laura. I might wake her. On the other hand, she might not be able to sleep for worrying about Marmalade. I hoped her phone wasn't set to make loud noises when texts came in. I texted, **Marmalade is in my apartment and fine. Let me know if you want me to bring him down to your room. He's welcome to spend the night here. Holly Miller**

That done, I showered, wishing I could wash away what had happened to Gustav. I slid into an oversized nightshirt. Even though I was weary from the events of the day, I couldn't get Gustav out of my mind, and paced through the rooms.

What a terrible death. Why had he gone out there near the river in the first place? And who would have wanted to strangle him? All I really knew about him was that he was opinionated and didn't know when to keep his tongue. I wondered if that had led to his demise.

Ben didn't return before I hit the sack. The two cats migrated to my bed, as did Trixie. But Huey stayed in the living room. I wondered if he was waiting for Ben.

I woke to loud whispering.

When I opened my eyes, two shadowy figures were in my bedroom.

NINE

I tried to scream, but nothing came out. In horror, I rolled off the bed, away from them, and fell to the floor. I jumped up.

They were between me and the door!

They screamed at the same time I finally screamed.

I flicked on the light next to the bed. Nessie and Sky stood in my bedroom.

"I told you that wasn't her snoring in the other room," Sky declared.

Nessie held up a green T-shirt with holes in it that looked like someone had tried to shred it. "Who have you been sleeping with, honey? Looks like some wild times to me."

I blinked, still trying to figure out what was going on. How did they get in? "Huh? That must be Ben's."

"My, my. He must be a wildcat!"

I wanted to shout, *What are you doing in here?* I glanced at the clock. It was three in the morning. I managed to choke out, "Is there something I can do for you?"

Nessie spat out, "Lulu and Duchess have been stolen!"

I could hardly think straight. "Who is Duchess?" I slid on my lush white Sugar Maple Inn bathrobe.

"A WAG dog." Sky brushed a wild cloud of hair from her face. "I'm in the If the Dog Fits program."

She seemed completely earnest, but I knew that had to be a lie. She hadn't made reservations, and she had checked in at nine o'clock without a dog. WAG would have been closed. Not to mention that the shelter would have notified me.

I blinked at her. "You didn't arrive until nine. WAG wouldn't have been open."

"I met the lady who runs the program last night, and she said she had just the dog for me, so we went and got Duchess. But now she's gone!"

Nessie seemed impatient. "I'm certain they were after Lulu. She's a retired champion. I bet somebody recognized her and knew he could get a lot of money for her. I called the police and they're on the way."

They followed me into the living room.

Putting aside the issue of the mystery dog, Duchess, I asked, "When did you see them last?"

"When we went to bed," said Sky.

"Lulu always sleeps with me." Nessie's fists were tight as knots.

Only then did it dawn on me that Trixie hadn't barked at them. I turned and looked around my apartment.

"What are you doing? Aren't you the least bit concerned about a thief in your inn?"

"Yes. Yes, of course I am. Would you excuse me

91

for just a moment?" I hurried back to my bedroom. No Trixie, no Twinkletoes, no Marmalade. I peeked in Ben's room. He snored, dead to the world despite the screaming, but Huey was nowhere to be seen.

I rushed back to Nessie. "None of my animals are here either."

Nessie pressed her palms on the sides of her face in horror. "It's worse than I thought. It must be a crook from a laboratory who wants them for testing. Ohhh, my poor Lulu!"

"How did you get into my apartment?" I closed the door and accompanied the two women down the stairs to the main lobby.

"Your door was open." Nessie said it without an iota of shame. "Your grandmother told us you live upstairs."

No one sat at the desk where Casey should have been. He'd been known to relax in the Dogwood Room before. Nessie followed me there, fretting aloud.

No sign of Casey.

But I heard something. Something that sounded like a yip.

"They're in a room being held hostage!" Nessie's eyes were wide.

"I don't think so." I passed the grand staircase and headed for Oma's private kitchen.

We surprised Casey when I opened the door. A book was open on the kitchen table, and he was eating leftover chicken salad.

"What are you doing up?" he asked innocently.

"We're missing dogs and cats. Have you seen any?"

Nessie couldn't contain herself. "They've been stolen for nefarious purposes. Did you see anyone dragging them out? I know my Lulu would never have gone willingly."

"Haven't noticed a thing. We had a lot of guests come in late, but it's been a quiet night. Hey, Holly? Marmalade's mom came in with Ben and went up to your apartment to get Marmalade. She said Trixie growled at Ben, so they decided to leave Marmalade there for the night."

"Thanks, Casey." I must have been sound asleep when Ben returned. The yip sounded again. I let the door swing shut. Following my instincts, I checked the inn's commercial kitchen, the only room where dogs and cats were not permitted in a nod to the health code.

It was silent and empty. But the next yip was closer.

"It came from there." Sky pointed at a door that was slightly open.

Oh no! The inn stocked an assortment of commercial cat and dog foods. Many of our guests preferred to feed their pets the same things they ate at home instead of the inn's gourmet food. As a courtesy, we asked their preferences when they made reservations so we could be sure we had their favorite brands on hand.

I strode to the pantry where we kept the commercial pet food and flung the door open wider.

If the dogs had worn hats, it would have looked like a wild party. Bags of kibble had been torn open and the yummy contents had spilled onto the floor, where Gingersnap, Trixie, Huey, Lulu, and an unfamiliar white dog, presumably Duchess, munched to their hearts' content.

As I stood there watching them, something pelted the top of my head. I looked up in time to step aside and avoid a shower of dry cat food that rained from above, where Twinkletoes and Marmalade sat on a high shelf, clawing open bags of kitty kibble.

"Lulu!" Nessie shrieked. She swooped down to grab the little dog, who made a panicked run for it. Her claws clicked on the floor as she scampered out the door and away from Nessie.

"I'm holding you responsible if she gets sick. She's on a very special diet. She's never eaten a morsel of grain in her whole life!" Nessie left to chase Lulu.

I focused on the other dogs. Gingersnap and Trixie had the decency to be embarrassed. Probably not for what they had done, but for being caught at it.

"Out!" I said it in my best scolding voice and pointed at the door. Gingersnap and Trixie pinned their ears back and hustled out of the pantry.

Huey and the other dog, presumably Duchess, continued eating like they'd never seen food. I should have been angry, but I felt sorry for them. I didn't know their histories, but maybe they had been hungry, like my Trixie, who had had to dig through trash for food to survive before she met me.

Twinkletoes and her friend grew bored once they ate their fill. They jumped down and paraded by me without so much as a whisker of regret. Their tails high, they stalked out of the pantry with feline confidence.

Sky called her dog, but if Duchess recognized her name, she gave no indication of it. She was a beauty. Her long white and tan fur gleamed. She reminded me of a border collie in size and shape. She gazed up at us and tentatively wagged her tail. The fur on it waved gracefully.

"Come here, sweetie. Are you Duchess?" I squatted to her level.

She approached me cautiously, carrying her head low.

I felt her neck for a collar. It matched Huey's WAG collar. "You must have been hungry!"

She wagged again and licked my face.

"Okay, you two. Hop on out so I can clean up." I nabbed them by their collars and escorted them out of the pantry.

A knock at the front door drew my attention. The entire pack raced there as though they anticipated excitement.

I unlocked the door and Dave stepped inside, looking exhausted. "A Nessie Jamieson called to report a stolen dog?"

"We found her," I said. "I'm sorry she got you out of bed. Nessie's a little high-strung."

Dave squatted to pet the dogs, who shamelessly kissed him with such gusto that Dave fell over backward. Laughing, he sat on the floor, petting all of them.

Twinkletoes and Marmalade watched from the grand staircase, their tails twitching.

"What's with all these dogs?"

I told him about the mismatch between Huey and Ben. "I think they're going to be the first couple to flunk out of If the Dog Fits. And apparently this pretty girl is also in the If the Dog Fits program. They executed a midnight raid on the dog-food pantry."

Dave scrambled to his feet. Speaking sternly and shaking his forefinger at them, he said, "I'm letting you off with a warning this time, but such behavior will not be tolerated in the future."

Huey sat very properly, didn't take his eyes off Dave, and offered his right paw.

"Okay, all is forgiven, pal." Dave shook his paw, dug treats for everyone out of his pocket, and rubbed Huey's head. "But I'm not forgiving that woman who called nine-one-one and woke me for this!"

Sky flushed red. "I'm so sorry. That was my roommate. It won't happen again."

When Dave left, I locked the door behind him.

Sky escorted Duchess upstairs, with Huey trailing along behind them.

I swept the floor of the pantry and put away the remaining kibble.

When I closed the door, I made very sure the latch caught properly. Gingersnap and Trixie lay just outside the door as though they were waiting for me. Huey had returned and waited by the stairs. "Everybody up to bed."

They raced up the stairs ahead of me. I picked up Twinkletoes and Marmalade and carried them, huffing and puffing. On the second floor, I made a brief detour to Oma's quarters to be sure her door was closed. Just as I expected, it stood ajar.

I set the cats down and tiptoed inside to check that she was all right. Even though the room was dark, I could make out the sound of soft snoring. I left Gingersnap inside and locked the door behind me.

I picked up the cats again and carried them. Halfway to the third floor, I wished I had taken the elevator. It felt like each of the cats gained a pound with every step I took. When everyone was safely in my quarters, I locked the door and double-checked the hidden dog door in my dining room. It was still closed.

Now I was seriously miffed with Ben. I could only imagine that he hadn't shut the door properly when he'd returned. But that didn't explain how

Lulu, Duchess, or Gingersnap had managed to join in the fun.

Glad that everyone was safe, I went back to bed but slept lightly, jerking awake at every tiny sound.

I gave up on sleeping when the sun rose, and I opened the French doors to my balcony. The chill in the early morning air didn't stop me from taking in the view.

Below me, early risers jogged with their dogs. A few walked cats, or sat on benches enjoying coffee.

Only the bakeries, coffee shops, and a couple of cafés were open at this hour. In the distance, the sun caught the mountains, bringing the lush greens of the trees to life.

Trixie turned her head, and with the tiniest, joyous yap, she ran through the apartment. I knew what that was about. Mr. Huckle delivered tea or coffee and prebreakfast treats five mornings a week.

The tiny old man stooped slightly but always looked impeccable in his formal butler's attire. After decades of service, through no fault of his own, he had lost his position as the butler of the wealthiest man in Wagtail. Oma had offered the wizened fellow a job. I couldn't imagine what might have happened to him otherwise. He was a wonderful addition to the staff. He walked dogs, brushed cats, delivered room service, filled in at the front desk, and even waited on tables when needed. Not to mention the personal favors he gladly undertook for our guests. Small wonder that they raved about him.

He set the tray down on the kitchen counter and slipped Trixie and Huey treats. "Miss Holly! You're up early. Is Mr. Ben awake as well?" He poured a cup of tea for me and added sugar and a splash of milk.

"I don't think so." I sipped the tea. "This is perfect. Thank you, Mr. Huckle."

"My pleasure, Miss Holly. I hear there was something of a raid on the pantry last night."

I shot Trixie and Huey a dirty look. "I can't imagine how they got in there. Probably a combination of lucky breaks. Doors that weren't properly closed or something."

"Is it true that there was a murder in the Shire?" He asked it with dignified casualness, as though he were inquiring about the weather.

"I'm afraid so. Are people gossiping about it already?"

"As you know, I don't gossip."

I almost spewed my tea. He was as guilty of gossip as everyone else.

"Then how do you know about it?" I asked.

"Officer Dave arrived first thing this morning to speak with your grandmother. Do we need to provide an alibi for her?"

"Mr. Huckle! It's nothing like that." At least I

hoped it wasn't. "The victim was supposed to be a guest at the inn and had a letter from Oma in his pocket. That's all. He never checked into the inn."

"That's a relief. Though I don't like having another murderous scoundrel on the loose in Wagtail. They say his wallet was stolen. I fear it could be one of the thieves from Snowball moving in on unsuspecting Wagtail tourists. We must put a stop to that immediately." He took his leave.

Feeling guilty for having it so good, I savored the creamy chocolate in the fresh-from-the-oven croissant he had brought.

I poured a second cup of tea, then showered and dressed in a navy-and-white-striped summer dress that I particularly liked because the broad stripes were on an angle that was slenderizing and becoming. The full skirt came to the top of my knees, which I liked because I often had to bend to pick up animals and things people had dropped or left behind in the inn. Short skirts were not practical in my job.

The green T-shirt lay on my bed. I picked it up to examine it more closely. One of the dogs must have dragged it out of Ben's room and played tug with it. I looked at Trixie. "Is this your way of telling Ben you don't like him? Huey, did you have anything to do with this?"

Huey cocked his head and wagged his tail. Too bad he'd been assigned to Ben. After the big middle-of-the-night feast, Huey had slept with us instead of with Ben. I sighed about it, but it didn't come as a surprise. Huey must have picked up on Ben's lack of interest in him immediately. Dogs are very perceptive about people. Fortunately, WAG didn't kill animals. He would be safe there when he went back. I made up my mind to keep an eye out for a potential new person for him.

I tossed the shirt on a chair. I would have to pick up a replacement in town.

I applied a little eye makeup, tied my medium brown hair back in a sleek ponytail, added dangling earrings, and slid my feet into white sandals. "Everyone ready to go?" I asked.

I carried the leash in my hand, wondering if I dared let Huey run loose with Trixie. Would he come if I called?

I opened the pet door and told the cats, "I think you had better eat downstairs this morning. Marmalade's mom will be looking for him."

They didn't seem upset by that and left with the rest of us, gladly springing down the stairs with the dogs.

The dining area was already packed. Hard as it was to walk by the smell of coffee and sizzling bacon, I accompanied the dogs outside.

Gingersnap already lay on the front porch, her favorite location. I suspected Gingersnap thought she would receive the most attention from guests there. But with no one around at the moment, she gladly accompanied us to the doggy toilet area around the side of the inn.

Two men in Indiana Jones–style fedoras waited for their dogs to do their business. As we neared, I recognized the dogs as Lulu and Duchess.

One of the men stood with his back to me but waved his hand around as he talked. Large diamond rings caught the sun's rays.

I cracked up laughing. It was Sky and Nessie, wearing jeans, men's shirts, and fedoras.

"Oh, look, Lulu," cried Nessie. "Here come the friends who got you into so much trouble last night."

Lulu and Duchess greeted the other dogs with great excitement.

"Think they're planning another escapade?" Sky watched them with suspicion.

"Don't even suggest it!" Nessie held up her palm in protest. "No more sleepless nights. I have enough worries about my daughter."

"Not that it's any of my business but why are you dressed this way?" I hoped I didn't sound rude.

Nessie mimicked a melody that sounded very familiar. "Dun dun, dun dun dun dun . . . 'Your mission, should you choose to accept it . . .'" Nessie and Sky laughed.

"You're too young to remember *Mission Impossible*, the TV show," said Sky. "Isn't this a stitch? We had the same idea and packed men's attire. Can you imagine, we even bought exactly the same hat online for this trip, thinking we could sneak around and spy on our daughters better."

Nessie pulled her hat down over her forehead a little more. "I think we make pretty good men. We're two moms engaged in Mission Impawsible!"

I wondered if I should mention that the dazzling rings Nessie wore might give her true identity away. Maybe not. She was having fun. It wasn't as though she was a real spy going into enemy territory.

An unfamiliar dog barreled toward us. The shaggy little dog had clearly gotten away from someone.

"Oh no!" Sky handed me Duchess's leash and ran like crazy.

TEN

Sky wasn't fast enough to outrun the determined black and gray dog. When the dog caught up to her and jumped playfully, Sky ducked behind a nearby hedge.

"Atticus! Atticus!" A young blonde woman ran toward us. "Have you seen a little dog run by?"

Nessie pointed in the wrong direction. "He was chasing a rabbit and went that way."

"Thanks!" The woman kept running.

"I'd have known Sky's daughter anywhere," whispered Nessie. "She's not as thin as her mom, but otherwise she looks just like her." She lowered her voice further and whispered, "Right down to the scruffy hair in dire need of conditioner."

Sky peeped over the hedge. "Psst. Here, hold on to Atticus and call her back."

"Honey? Maddie? We found Atticus!" called Nessie.

I grabbed Atticus and snapped the leash onto his collar. Sky crouched behind the hedge again.

Maddie returned, panting. "Thank you so much!" She swapped her leash for mine and handed it to me. "Oh, Atticus," she cooed, "you'll get lost if you run off like that. And that would make me very, very sad." She picked him up and held him close. "He's usually so well behaved. I don't know what came over him."

"I'm glad we were able to catch him." Nessie was right. Up close, the resemblance to Sky was remarkable.

Maddie stopped fussing over Atticus and studied Nessie. "Do I know you?"

Nessie held out her hand. "I don't believe so. I'm Nessie Jamieson, and this is Holly Miller."

Maddie eyed us. She maintained a pleasant expression but asked, "Then how did you know my name?"

Nessie's smile faded fast. "The tag on Atticus's collar."

"I see. Well, thanks again for catching him for me." Maddie walked away, glancing back at us a few times.

"That was close! How stupid of me to have called her by her name." Nessie sighed with relief.

Sky joined us again. "I don't think I have the nerves to be a spy. I should have realized that Atticus would give me away. I need a strong cup of coffee."

We all returned to the dining area. Nessie and Sky opted for a table outside on the patio overlooking the lake. I made a beeline to Oma, who sat at a table with Officer Dave.

I scooted into a chair without asking if I could join them, hoping Oma and Dave would be less likely to shoo me away if I simply sat down.

Oma's floral dress in happy shades of pink and yellow contrasted with her worried face.

"What's wrong?" I asked.

Oma frowned. "Dave says the egg and avocado toast is delicious."

She'd sidestepped my question, and I didn't like that at all.

Dave glanced at her. "I've been hearing about avocado toast. It's supposed to be very healthy, and it tastes better than I expected." He took a swig of coffee and started to say something else but stopped when Shelley came along with coffee for me.

A proper breakfast was one of the many luxuries of living in an inn. No more hurried yogurt or dry toast on the run. Not to mention the bliss of not having to sit in traffic for an hour to get to work.

"Avocado toast special?" asked Shelley.

"Yes. Thanks, Shelley." Trixie placed her front paws on the edge of my seat as though she didn't want me to forget her. "Is there a dog version?"

"They weren't excited about it, but dogs love it now that we swapped the avocado out for chicken livers," she said.

Trixie yelped and danced in a circle. "Sounds perfect. For Huey and Gingersnap too, please. Have you seen Twinkletoes and her friend, Marmalade?"

"Oh, sure. Twinkletoes brought him by for breakfast. I gave them Loverly Liver, which is a fancy way of saying chicken livers and chicken. Last I saw of them, they were out on the terrace lounging in the sun."

What had happened to Marmalade's mom? She had probably been out late partying and was still catching up on beauty sleep.

As soon as Shelley left, I demanded, "What's the big secret?"

"It's not really a secret. We just don't want this getting around town," Dave said. "I like Shelley a lot, but, you know, she sees and talks with a lot of people."

In other words, Shelley was a gossip. "So what's up?"

"We think Gustav must have been mugged, because his wallet and money are missing," Dave said. "If it hadn't been for the letter from your grandmother, we wouldn't even know his identity. He was probably on his way over to the Alley Cat and someone was lying in wait. You know how poor the lighting is there."

I looked at Oma. "Why would that have to be such a big secret?"

"I am not the one who wishes this." Her lips drew thin in annoyance.

After I'd joined Oma as her partner at the Sugar Maple Inn, she had run for mayor and won. I was happy for her, but it meant that all of tiny Wagtail's problems were her problems, too. And to some extent, *my* problems, since she expected me to help her.

"We're going to bring undercover cops over from Snowball to patrol there for the next few nights in the hope of catching our killer. Obviously, if word got out about that, the killer wouldn't lurk around in the Shire."

"You really think he'd go back to the same place?" I asked. "Seems kind of stupid to me. I'd be glad I got away with it once and wouldn't try again."

Dave almost smiled. "Criminals usually don't think these things through. If they did, they wouldn't commit a crime in the first place."

I shrugged. "Maybe. Have you notified Gustav's family?"

Oma placed her palm flat against her cheek. "All we have are his mail and e-mail addresses. I know that he has a daughter named Trudy and a son called Michael. But that doesn't help much."

"I'll be contacting the police in Tucson, where he lives. Lived," Dave corrected himself. "They can probably help us track down his next of kin."

Shelley arrived with breakfast for Trixie, Huey, Gingersnap, and me.

Dave thanked Oma for breakfast and excused himself.

I hated seeing my grandmother so down. "Oma, we've been through these kinds of things before. Dave will get to the bottom of it."

Oma shook her head in dismay. "Another murder in Wagtail. And it was someone who was supposed to be a guest of the inn. This is very bad."

"I'm sure Dave will catch him."

Oma changed the subject and got down to business while I savored the creaminess of the avocado, which went surprisingly well with the soft egg yolk. "I have a meeting this morning," she said. "You can take care of everything here and fill in for Zelda when she goes to lunch?"

"Absolutely. Is this a mayoral-type meeting, or are you participating in one of Macon's events?"

Oma didn't laugh. "Please. Of course it is about Wagtail."

"Oma, what's wrong?" I stopped eating and looked her in the eyes.

She averted her gaze. "You like this John Adele?"

"I don't really know him very well. So far our relationship consists of finding a dead man together."

"Lesser things have helped couples bond. And he is better than the Ben. Where is the Ben?"

"Probably still in bed. Did you hear about the dogs getting into the food?"

My description of the pantry raid in the middle of the night had her in stitches. I was glad to see a smile return to her face.

"I can only think that Ben didn't close the door properly. Otherwise I can't imagine how they managed to get out."

"But this does not explain the presence of the other dogs, like my Gingersnap."

"It's a mystery!"

Oma seemed more like herself when she headed off to her meeting.

But I was disturbed because so many doors had been opened during the night. Almost as though someone had gained access to the master key. Ben stumbled down the stairs and joined me. He'd visited often enough that Shelley came over to say hi and bring him coffee.

After she left with his order, I told him about the dogs escaping, and concluded with, "So one of us must not have closed the door properly."

Ben grimaced. "You're so passive-aggressive. Just come out and say I didn't shut the door. I admit that I came in a little late, and I might have had—"

"May I join you?" I hadn't noticed Laura Pisani, Marmalade's mom.

"Yes, of course." I started to introduce her to Ben, but she interrupted me.

"We've met. We had the best time last night."

I was stunned to see Ben blush. He actually ran his hands through his hair like he was primping for her. I wouldn't have admitted it to him, but it did feel a little odd to see my former boyfriend interested in another woman. Still, as they carried on, laughing about something like old friends, I was genuinely happy for him. Laura was very attractive. Maybe she even had a slightly nerdy side.

I finished my tea, handed Huey over to Ben, and found I was smiling as I set off on my morning walk-through of the inn to make sure everything was in order.

I began in the main lobby, which bustled with Animal Attraction participants, then made my way to the small library. One lone woman was curled up in the window seat with her cat, reading a book. The library connected to the cats-only wing, where the rooms were outfitted with screened porches, a real tree to climb, and a catwalk near the ceiling that ran around each room. I picked up an umbrella that someone had dropped and continued upstairs. I couldn't help noticing quite a few *Do Not Disturb* signs. A lot of guests must have been up late the night before.

I walked through the second floor, pausing briefly at the grand staircase to gaze down at the lobby. Still busy. I kept going to the other end, where Oma's apartment was. The hallway ended at a balcony that overlooked the reception lobby. I trotted down the stairs to the desk where Zelda worked and placed the umbrella in our lost and found box.

"Did you meet an interesting guy last night?" I asked.

"I don't think I'm the only person in Wagtail with a hangover this morning," she groaned. "Macon matched me up through Live Love Meow. I brought my cat Leo along for our meeting because everyone loves him. My guy, Axel, turned out to be adorable. He had the most open, friendly face and sweet blue eyes that just melted my heart the minute I looked into them. But my good-for-nothing ex-husband, Hank, showed up at the bar of the restaurant. So then, of course, I acted like a complete idiot, trying to avoid being seen by him."

"Did you tell your date what was going on?"

"In spite of my best efforts, Hank spotted me and had the nerve to pull a chair up to our table. Naturally, he was a total jerk and made it sound like we were still together! Holly, it was a nightmare. And even worse, Hank made some thinly veiled threats! So I tricked him into going to the bar for more drinks, grabbed the cats, and told my date we were on the run."

Uh-oh. "I hope you paid your check?"

"Luckily, our waitress was a friend of mine. She knew all about Hank and could see what was happening, so she said, 'Go, go, go!' After that the date was very romantic. I'm seeing him again when I get off work."

"How are you going to dodge your ex?"

"I wish he didn't know where I live. That creep came around and banged on my door in the middle of the night. Good thing I changed the locks when I got rid of him. I didn't let him in, of course, but I didn't get much sleep knowing he was hanging around out there. I even saw him looking where we used to keep a spare key! Today I've outsmarted him. I rented a boat and ordered a picnic! The only way Hank is going to be able to bug us is if he swims out to the boat." Zelda cackled with glee.

"Are you taking your cats?"

"You bet! Well, not all of them. Only Leo. The inn chef is making them Something Fishy, which is Leo's favorite."

I retreated to the office to take care of some paperwork. Sunshine streamed through the open French doors. Twinkletoes sat on the desk trying to open a drawer, and Marmalade assisted her from the desk chair.

"What are you two doing?" I asked. "There are no treats or catnip in there."

That information didn't stop them. Marmalade managed to pull the drawer open slightly. From above, Twinkletoes immediately jammed her paw into the drawer and felt around.

I was so amused that I watched to see what she would find. She dragged out a plastic bag of catnip with her claw, seized it in her mouth, and jumped off the desk.

"I stand corrected." I dashed after her to rescue the catnip.

Marmalade and Twinkletoes followed me back to the desk, desperately trying to snag their catnip booty again. I put it back in the drawer and located two catnip-filled mice for them to play with.

Thrilled, they seized their toys and ventured outside into the sun. I could see them rolling on their backs with the mice clutched in their front paws.

Trixie settled near me. I tried to concentrate, but my thoughts kept turning to Gustav and the abrupt end to his life.

An hour later, Zelda showed Laura into the office. Apparently, they had met the night before too, because they were carrying on about how much fun they'd had.

"Marmalade!" cried Laura. She ran to the terrace, scooped him up in her arms, and carried him inside, holding him like a baby. "Thank you so much, Holly. I saw him briefly this morning, but then my little sweetie took off again. I was worried sick about him yesterday until I received your text."

"And then we sang 'Don't Go Breakin' My Heart'!" Zelda laughed.

"I've never sung karaoke before," said Laura. "It was a blast."

I could hear Marmalade purring in her arms.

"Thanks again for letting him spend the night, Holly. We're on our way to a cat store. Marmalade has never been shopping before. Then Marmalade and I have a lunch date!"

Zelda walked out of the office with Laura, still gabbing about the previous night.

I spent the next couple of hours catching up on paperwork.

At eleven, Zelda popped her head in. "Mind if I take lunch now? I'm leaving at three."

"Sure. Perfect timing. Seems like things are pretty quiet."

Zelda sat down in the chair opposite me. "Holly? I've been debating whether to tell you this, but I think maybe you should know."

I tensed. Had she seen the killer? Was Zelda in the Shire last night?

"I met Laura at Hair of the Dog last night. She was with Ben."

I stared at her for a moment, waiting for the bad news, then laughed aloud when I realized she was done. "That's fine. I'm glad Ben met somebody nice. I was afraid you knew something about the murder."

"Murder?" she screeched.

I told her about finding Gustav and warned her to be careful.

Zelda took off, shaken by the news. Minutes later, I heard the sliding glass doors to the reception lobby slide open. Trixie jumped to her feet and ran out to see who it was before I had left the office.

An older gentleman walked in. He carried himself quite erect but shuffled a tad and relied on a walking stick that was covered with medallions. I was familiar with them. Many of our hiking guests had similar walking sticks with badges marking the places they had visited in Europe.

"Good morning!" I said.

"Good morning. I should like to check in," he said with a pronounced German accent. "I have a reservation under Gustav Vogel."

ELEVEN

My breath caught in my throat. How could this be happening? All kinds of strange scenarios ran through my head. Was this the real Gustav Vogel? Was he an impostor? Could there be two people by that name?

I swallowed hard. Maybe I had misunderstood. I didn't think so, but I asked anyway. "I'm sorry? Your name again?"

He spoke slowly. "Gustav Vogel. V-O-G-E-L. I was supposed to be here yesterday but was detained because I was mugged."

That sounded way too familiar. Two Gustav Vogels, and both were mugged? "I'm sorry to hear that." I faked a smile. "Thank you. Would you excuse me for a moment?"

I hurried into the office and phoned Officer Dave, all the while keeping an eye on Mr. Vogel through the open door.

"Dave," I whispered. "I have a Gustav Vogel trying to check in."

After a moment of silence, he said, "That's not funny."

"I'm not trying to be funny."

I heard him suck in a long breath. "I'll be there in a few minutes, but this better not be some kind of gag."

I hung up, feeling annoyed. I had never tried to trick him before. This wasn't in the least bit amusing for me either.

I returned to the desk.

"Is there a problem?" asked Mr. Vogel. "Perhaps I could speak to Liesel Miller. She is expecting me."

"She's out at the moment but should return soon. There's just a little bit of confusion. May I see your identification?"

There. That should solve it.

"As I mentioned, I was mugged. I do not have my driver's license because my wallet was stolen. The police were kind enough to give me a copy of their report. Perhaps that would help you?"

He handed me a pink sheet of paper. The writing was faint, as though it had been the third carbon sheet and the officer hadn't pressed quite hard enough. "This is dated yesterday."

"That is correct. Had it not been for this misfortune, I would have arrived here yesterday. But I was hospitalized for the night."

"I'm so sorry. Perhaps you would like to sit down?" I gestured toward the love seat.

"I should like to lie down if I could please be shown to my room."

Dave turned up at that exact moment, panting like he had run from wherever he had been. I was relieved to see him because he had spared me having to tell this man, assuming he really was Gustav Vogel, that we had given his room away.

Dave asked if he could borrow the office. Naturally, I consented. The two men entered the little room behind the desk and the door closed.

I picked up the phone and called Oma's friend, Rose Richardson, who owned several rental properties. "Rose, I'm in desperate need of a room. Are all your places full?"

"Funny you should mention that. I have a darling one-bedroom bungalow that wasn't rented this week. Seems most of the people came to Animal Attraction with friends and needed more than one bedroom. I was just telling your grandmother about it."

"Oh! She's there?" I should have realized. Rose and Oma were thick as thieves. "Where are you? Can I send someone over to pick up the key?"

"Liesel is just on her way back. I'll send it with her." Her voice faded as though she was talking to Oma and not into the phone. "It's the yellow cottage on Pine Street. Close to Hot Hog."

I heard Oma say, "I know the one. It's very cute. Tell Holly I'll be back in five minutes."

I thanked Rose, hung up, and let out a heavy breath. One crisis resolved. Sort of.

Ben walked in at that moment with Huey. "There you are! Holly, we need to talk."

We certainly did. But Dave would surely be finished with the second Gustav Vogel shortly, and Oma would be back any minute. It couldn't have been a worse time. "I'm a little busy at the

119

moment. Maybe we can meet for coffee or lunch in an hour?"

He flushed pink. "That's what I wanted to talk about. Actually, I have a lunch date. I want to borrow Twinkletoes, but I can't find her."

I smelled a rat. Twinkletoes and Ben did *not* get along. Not at all! "For heaven's sake, take Huey. You've ignored him since last night. And he's such a great dog. He has behaved like a perfect angel."

"Um, no. It has to be Twinkletoes."

"Why? You do recall that you don't like each other. Right?"

"I may have told Laura that Twinkletoes was my cat."

"May have?" I giggled.

"Okay, so she's a cat person, not a dog person."

"What a great start to a relationship. You're lying to her already. And the only cat you know is Twinkletoes, who hates you!"

"*Hate* is such a strong word."

"Don't you think Laura will notice when Twinkletoes spends lunch hissing at you?"

The door behind me opened. Dave and the second Gustav Vogel exited the office. Just as Mr. Vogel rounded the desk to the reception lobby, Oma walked in through the sliding glass doors.

They looked at each other, and if it had been a movie, heavenly music would have played. Maybe Macon was right about us making up our minds in ninety seconds to four minutes. I wasn't sure it had taken them that long.

Gustav nodded at Oma and held out his hand. "Gustav Vogel. You must be the lovely Liesel."

I hoped Oma wouldn't faint. In a big rush that alarmed the dogs, I hurried to her side, ready to catch her.

Oma stared at Gustav for a long moment as though she were looking at a ghost. She shook his hand. "I thought you were dead."

Gustav laughed. A nice, hearty chuckle. "I must misquote Mr. Twain. As you can see, reports of my demise have been greatly exaggerated."

"I have to sit down. I did not expect this."

I walked with Oma to the love seat just in case she should topple. Gustav promptly sat next to her.

Trixie and Huey, probably sensing treats from Oma, wagged their tails and sniffed them.

I hustled over to Dave and whispered, "So, what's the story?"

Ben sidled up to us to hear what was going on.

"I called the police to confirm. He's on the up and up. On his way here, Gustav was jumped and mugged. They took him to the hospital as a precaution because the mugger did a number on him."

"So who is the other guy?"

"What other guy?" asked Ben.

Dave raised his eyebrows and shrugged. "Beats me. How am I supposed to investigate a murder if I don't know the identity of the victim?"

TWELVE

"Murder? There's been a murder? Why didn't you tell me?" Ben glared at me.

"Did you expect me to wait up all night for you, or did you want me to wake you early this morning to share that news?" It was a little testy of me, but I hadn't had much of a chance to talk with him privately.

Dave seemed annoyed. "If you'll excuse me, I don't have time for your petty bickering."

He put us in our place with that one sentence. "I'm sorry, Dave," I said. "If there's anything I can do to help, please let me know."

Dave's mouth twisted to the side. "Do you know if the dead guy signed up for any of Macon's matchmaking? That might be a good place to start. Maybe Macon has the guy's real name and address."

"It could assist in identifying the killer, too," Ben pointed out.

Dave flashed him a look.

"What? Maybe he didn't like the person he was matched with."

"Right, he meets someone for half an hour and she already wants to kill him?" I doubted it.

"What exactly did the now dead Gustav Vogel say to you and Liesel yesterday?" asked Dave.

I motioned for him to follow me. "I'm sorry to interrupt, but Oma, could you help me remember what that odious man said about dog and cat lovers yesterday?"

"*Ja*, of course. He said that cat lovers were neurotics and dog lovers were replacing their need for human companionship with dogs. And that dogs don't understand what we say."

Ben snorted. "The guy was right. He was just telling the truth. Who would murder him for something like that?"

I couldn't believe my ears. Why did people who had never had a dog or cat think they knew more about animals than those of us who spent time with them?

"Ben, why did you come here this weekend?" I asked. "Don't you think you would be better off with a woman who is like you and doesn't want pets?"

The broad grin on Oma's face was irritating. "Holly is correct. You will meet the wrong women for you here in Wagtail."

Ben scowled at me. "Look who's giving advice on romance. I don't see you hooked up with anyone." His eyes widened. "That's why you're so short with me. Have you changed your mind? You want to marry me after all?"

Why were we having this little scene in front of an audience? I could feel my ears getting hot. "Ben, go on your date and tell her the truth. Dave, Gustav number one recognized Macon. Maybe

Macon would know who he is? Oma, would you like to show Gustav to his cottage? Or should I take him over?"

A scant five minutes later, everyone had cleared out, but Ben left poor Huey with me again. Zelda returned, and I headed for a much-needed lunch.

The dining area still buzzed with visitors. It was fun to watch people getting to know one another. I considered eating in Oma's private kitchen, but Huey and Trixie found Lulu and Duchess.

Through the window, I spied Ben dining with Laura on the terrace. Laura appeared interested in what he was saying. Twinkletoes and Marmalade watched activities on the lake from a spot near the terrace stairs that led to the lakefront. At least Twinkletoes wasn't embarrassing Ben by hissing at him.

Sky and Nessie worked on a laptop at the table where I usually sat when I was alone. It was partly hidden, back by the window where Shelley placed and picked up orders.

They called me to join them.

"This is such fun!" Nessie typed something into the computer. "There she is. My sweet angel, Celeste. Oh no! This won't do at all. I knew there was something wrong, wrong, wrong about that guy she was with last night. Macon has matched her to a musician!"

"What's wrong with that?" asked Sky. "Musicians are very creative and kind."

Nessie glared at her new friend. "Stick with me, Sky. I swear I never met anybody so naïve. I would love it if she were being matched to someone kind, but honey, *musician* is code for poorer than the proverbial church mouse. No, no, no. That won't do at all."

"What are you looking at?" I asked. "Celeste's Facebook page?"

Nessie ignored my question. Her fingertips hit the keys rapidly. "Ohh. Here's a doctor. Now, that's much better! Okay, let's see what's happening with Sky's daughter, Maddie."

Shelley waved at me as she picked up an order. "Steak salad, peppered trout, or barbecue chicken pizza?"

They all sounded so good. "Steak salad, please. With iced tea. Is there a dog version of the steak salad?"

"Of course." Shelley grinned. "Theirs comes with sweet potatoes and cooked kale."

"Trixie and Huey will have that. Thanks, Shelley."

Nessie gasped. "Oh my! Look at this—a dot-com entrepreneur. He's perfect for Maddie."

"Did Macon post a list of participants online?" I asked.

"No, darlin'." Nessie winked at me.

Sky looked over her shoulder. "Who did Macon match her to?"

"Oh, good grief. First it was an artist. I guess

125

Maddie was smart enough to bail on him. Oh no! Her second match was a writer!"

"What's wrong with that?" I asked, thinking of John.

Nessie shook her head and tsked at me. "Darlin', listen and learn. When they put down *writer, actor,* or *musician* as a career, it means they have no money and no prospects. They're probably waiting tables while they hope for their big break. Always walk away from them."

"But the musician or writer could be a very nice guy," I protested.

Nessie gave me a look over her reading glasses. "Nice won't pay the bills, sugar."

"Where are you getting all this information? Did Macon give you access?" I asked.

"You might say that." Nessie focused on the computer screen and groaned. "Sky, is your daughter really a dog walker?"

"Let me see." Sky turned the computer so she could view the screen. "That's odd. Maybe he confused her with someone else. Maddie sells real estate."

Nessie took control of the laptop again. Her fingers clicked the keys rapidly. "There, that's better. Maddie is now set up with the dot-com guy. A far better match for her, don't you think?"

Sky's eyebrows dipped in worry. "I don't know. The writer might be a really terrific and interesting fellow."

The chef waved at me from the open window. I rose to collect our lunches. Behind me, I heard the whooshing sound of e-mails being sent.

Trixie and Huey wasted no time scarfing up their lunches as soon as I set them on the floor.

Nessie flipped the laptop shut. "I'm sure the writer is nice. But there's no reason the dot-com guy isn't every bit as wonderful, and he's probably a lot better off. Now let me get this back before Macon notices it's gone."

"What?" I ignored the rosy slices of steak on a bed of greens. "That's *Macon's* laptop? You stole his computer?"

"Borrowed. And you can see why. I'm not letting Celeste end up with an unemployed musician of some kind. She can just as easily fall for a lovely doctor." Nessie stood up and scurried away.

"I don't believe you two. How did you get his password?"

Sky blushed. "*Matchmaker* wasn't too hard to guess. Nessie doesn't mean any harm. And we didn't steal it. Macon left it outside on a rocking chair. She's returning it to him."

I was supposed to be nice to the guests no matter what. *No matter what,* I reminded myself. They had done something so wrong!

Sky leaned toward me across the table. In a low voice that I could barely hear, she said, "When my husband died in a car accident, I was devastated. He'd had too much to drink and ran off the road.

127

Everyone said, 'Sky, he was coming home to you. He loved you.' But you know who showed up at the funeral? The mistress he was drinking with before he got into his car and drove off the road. I don't want Maddie to go through that."

She sat up straight. "I'm not a total loony, Holly. I just want to spare Maddie the pain I went through."

"Does Maddie know that about her father?"

"I've never told her. It was certainly public knowledge when that woman turned up, though. I expect someone could have mentioned it to Maddie. Or maybe people are decent enough not to tell a young woman that kind of thing about the father she lost. It's probably hopeless to wish that she'll never know."

"Is that why you never remarried?"

Nessie hurried up to the table, panting. "Did you know someone was mugged and murdered last night?" She showed us her hands. "And me with expensive jewelry! That could have been me! Holly, is there a safe in this inn?"

"Yes, there's one in Oma's office."

"Did you know about this?" Nessie fixed a stern glare on me.

"I did. But I don't think you have anything to worry about. Officer Dave is very good. He's on it already." They didn't need to know that Dave had no idea who the victim was.

"Officer Dave? You call the investigating

officer *Dave?* Good grief. I think I should hire a bodyguard to follow Celeste."

Sky turned sympathetic eyes on her new friend. "Nessie, *we're* already following them."

Nessie's eyes grew large. "Not right now we're not!"

"Then let's go." Sky pulled a schedule out of her pocket. "Umm, looks like there's an ice cream social at two o'clock. Sounds like something Maddie would like."

"Celeste, too."

"Sorry to leave you alone, Holly." Sky glanced at Nessie, who stared at the rings on her fingers.

"Where do men carry everything without a purse?" asked Nessie.

"Just put them in your fanny pack." Sky winked at me.

"I'll never forgive myself if I lose them."

"Come on, already!"

The two of them left, squabbling good-naturedly like old friends.

I noticed, though, that Duchess seemed reluctant to go with them. She had such a pretty face, with sweet eyes and perky ears that flopped forward. The fur on her ears darkened to a light caramel at the base. She looked back at us as if she didn't want to go when Sky called her. Ultimately, she went anyway.

I was just finishing my lunch when Cooper bounded in. He wiggled from end to end with excitement. I patted him and even received a few sloppy dog kisses in return.

John pulled out a chair, leaned toward me, and whispered, "Is it wrong of me to want to go back to see the scene of the crime in daylight?"

THIRTEEN

"I feel kind of guilty for wanting to go back at all." John paused and waved his hand slightly. "Not guilty like I had anything to do with Gustav's murder." His eyes grew wide. "They always say the criminal returns to the scene of the crime!"

He ran a hand through his hair. "I'm sorry. I hardly slept last night. I couldn't get Gustav out of my head. I just saw his face over and over again. The way he was laying there, and the mark on his neck."

I had to break it to him. He was already so agitated that I hoped John could take the news. I spoke in a low tone so no one else would hear. "He's not Gustav. The real Gustav Vogel showed up this morning."

"What? But he had that letter. How did he get a letter that was written to Gustav?"

"Good question. Gustav was mugged on his way here. Maybe the victim was Gustav's mugger?" I wondered if I should call Dave to tell him about that possibility, but decided it was too obvious. Dave would have already considered that.

John sat back in his chair. "This blows my mind. But I still want to see it in daylight. Will you go with me?"

I had to admit that I was a little bit curious,

too. "Don't be disappointed if it's roped off."

"I guess that's to be expected. So, who is the victim? Do they know?"

I told John about the man recognizing Macon.

On the way out, I let Mr. Huckle know where I was going in case Oma needed me. "I have my cell phone." Though I knew that wouldn't do much good.

Although we issued an invitation to join us, Gingersnap declined. That didn't surprise me because there wasn't a single empty rocking chair on the porch. She knew where she would get the most attention.

Dave was allowing Cooper to run off leash, which made me feel sorry for Huey. He turned those heart-melting brown eyes toward me, and I reluctantly unsnapped his leash. After all, he still wore his Sugar Maple Inn GPS collar.

The crowds thinned as we walked toward the road on the east side of Wagtail. Once again, it was quiet. Not surprising since most cars parked outside of Wagtail.

We crossed the street, and as we walked deeper into the Shire, John exclaimed over the quaint architecture. "It's like a country village. I couldn't see all the flowers and blooming bushes last night. But the houses look small."

"They are. No mansions allowed in the shire."

We turned off onto the trail that led down to the river and the location where we had discovered the body. In daylight, it didn't look one bit sinister. Bright yellow buttercups waved in a soft breeze, and hundreds of big, orange clusters of butterfly weeds dotted the green grass.

"There's no tape keeping us out," John whispered.

"It wouldn't have been difficult to drive in a few stakes and swing it around that tree."

"Must mean they're confident that they got everything. Where do you think he was?"

"From the way all three dogs are sniffing right there, I'd bet that's where he was lying."

John sucked in air and let it out slowly. "This is really awful of me, but I feel like it never happened. I thought it might be hard to come out here, but the sun is shining, and the flowers are blooming, I'm with a really pretty girl, and I'm not feeling shock at all."

A couple holding hands passed us on their way back from the river with their two dogs.

We nodded in greeting. "I understand what you mean. Something sinister and vile took place right here. But today, life goes on like nothing ever happened. If we hadn't seen him, we might never have known about it."

"I'm glad you understand. I was afraid it was just me. There's something very sad about the fact that people who walk by here will never have any idea of the horror that took place in this spot."

We took a stroll down to the river, where

Cooper and Huey jumped in for a swim. Trixie declined and barked at them from the safety of the riverbank.

John grabbed two sticks and threw them for Cooper and Huey to fetch in the water. "Trixie didn't even watch. Doesn't she fetch?"

I told him the story of finding her. "She was a sad mess. She likes toys, but I guess she never learned to fetch as a puppy."

John sat down on the big, flat rock beside me. "You know what I did last night?"

I looked at him.

"It was too late to call anyone, so I e-mailed my parents and told them I would check in with them every day. If I didn't, they should come looking for me."

"Don't they know where you are?" I asked.

"Not really. Now that everyone has cell phones and e-mail, you can stay in touch without knowing a physical location. I had simply said I was writing in a cabin in the mountains. Finding a corpse really shook me up. That could have been me! Even worse, nobody knows who the guy is. It could be days or weeks until somebody notices that he never came home. I wonder if he told anyone he was coming here. He might end up being labeled a John Doe. One of those faces you see on the Internet with the word *Missing* in huge letters."

"I would have looked for you."

"No, you wouldn't have. You would have assumed that I'd left town. You wouldn't have given me another thought."

"I would have thought about you, but you're probably right about me believing that you had left town. Poor Cooper! He would have been all alone."

Cooper and Huey bounded up to the rock and shook like crazy, splashing both of us with droplets of water and breaking the gloomy feeling that hung over us.

"How about some ice cream?" asked John.

We headed back, skirting the spot where we thought the body had been.

Huey stayed with us and joined in the fun, romping with the other dogs when we reached the ice cream social.

We loaded up our bowls with chocolate, peppermint, and sea salt–caramel ice creams and drizzled them with butterscotch. That was enough for me, but John sprinkled his with chopped peanut butter cups. I handed John my bowl and fixed three bowls of peanut butter ice cream made especially for dogs.

We settled on a bench near the big gazebo and dug into our rapidly melting, sinfully delicious treats. Huey and Cooper finished theirs first. Trixie nosed her bowl under the bench, where it would be harder for the big dogs to steal her ice cream.

Macon Stotts spied us and toddled over. "You

can't imagine where I've been. At the morgue! There's something I never thought I would do in my life. They took me in to see if I recognized the man who died."

"And did you?" I licked butterscotch off my spoon.

"I did! And I'm not one bit sorry he's dead. Isn't that just awful of me? I wish I had never seen the man dead, but I can't say I'm sorry he's gone."

"Who is he?" John stopped eating.

"Randall Donovan. A highly disreputable psychiatrist prone to writing hogwash and pretending like it's fact."

So they *had* known each other. As casually as I could, I asked, "Was he one of your matchmaking customers?"

"Good Lord, no! I wouldn't dream of matching some innocent unsuspecting person with a crosspatch cynic like Randall."

"I get the feeling you didn't like him," joked John.

"I certainly will not miss him. I guess he ran his mouth one too many times. He must have really ticked somebody off this time. His vile nature finally caught up with him." Macon dabbed his forehead with a handkerchief. "It was a good thing he was dead. He'd have croaked for sure at the thought that *I* might be the one identifying his remains. Oh my! He was a prophet of doom intent on sucking the joy out of everyone's

136

lives. Seriously, if there were no love and no appreciation of the pleasures in life"—he bent to stroke Trixie's head—"then the world would be gray and without laughter. Except perhaps for his contemptuous cackle."

I didn't know Randall, but from what I had seen, Macon described him well.

"Where's Huey?" asked John.

FOURTEEN

I looked around. Trixie and Cooper lay side by side, but Huey was nowhere to be seen. "Oh no!"

In a panic, I excused myself, called Trixie, and ran for the inn. John caught up to me. We were breathless, and the dogs were panting by the time we reached the reception area.

"What's wrong? Is it my ex-husband?" Zelda ducked partway down behind the registration counter.

"No," I gasped. "I lost Huey."

Zelda pulled out the iPad and brought up a map. "Okay. Catch your breath. Unit number four? There he is. I love this gadget. Saves so much worry."

I staggered toward her. "Where? Where is he?"

Zelda bit back a smile. "Looks like he's out on the lake side of the inn."

I barged through the office and out the French doors onto the immaculate lawn. Zelda, John, and the dogs followed me. I did a panoramic sweep in search of Huey. "Do you see him anywhere?"

They both said no.

Desperation welled up inside me. I couldn't lose that sweet dog. I walked forward, toward the lake.

"There he is!" John pointed at the dock, downhill from where we stood.

"Thank goodness." Zelda patted me on the back and walked inside.

Huey jumped into a boat with two men.

I ran down the hill. "Stop! Huey! Stop! That's my dog!"

But as I neared them, I recognized Lulu and Duchess. Huey was with Nessie and Sky. I arrived at the dock seconds after they cast off. The pontoon boat was only a couple of feet away. Huey's tail wagged like crazy, and he lifted his nose in the air to catch scents.

Sky waved at me. "Hope you don't mind Huey tagging along."

I guessed it was okay. He certainly seemed happy. As long as he didn't jump off and swim to shore, he should be fine. "Don't lose him!"

Nessie waved and gunned the boat forward, crying, "Yeehaw!"

John wrapped his arm around me. "He'll be all right. They seem like nice women. A little crazy, but nice."

"It's a shame Ben isn't interested in Huey."

John's arm dropped, and he turned toward me. "You know, most people would have taken him back to the shelter by now."

"Look how much fun he's having. I can't bring myself to take him back to a cage. WAG is amazing, but he'd still be in a cage."

"Maybe someone will meet him this weekend and want to adopt him."

I sighed. "I wish."

We walked back up to the inn on broad stone steps. Masses of red geraniums and giant daisies mingled with cascades of purple-blue petunias lining the stairs. A few guests in bathing suits were carrying towels on their way to the lake for a swim. It wasn't as if I hadn't known it was summertime, but except for our ice cream outing today, I'd spent so much time working that I hadn't taken advantage of all summer had to offer yet.

"Dinner tonight at six?" asked John.

I hated to say it, but I had to. "Can I give you a call? I'll have to check to be sure the inn is covered. Oma may have plans with Gustav."

"Sure." John wrote down his number and handed it to me.

Officer Dave arrived at the door to the inn at the same time we did. He nodded a greeting to John, who said, "See you later," to me.

When we were inside, Dave turned around to watch John walk away with Cooper. "So, you like this John Adele guy?"

Hadn't Oma asked me the same thing? "He's kind of sweet."

"He tell you where he works?"

I frowned at Dave. "For himself, I think. He edits history textbooks. What are you getting at?"

"Nothing."

I didn't like the way he said that. "Are you here to see Oma?"

He nodded. "Need to update her a little."

He didn't ask me to join them, but I followed him anyway. He must have called ahead, because he said *hi* to Zelda and walked through the inn to Oma's private kitchen.

I couldn't believe the transformation in my beloved Oma. The worried expression was gone. She hummed as she poured hot water into a teacup.

"Excellent timing. Would you like hot tea or should I have Shelley bring coffee?" She delivered a plate of cream puffs and chocolate-dipped strawberries to the table.

"Iced tea for me, thanks."

"I'll get Dave's tea, Oma." I hurried out to where people were enjoying afternoon tea, grabbed a tall glass, and filled it with ice cubes and cold tea. I rushed back in, set it in front of Dave, and stepped away to make my own hot tea.

"I have a little bit of news, Liesel." Dave took a long drink. "Good news and bad news, unfortunately. The victim was a psychiatrist named Randall Donovan. Your letter was full of fingerprints. They haven't identified all of them yet, but interestingly, the prints of a small-time thief came up, too. A guy named Mick Huff. He has a long record, mostly for petty crimes, but he has also burglarized homes and businesses."

Dave slid a picture across the table to Oma. "Recognize him?"

I spooned sugar into my tea and brought it to

the table so I could see the picture. Mick wore metal-rimmed glasses that looked too big for his face. A thick mustache covered his upper lip, but his mouth hung open. His hair was cut short in front but curls in the back touched his shoulders.

"Such a man killed Randall?" Oma shook her head. "He looks small, and, please forgive me for saying this, but he doesn't appear very intelligent."

Dave selected a strawberry. "Most petty thieves don't have PhDs, Liesel. And we don't know that he murdered Randall, but it's a pretty good guess."

"What's the bad news?" I picked out the smallest cream puff and bit into it, savoring the insanely decadent cream.

"No one knows where he is."

Oma gasped. "Holly, would you please make copies of this photo and be sure all the employees see it? Perhaps post it at the registration and concierge desks?"

"Of course." A bit reluctantly, I left my lovely cream puff and afternoon tea behind to make copies. I hurried down to the office.

"So, what's the scoop?" Zelda tossed back her hair.

I held out the photo. "Small-time crook. His fingerprints are on the letter."

Zelda frowned. "I saw him! Seriously. I saw him last night at Hair of the Dog."

"Go tell Dave. He's in Oma's kitchen."

While I was making copies, Ben returned.

"Is this a better time to talk?"

"Not really." I showed him the photo. "I saw him last night."

"So did Zelda. Where did you see him?"

"At Hair of the Dog."

"You better go tell Dave."

"Holly?" Ben asked.

"Hmm?" I removed the original photo from the copy machine.

"I have a confession. I came here and filled out one of Macon's forms in a way that I thought would match me to you."

"You what?"

"I filled out my form the way I thought you would fill out your form because, well, I thought if we were matched up you might have to reconsider our relationship."

"Oh, Ben. That's about the sweetest thing you have ever done."

"Then last night, I met Laura." Ben looked down at the floor. "Now I feel kind of conflicted."

"Did you have a good time?"

"Surprisingly, yes. Did you know that she's a professor? She's smart and funny. She's a pun genius. You know how I love puns. She even talked me into singing karaoke."

"That's nothing to feel guilty about."

"We're having dinner tonight."

"I think that's great. I won't have to worry about you sitting around my apartment all by yourself.

You better hurry to the kitchen before Dave leaves. He needs to know what you saw."

"Yeah, okay."

"Go on."

He left with his head slumping down, which made me wonder if he had expected me to throw myself in his arms and beg him to reconcile with me. I hoped that wasn't the case. I wanted him to be happy.

When Zelda returned, I went back to the kitchen. Dave, Ben, and my cream puff were gone, but Oma still sat at the table with her cup of tea.

"Do you feel better now? I'm sure they'll catch this Mick guy tonight."

"Holly, I have a confession to make."

FIFTEEN

Why was everyone saying that to me? I took a deep breath and sat down opposite her.

"In Germany, it has long been acceptable to place personal ads in newspapers and magazines. This is considered quite normal. It is not really very different from meeting a potential date through one of your modern computer dating services."

I had no idea what she was getting at. "Uh-huh."

"I didn't think there would be many men in my age group here this weekend, so I placed a personal ad in one of the magazines for Germans living in America. This is how I met Gustav."

"Oh!" I hadn't expected that. I studied my grandmother. Somehow I had thought she was happy with her life. How utterly clueless of me. "I thought you were interested in the owner of the Blue Boar."

"Ach. He is a friend, but there is no spark. I thought perhaps I should meet someone with a similar background to mine. This is why I knew something was very wrong. The dead man wasn't old enough to be Gustav Vogel."

That made sense. "Why didn't you just say so?"

"I felt like a fool. Here I was expecting a fine, older gentleman, and when he turned out to be that dreadful man we met on the plaza, I thought

I had been tricked and that I had believed the lies of a con man. I feared you would think me a silly old woman."

"That's why you were so troubled. I can understand that. But you weren't sucked in by a con man." I hoped not. After all, I didn't know anything about Gustav. But as that thought crossed my mind, I realized that I knew just as little about John. "Do you like Gustav now that you have met him?"

"He is a nice man. Tonight we will have dinner at the Blue Boar, and tomorrow morning, we are taking a picnic lunch and hiking up the mountain. I look forward to it!"

"Then it all worked out okay."

Oma tapped her teacup with a fingernail. "You don't think I started this dreadful chain of events? If I hadn't invited Gustav, then he would never have been mugged, and . . ."

"And what?"

"And perhaps Randall would never have been attacked. That man, Randall, he was looking for someone. Do you remember? What if he was looking for Gustav?"

"Why would you think that? Because he had the letter on him that you sent to Gustav?"

"Exactly. Why would he be in possession of a letter to Gustav? Now Dave is looking for this Mick Huff, but still something is not right."

"Maybe Randall was looking for Mick."

"*Liebling*, I want very much to imagine that some small-time crook intended to mug Randall and somehow ended up killing him. But I have a feeling that I cannot explain. There is something more to this." Oma reached across the table and laid her hand over mine. "You help me, *ja*? You help me figure out what happened so this ugly crime isn't hanging over our beloved Wagtail, besmirching its reputation?"

"Of course, Oma. You know I'll do anything I can."

"Very good." Oma sipped her tea. When she set her cup down, she leaned toward me. "So far, it appears that the only person who knew Randall was Macon. Let us begin there."

When Oma renovated the inn, she had installed two hidden stairways. One led from the kitchen to the dining room in my apartment. I left Oma in the kitchen and sprinted up the stairs to retrieve my iPad. I startled Twinkletoes when I dashed in, but she accepted my presence with feline aplomb, raising her head to see who it was, then curling into a tighter ball. She even had the nerve to slide a paw over her eyes, clearly shutting me out.

Trixie followed me up the stairs and back down to the kitchen again.

I turned on the iPad and searched the name *Randall Donovan*. I recognized his photo as soon as it appeared. He had a website. I clicked on it and showed it to Oma.

"He was famous, this Randall Donovan?" she asked.

"Anyone can have a website, but it appears that he blogged a lot and was a speaker, too," I said.

On a hunch, I searched *Randall Donovan and Macon Stotts*. And there it was—the smoking gun. "Good grief. He didn't like Macon. Oma, he goes on and on about Macon. First he says there is no such thing as love. He goes on to say, 'Romantic love is a hoax perpetrated upon us by our culture from birth. What we perceive as love is a temporary infatuation that wears thin after marriage, explaining the high rate of divorces.'"

I scrolled down a little and read aloud. "Aha! 'Make no mistake that romance is big business. From major corporations that sell products designed to enhance our attractiveness to charlatans like Macon Stotts, who hoodwink people into believing that they can find our perfect mates, romance is all about money.' And then he goes on to blast Macon. Wow. He really hated Macon."

Oma placed her hand against the side of her face. "What have I done?"

"Stop that! You didn't do anything wrong. I met someone. Zelda met a nice guy. Hey, even Ben met a girl that he likes. Can you believe that?"

"*Ja?* The Ben? This is truly amazing."

"Randall was clearly a sourpuss. I doubt he had anything good to say about anyone."

"And Macon might have murdered him. Perhaps I should not have brought Macon to Wagtail."

"Oma, it's not your fault that Randall and Macon had issues with each other. But now we know Macon had a motive. If we ask around, maybe we can find out where he was between the time we saw Randall on the plaza, after six, and the time John and I found his body, probably around ten o'clock that night."

Oma nodded and stood up.

"And you go right ahead and enjoy Gustav's company. I'll watch the fort." I knew it meant skipping dinner with John, but that was okay with me. I'd much rather see Oma be happy.

I checked my watch. Five o'clock already! I pulled up the schedule of events to see where Macon might be. Yappy Hour. Of course!

"C'mon, Trixie." The inn was silent. But just outside the front door, the hooting and applause were loud. We joined the onlookers who watched from the porch.

The town had passed a special exception allowing people to drink in public during Yappy Hour. Oma had very reasonably decided not to serve dinner at the inn so guests would go out and enjoy all the town had to offer. The drinking exception allowed people to buy their cocktails elsewhere but enjoy the Yappy Hour parade from the best vantage point in town—the front porch of the Sugar Maple Inn.

I watched as proud dog and cat parents paraded with their four-legged friends. A few small dogs and one Great Dane wore tutus. At least two cats sported tiaras, and one bulldog waddled along in a top hat. I wondered how they had secured it to his head. Laura had joined the fun with Marmalade, who walked on a leash, oblivious to the dogs, but it looked to me like he had his eye on the cockatoo sitting on the shoulders of the dog who walked in front of them. As usual a few other species showed up. Miraculously, none of the dogs were eyeing the squirrel that perched on a man's shoulder. The cat who rode a miniature horse got the most applause—or maybe it was for the cute horse who tolerated a cat on his back.

I spied Macon at the end of the porch with a small crowd of people. But before I could edge my way over to him, Huey bounded up to me, followed closely by Duchess.

"Hi! How did you like your boat ride?" I asked Huey.

He shook his body nose to tail, sending droplets of water all over.

I took that to mean he'd gone swimming too, and had a grand time.

Duchess was more demure about it and licked her wet fur.

Sky and Nessie laughed as they walked toward me with Lulu.

"Did you have fun?"

Sky's phone rang, and she excused herself, but Nessie smiled and gestured dramatically. "It was a hoot. We pretended to fish so we could watch both of our girls on boats. Sky's a little worried about Maddie. She thinks Maddie might have had too much to drink because she wasn't acting like herself at all. Or worse—it could have been rohypnol. Honestly, it's not like when we were young. These girls have to watch out for so many dangers! But we saw them make it safely back, so we know they survived their boating adventures this afternoon."

Sky returned, pale as a ghost.

"Honey!" cried Nessie. "Is something wrong?"

"My sister has been trying to call me all afternoon. I can't believe this. Her husband was murdered!"

SIXTEEN

Nessie gasped and slapped a hand against her chest. "Oh my word. What happened?"

"He was strangled. Right here in Wagtail."

"Your brother-in-law was Randall Donovan?" I squeaked.

"You know about this?" Sky took off her fedora.

"He's the guy who was mugged. The one Nessie was referring to earlier today. I didn't know you were related to him. I'm so sorry."

"Oh my. I'm sorry too, Sky." Nessie's eyes narrowed. "What was your sister's husband doing in Wagtail on a singles weekend?"

Sky sighed. "My sister didn't even know he was coming here. She thought he was giving a talk in Boston. Then she received a phone call about his death out of the blue."

"Ohhhh." Nessie shook her head slowly. "That does not bode well for him. Lying to his wife is bad enough, but coming here right now, when there are a lot of single women? That just spells trouble. He was up to no good."

Furrows worked their way onto Sky's forehead. "I bet you're right. Why else would he come here? He sure wasn't a dog or cat kind of guy."

"He was looking for someone yesterday. Someone participating in the matchmaking events. Do you know who that might have been?" I asked.

"I don't have the first clue. But I'll talk to my sister to see if she knows anything."

Nessie snorted. "They never do. The wives are always the last to know about these things."

"Will you be leaving?" I asked Sky.

"I haven't decided yet. Apparently, his body has been shipped to the coroner in Roanoke for an autopsy, so there won't be a funeral immediately. She's going to call me back. As you can imagine, she's in a state of shock. She never imagined that anything like this could happen. Randall was a very difficult man, but murdered? No one deserves that."

"Come on, Sky. Let's go up to our room."

"Huey!"

I recognized Ben's voice and turned.

Panting, he rushed toward the staircase. "Huey! Come with me," he gasped.

Huey paid him no attention at all. He had already reached the landing on the stairs with Duchess and Lulu.

Sky and Nessie called him.

Huey looked at us but made no move to return down the stairs.

Ben was going to need a leash. I headed for Oma's kitchen, where we kept extra leashes in case they were needed in a hurry. I brought it out to Ben. "What do you want Huey for?"

"You're the one who told me I was ignoring him."

"You're avoiding my question."

Ben blinked and said somewhat sheepishly, "I want to give him a chance and get to know him."

Sky had Huey by the collar and escorted him down the stairs to Ben.

I longed to believe Ben, but nothing in all the years I had known him led me to accept that response. Ben was a good guy. He would never hurt Huey. He just wasn't an animal person. Still, he had requested a dog, and both of them deserved the chance to get to know each other.

I watched him walk out of the inn with Huey before I skedaddled into the kitchen and prepared a pot of strong black tea for Sky and Nessie. I threw a white cloth over a room service cart and loaded it with cream, sugar, lemon slices, teacups, napkins, forks, spoons, and tiny plates. In the cooler, I found the leftover cream puffs, chicken salad, rolls, butter, and steak, which I carved into thin slices, arranged on top of lettuce, and garnished with savory olives and salty mini-pickles. It wasn't much, but a little finger food might make them feel better. After one last glance at it, I added a vase of gladioli and dahlias.

I rolled the cart up to their room and knocked on the door. Sky was on the phone again, but Nessie thanked me for bringing them goodies. She tried to tip me, but I refused.

Trixie and I headed down the grand staircase. With everyone out to dinner or dressing to go out, the inn was quiet. That suited me fine because my head was reeling with the most awful thoughts. I liked Sky so much. She impressed me as a gentle and lovely person. Surely she couldn't be the one responsible for Randall's death.

Suddenly, it occurred to me that I hadn't called John. I rushed to the phone in the kitchen, pulled out his number, and dialed it. His line rang for a long time. Just as I was giving up, John answered the phone.

I explained that I had pulled inn duty and wouldn't be able to have dinner with him.

"Okay. Thanks for letting me know."

"Maybe we could meet later for a drink?"

"I don't think so. I'm bushed. But thanks anyway." He hung up.

I frowned at the phone. "Now was that my imagination, or did I just get the brush-off?" I asked Trixie.

She ignored me and stared at the entrance to the hidden staircase.

"What is it?" I whispered. I hoped no one had hidden there.

Tiptoeing, I walked over to the door disguised as a bookcase. On the bottom shelf a pet door allowed Twinkletoes and Trixie to go home to our quarters if they felt like it.

Trixie growled softly, almost a hum.

An orange paw darted out at us.

I bent to see better. I caught a glimpse of Twinkletoes and Marmalade before they scampered back up the stairs. "I think they were spying on us!"

Trixie gave the pet door one last glance before she followed me out through the lobby and onto the porch. I sat down in a rocking chair.

My mind went straight back to John. I wanted to think I was being overly sensitive. Maybe he had been writing and I had interrupted him. Or maybe he was moody. If that was the case, it was just as well that I knew it now.

I tried to put him out of my mind and focus on Randall. Gingersnap left her cherished position by the stairs, came to me, and nuzzled my hands. "Hi, baby girl. Just because Sky was related to Randall doesn't mean she murdered him. Does it?"

Gingersnap wagged her tail slowly. She probably didn't know either. As I stroked her silky head, it dawned on me that Randall might have been looking for Sky or her daughter, Maddie. His wife could have mentioned they would be in Wagtail. Maybe she'd even made fun of Sky for keeping tabs on Maddie. I hated that the scenario involving Sky was more logical than the one about Randall looking for a small-time crook.

And where had Randall's wife been the night of his murder? Was it possible that the two sisters had conspired to murder him? People did a lot of strange things for family.

A man who didn't believe in love had to have been a nightmare as a husband. In fact, I wondered why he would have married at all if he really believed that love was only a cultural delusion. What had Sky called him? *Difficult*. A very polite way of saying he was a problem.

As I pondered the relationship between Sky and her brother-in-law, my gaze fell on a young blonde who marched toward the inn with a grim expression. Her little dog kept pace beside her.

Maddie Stevens!

I jumped to my feet and dashed inside to the concierge desk. Moving lightning fast, I picked up the house phone and called Sky's room.

The phone rang and rang. And was still ringing when Maddie Stevens entered the inn and walked up to me.

"Excuse me, do you have a guest by the name of Sky Stevens?"

I didn't even have time to debate what to do before Maddie shouted, "Mother!" Half of Wagtail must have heard her.

Sky stopped midstep on the grand staircase. To her credit, she didn't turn tail and run back upstairs. Calmly, Sky walked to her daughter, placed a gentle hand on her arm, and said, "I'm glad you're here. We need to talk."

Maddie scowled at her mother and the two

of them ducked into the library with Atticus, Duchess, and Lulu.

Nessie barreled down the stairs. The two of us bounded after them. We stopped at the open entrance to the library and lurked to hear their conversation.

"What do you think you're doing? Have you lost your mind?" Maddie was mad as a yellow jacket.

"Honey, I was just looking out for you."

"Did you really think I wouldn't recognize you on that pontoon boat today? And what was that? A boat full of dogs and two women in Indiana Jones hats, pretending to fish?"

"We caught one. Did you see that? With just a hook. We didn't even have bait. I didn't know a fish would do that!"

"Don't change the subject. Aww. Who are these doggies?"

"This one is Duchess. She's a shelter dog. I'm going to adopt her. Isn't she sweet?"

"She's beautiful. Okay, Mom, listen. You have to back off. I met a guy I really like."

"The one on the boat? Were you drinking? I've never seen you so inept on a boat."

"I was pretending that I didn't know anything about boats. He doesn't know who I am, and I don't want him to know. But if you keep this up you're going to give me away."

"Maddie, why would you do that? Honey, you're such a lovely girl. Be yourself, and he'll like you."

"Do you remember Kyle? Don't look so worried. I'm not getting back together with him. But I don't want someone like that. I want someone who likes me for me."

"Sweetheart, I understand that. But pretending to be different will only backfire on you."

"Mom. I'm not a kid. I'm mortified that you're here at all. I may never forgive you for this. I'm an adult, Mom. You're—you're stalking me!"

"Maddie, there's something I need to tell you."

"What could it possibly be? You don't know Chad." Maddie gasped. "Oh no. You didn't hire a private investigator to check him out, did you?"

"No. It's not about Chad."

"If you don't stop spying on me, I swear I will never speak to you again."

Maddie stormed by us and backed up. "You!" She pointed at Nessie. "I *knew* you didn't get my name off of Atticus's collar." She gestured toward me. "And you, too. My love life is none of your business. Come on, Atticus."

Sky emerged from the library. In a soft and patient voice, she said, "Randall is dead."

SEVENTEEN

Maddie stopped midstride. She swung around and looked at her mother. "Is Aunt Cate all right?"

Maddie walked toward her daughter. "She's fine. Quite shaken, as you might imagine."

Maddie hugged her mother. "What happened?"

"Honey, he was murdered."

Maddie clapped a hand over her mouth. As she absorbed the information, her hand dropped. "We always said he would cross the wrong person someday."

Mother and daughter walked out to the porch together.

"Do you get the feeling they didn't like him very much?" I asked Nessie.

"My mama brought me up never to speak ill of the dead, but it sounds to me like the wake might be a celebration," Nessie said. "Pity that he won't have a chance to mend his ways." She called Lulu and went outside.

I walked to the bay window in the library and watched the three of them stroll away from the inn.

Sky and Maddie may not have been fond of Randall, but news of his death had caused Maddie to put aside her anger. Death always put things in perspective.

For the next couple of hours, the inn was quiet as a tomb. I paid some of the inn's bills. When the sun set, I hit the magic refrigerator for dinner. Trixie, Gingersnap, and I polished off leftover crab cakes and three-bean salad. I was washing dishes when the phone rang.

"Holly!" Zelda cried. "I need a favor."

"Sure." The word slipped out of my mouth before I considered the possibilities. Zelda was part of the Sugar Maple Inn family. There wasn't much I wouldn't do for her.

"Hank has been a pill all day—"

"Even when you were on the boat?"

"Ugh. He rented a boat too, and was out there with a pretty date. The poor girl was much younger than us. She has no idea what she's getting herself into with Hank."

"Maybe that's a good thing. Maybe he's moving on."

"I don't think so. I'm at my house, and Hank is outside right now, lurking in the shadows. I'm supposed to meet my date at Tequila Mockingbird, but I'm afraid Hank is going to follow me. Could you come over here and help me?"

"I can as soon as Oma comes back. What do you want me to do?"

"Wear a hat or a hood or something to cover your hair. You can leave through the front door while I sneak out the back. Hopefully, he'll follow you and won't know where I went."

I wasn't excited about the prospect. Zelda didn't live too far from the stores and restaurants on the green, though. If I headed in that direction, there would be loads of people around.

"Please, Holly? I don't know what else to do."

"Why don't you just leave lights on so he'll think you're home and then sneak out the back?"

"He's circling around the house. I've seen him watching from the neighbor's yard. I need you to distract him. If he thinks you're me, then he'll follow you, and I can make a clean break."

"Okay. I'll be over as soon as Oma returns." I didn't relish it, but we all did things for our girlfriends.

It was past nine when Oma and Gustav walked into the private kitchen.

"Did you have a nice dinner?" I asked.

"It was delicious." Gustav bestowed a fond smile on Oma.

"Of course, we talked about the murder of this Randall Donovan." Oma took out two wineglasses. "We have concluded there are two possibilities. Either Randall mugged Gustav or the person who mugged Gustav murdered Randall and planted the letter on him. These are the only two explanations for Randall having it in his possession."

Made sense to me, except for one thing. "Why would a psychiatrist mug someone? Aren't most muggers after money?"

Oma handed Gustav a bottle of wine. "We have

considered this but have no satisfactory answer. Perhaps he was broke. Or maybe he wished to have identification other than his own."

"We believe that the murderer must be the person who mugged me," said Gustav, "because there is no logical reason for planting the letter."

I considered telling Oma about Sky Stevens's connection to Randall but decided not to say anything in Gustav's presence. I wasn't sure why I was hesitant. Because it all seemed to begin with him? Could Gustav somehow be at the root of Randall's murder?

I smiled at him and changed the subject. "Zelda's obnoxious ex-husband is lurking around her house. She wants me to come over and distract him. I'm supposed to pretend to be Zelda and lure him away so she can leave the house without him following her."

"Ach. I do not like this man, Hank." Oma looked at me and began to laugh. "Zelda is much more zaftig than you, and taller. And your hair is the wrong color. Even this stupid man Hank will not be fooled."

"Liesel, perhaps Holly can wear extra clothes to bulk her up," suggested Gustav.

"I think I have a blonde wig somewhere!" Oma said. "Come with me, Holly."

The three of us, Gingersnap, and Trixie walked to the office. Oma pulled a life vest out of a storage closet and then produced a blonde wig and a black coat. By the time she was through with me, I had more girth and blonde locks. We couldn't change my height, of course, but in the dark, maybe I could pass for Zelda.

I looked down at Trixie. "But you would give me away, sweetie pie." I took her up to my apartment, closed the pet door, told her to behave, and locked the door.

I approached Zelda's quaint house from the rear by sneaking through the yard of the house that backed up to her lot. Dense pines and shrubs separated the homes. I crouched among the trees and watched for Hank.

In the darkness, every shape seemed sinister. I had spent many happy hours on the brick patio in Zelda's backyard, which seemed enchanted when the little fairy lights hanging from the trees sparkled. She had built special structures with hammocks and perches for her cats. Lavender, sage, rosemary, and catnip-filled giant pots around the patio. But the fairy lights weren't on, and the kitty play structures were frightful blobs that could be stooped people.

Lights glowed in Zelda's windows. Quaint and old, her house featured diamond-paned windows and dormers on the second floor. But in the night, knowing that Hank lurked outside somewhere, her fairy-tale-style house seemed spooky.

I wished I had night-vision glasses. As I scanned my surroundings, a figure sneaked along the side of the neighbor's yard. What a jerk Hank was! I held my breath and remained as still as possible.

I recoiled and drew in a sharp breath when Zelda's big tabby, Leo, rubbed against my knees. My gaze snapped to Hank. Had he heard me? It didn't look like it. He disappeared toward the street. I tickled Leo under his chin and made a mad dash for Zelda's back door.

It was unlocked. I let myself in and waited for Leo to amble inside. Crouching a bit, I hissed, "Zelda?"

She emerged from the living room and gave me a big hug. "Oh my gosh! Who dressed you? I hope I don't look like *that*."

"Oma was having fun. You're going to have to move fast, because it won't be long before he realizes that I'm the wrong height."

"Gotcha. Don't worry too much, though. I've noticed that it's sort of difficult to determine a person's height at night. Especially when that person is creeping around. There's a tendency to hunch over."

I could believe that. "So what's the plan?"

"You leave by the front door. Pretend you're locking it. Then walk toward the center of town, keeping your face in the shadows. Okay? Do *not* look back. It's only a couple of blocks. If you look back, he's likely to get a glimpse of your face under a streetlamp. Meanwhile, I'll hustle out the back way. I don't need much lead time. He'll probably recognize you by the time you reach the green." Zelda grinned at me. "But by then, I'll be long gone!"

"I can't believe I'm doing this." I chuckled. "I hope the new guy is a winner."

"Trust me, Holly. Hank taught me not to assume good things are in pretty packages. I'm being very careful about who I date."

"I hope so. Have fun." I walked to the door and looked back at her. "Tell me when he's watching."

Zelda turned off the lights in the living room, and peered between the curtains. "Okay," she whispered. "Go!"

As I turned the knob, I decided I would make a lousy spy. This wasn't a big deal, more of a game than anything else, but adrenaline pounded through me. Still, I hoped it would get Hank off Zelda's trail, if only for a little bit. I stepped outside, pretended to lock the door, and headed for the street, taking care to keep my face down. In spite of that, I could see Hank's shadowy figure lurking at the side of Zelda's yard. I didn't dare look back to see if he had taken the bait. I picked up my pace to move him farther away from Zelda's house in case he figured out what was happening.

In minutes I was at the green and turned right on the sidewalk that ran along it. Merchants were open late, and the dining tables on the sidewalk were swamped. People mingled with drinks in hand as though the restaurants had overflowed.

Their dogs and cats roamed underfoot. It was a perfect setup for getting lost in a crowd.

I dodged into Hot Hog, which was always packed with people. I slid the wig off my head as I wedged between patrons in the bar and worked my way over to a view of the sidewalk. I shed the hot coat and the life vest without taking my eyes off the window.

But I didn't see Hank. Time crawled by as I waited anxiously for a glimpse of him. The crowd was dense, though. I could have missed him. What if we hadn't fooled him? What if he had turned back and caught Zelda sneaking out the back way? I pushed my way through the crowd again and leaned out the door, looking for Hank.

But then I saw something I hadn't expected at all.

EIGHTEEN

Trixie trotted along the sidewalk with her nose to the ground. Without looking up, she walked straight to my sandals and wriggled with happiness end to end.

"What are *you* doing here?" I scooped her up and was rewarded with a kiss on my nose.

"You scamp. Who let you out? This was supposed to be a solo mission." And then it dawned on me that if Hank had seen Trixie, he might have realized that he wasn't tailing Zelda.

Oh no. It wasn't easy carrying the coat, life vest, wig, and Trixie, but there were so many people on the sidewalk that I feared she might be stepped on or get sidetracked.

I turned right onto a quieter residential street and set Trixie on the ground. For a long moment, I considered returning to Zelda's house to find out if she'd escaped from Hank. "Maybe we should stop by Tequila Mockingbird instead?"

Trixie hummed at me. It wasn't quite a growl, more like her version of speaking.

I dug in my pocket for a mini-treat. "That way, if Zelda made it to Tequila Mockingbird, but Hank is still hanging around her house, we won't lead him to her."

We set off for the lake. It wasn't far, just across

the main road on the west side of Wagtail. We passed several couples walking hand in hand, their dogs and cats strolling with them. One poor man sobbed into the fur of a cat that he held tightly. I guessed his date hadn't worked out well.

We crossed the empty street and walked over to Tequila Mockingbird. It was made of post and beam construction, and its heavy timbers supported a charming rustic entrance. A wide peaked roof jutted out over double glass doors, and benches on both sides offered seating. The lights in the ceiling of the cedar plank roof illuminated the area and small canned up-lights showed off giant elephant ear plants and lush red geraniums.

I held the door open for Trixie. The vaulted ceiling inside was supported by more beams, giving it an open and airy feeling. A wall of windows faced the lake, where boat lights bobbed in the distance.

The restaurant and bar were full, as was the outdoor seating. I wondered if I would be able to find Zelda in the crowd.

But my little sidekick, Trixie, led me straight to Zelda at a table in the corner. Zelda bent down to pet Trixie. When she looked up and saw me, she waved me over.

"This is Axel, Holly." Zelda smiled at him. "Would you like to join us?"

He was as lean as she was robust. Yet they made a stunning pair. His hair was as fair as hers, and his blue eyes gave me the impression he was honest and sincere. I liked him right away. But I knew Zelda wanted to get to know him better, and I wouldn't dream of interfering now that she had eluded Hank's watchful eyes.

"I don't mean to interrupt, but I never saw Hank once I got to the green. I just wanted to be sure you made a clean getaway."

"No sign of him yet. I think our plan worked!" Zelda beamed at me.

I wished them a good time, intending to leave, but Trixie had run off. I found her kissing up to Sky, who sat at an indoor table with Nessie and Macon Stotts. Duchess and Lulu lounged at their feet.

Macon pulled up a chair for me. I joined them and told them briefly about the little prank Zelda and I had played on Hank.

"You have to be so careful these days." Nessie sipped what I thought to be a mint julep, judging from the garnish.

"That's why Sky and I are here. To make sure our girls don't get tangled with the wrong men."

Sky tapped her fingers on the table. "Even though I'm here to protect Maddie, she won't listen. Why can't she see that she's going about this all wrong by lying to this young man?"

"What happened with her old boyfriend, Kyle? You never did tell me." Nessie sounded like she could hardly contain herself.

170

"He seemed like such a nice young man. He was polite and good-looking. I thought the world of him. And then he started hitting us up for money. It became painfully clear that he was more interested in the bank of Stevens than in Maddie. She was devastated."

"That's so sad. You'd think he would have targeted someone with more money." Nessie drained her drink. "I have to worry about that. Divorce can cost a bundle. Sky, you tried to tell Maddie to be herself. I hope she listens to you."

Macon patted Sky's hand. "I set her up with the right guy. Trust me on this." He frowned at me. "Where's John Adele? I hope you're meetin' him here."

"Sorry, Macon. In spite of you, Trixie, and Oma, I don't believe that match is going to take." Part of me was sorry to admit that. I wasn't going to weep about it, but I had been surprised and disappointed to detect John's clear disinterest when I phoned him.

Macon lifted his forefinger and shook it. "I don't believe that. I was there with you two last night, and I know sparks when I see them. I'll have a talk with that young man."

"That's very kind of you, but you also matched him to Maddie Stevens. Maybe that match will work out after all."

"Not a chance. That was to prove to them that my original matches were correct. Do you really think I'm so stupid that I would mismatch people like that?"

Sky's mouth dropped open. "Why, you rascal. You're like a puppet master pulling all our strings."

Macon grinned with pleasure. "Honey, I'm good at what I do. Don't ever doubt Macon."

That simple sentence, which I was certain was nothing more than puffery, sent chills up my arms. Randall hadn't just doubted Macon. He had belittled and insulted him publicly. Had he paid for that with his life?

"So did you set up Maddie with that young man she likes?" asked Sky. "Or was it just a coincidence that they met?"

"Of course I did. They're perfect for each other."

"Not the artist?" Nessie turned up her nose.

"There's much more to making a good match than careers, Nessie," Macon said.

Sky appeared doubtful. "What happened to good old-fashioned meeting someone and having that marvelous feeling about him?"

"Why, nothin', Sky. That's still what happens. I just steer the right people toward each other so they don't waste a lot of time on the wrong ones. Look around here." Macon gestured with a wide sweep of his hand. "I can tell which couples are going to work out. The big problem for me is when people lie—when they're too ashamed to admit the truth about themselves, and they fill out my questionnaires incorrectly. Then I can't do my job."

"You mean like where their dog or cat sleeps?" I asked.

"That's an excellent example. A woman who thinks the cat or dog should sleep in the garage will end up fightin' with a partner who allows the animals to sleep on the bed. It might not *seem* like an earthshaking thing, but it goes to fundamental differences. Trust me when I say that won't be the only thing they disagree on."

"Macon, I hate to hurt your feelings, but you were terribly wrong about my Celeste and that musician. They would never have worked out. You have to see how happy she is with the doctor I matched her up to." Nessie pulled out her phone and her face contorted. "Oh no! Someone tried to snatch Celeste's purse. The doctor punched him out! Look at this."

She held the phone out to Macon.

"Is she okay?" Macon reached for it leisurely, but when he looked at the photo, his demeanor changed. "Celeste is a beautiful girl, Nessie. You must be very proud of her."

He handed me the phone, but I caught the concern in his eyes. I took one look and my heart sank. I knew the man with his arms around Celeste. I recognized the cunning grin and cagey eyes. "That's no doctor. That's Zelda's good-for-nothing ex-husband."

Nessie scooted her chair back so fast that she nearly toppled over. "That is not amusing."

"But it's true. Zelda is sitting right over there. You can ask her."

Nessie hurried over to Zelda with Lulu at her heels. I watched as Nessie showed Zelda the photo.

When Nessie returned, her lips were bunched tight in anger. "I'm putting a stop to this right away. Imagine my baby in the hands of that man. I don't care if he did defend her from a purse snatcher." She slapped money on the table. "Sky, you coming with me?"

Sky rose from her seat and added money to the pile. "Sure."

Nessie was already marching toward the door.

"Good night," said Sky. She and Duchess caught up to Nessie and Lulu. We heard Sky ask, "What are you going to do?"

"You knew Nessie changed your matches?" I asked.

Macon shook his head and *tsked*. "She came right out and told me. Said she was a better matchmaker than I. One presumes she might be reconsidering that just about now. Mama Nessie should not have butted in. I would never have matched an innocent young woman like Celeste to a man ten years her senior, and a con artist at that."

"How did you know he was a con artist?" I

174

asked. "He's the kind of guy a lot of women find attractive."

Macon appeared surprised by my question. "I have met some very handsome doctors. But not one of them has ever filled out his or her occupation as *doctor*. They always write their specialties. You know, cardiologist, radiologist, podiatrist, dentist. In my experience, only the pretend doctors fill in the form with the word *doctor*."

I smiled at him. Maybe Macon really did know his stuff.

It was surely getting close to midnight, and I had had a long day on not much sleep. I bid Macon a good night, called Trixie, and walked home to the inn.

Casey greeted us when we entered through the front door.

Twinkletoes dashed by me dragging a blue cloth adorned with white paw prints that did *not* look like a cat toy. Marmalade was right behind her, grabbing for it with his claws.

"Hey, you two!" I started after them, but they were too quick for me.

"Casey! Have you been letting them tear that?"

"Sure. Why not?"

"It looks like a scarf."

He shrugged. "It has paw prints on it. I thought it was some kind of cat toy. They've been having a lot of fun with it."

I made sure the other doors around the inn were

locked and trudged up to my apartment. When I opened the door, Huey greeted us, his tail wagging like we were long-lost friends. Twinkletoes and Marmalade must have come up through the pet doors because they sat very innocently on the hearth. But I spied the scarf in my dining room and picked it up.

Beat as I was, I stopped in the kitchen to feed the cats. "Salmon?" I asked. "It's very trendy and popular in fancy restaurants." From the way they snarfed it, I assumed I had made a good choice.

Huey watched them with a tiny bit of drool edging out of his mouth. Trixie eyed the cats enviously. I dug into the dog cookie jar and found two crunchy cookies in the shape of dog bones. I handed Huey the large one and Trixie a small one.

When the cats finished, I let the dogs lick their bowls, then washed them. I tiptoed to the guest room and peeked in. Ben snored as though he'd been asleep for quite a while.

On Saturday morning, I stretched, opened my eyes, and realized that not a single cat or dog lay on my bed. I scrambled into my bathrobe and ran into the living room of my apartment. They weren't there either. *Not again!*

I barreled into the guest room. "Ben! Ben!" I shook his shoulder.

"Mmmpf. Whaaat?"

"Did you let the animals out?"

"No." He flipped over and pulled the pillow onto his head.

I couldn't believe he had done it again. I ran down the stairs. No sign of the dogs or of Casey.

I heard sounds in the commercial kitchen, though. I pushed the door open.

Shelley and the cook chirped, "Good morning!"

"Morning! Have you seen any dogs or cats walking around?"

They hadn't seen any of the animals. They didn't know where Casey was either.

I walked back to the desk in the lobby. "Casey?" I called softly.

I thought I heard something, crossed the room, and flung open the door to Oma's kitchen. Casey napped in an easy chair, surrounded by Huey, Duchess, Gingersnap, Trixie, and Lulu. Twinkletoes and Marmalade were curled up on the hearth. *Not in the chair next to Casey?*

The dogs wagged their tails at the sight of me, but none of them bothered to get up. They appeared exhausted.

On a hunch, I left the room and checked the dog and cat food storage room. I couldn't believe it. The door was wide-open, and they had had another party. How had they done that?

I got out the broom and dustpan and, once again, swept up the kibble mess on the floor. I took the time to make a quick inventory of the bags that had to be replaced.

My frustration with Ben grew as I worked. I knew *I* had not opened any doors during the night. It had to have been Ben who'd let the dogs out. Why would he do that? Was he sneaking out at night? As I fumed about it, I realized that he might not want to admit it to me if he was slinking out to spend his nights elsewhere. I had seen him in bed, but he could have had a rendezvous after that. A normal person would slip in and out without allowing the dogs and cats to escape, but Ben was inept and not used to animals. Maybe he couldn't control them.

But how had Gingersnap, Lulu, and Duchess gotten out? I started laughing and bent over double as I realized what must be happening. It was matchmaking week! A whole lot of people were sneaking around at night. No one cared if they didn't sleep in their own beds—after all, they were adults—but by escaping, the animals were giving away their nocturnal escapades!

Where had Ben been going? To Laura's room? And which of the snoopy moms was sneaking out—Nessie or Sky? And my own Oma!

I tried to control my laughter. Happily, Mr. Huckle had arrived. I stole a chocolate croissant and a mug of tea and headed upstairs. I didn't see the point in waking Oma, Nessie, or Sky, because all the dogs were safe. Besides, they all probably needed their sleep. I did close their doors, though.

When I returned in a sleeveless white top, belted

red skirt, chunky necklace, and drop earrings, guests were already drinking coffee in the dining area and out on the terrace.

The dogs hadn't budged from Oma's kitchen, and they certainly weren't getting any breakfast after their midnight buffet, so I let them snooze.

Shelley bustled up to me. "Is it true what they're saying?"

I blinked at her. "About what?"

"About Bob Lane."

"The pharmacist?"

She tilted her head. "Do you know any other Bob Lanes? Of course I mean the pharmacist. Do you think he murdered that guy Randall?"

"Why would anyone think that?"

Shelley lowered her voice. "Because he slugged Randall."

"That seems unlikely. Bob is such a mild-mannered man. I can't imagine him punching anybody."

"That part is for sure. There were witnesses. The question is whether he killed Randall that night. You're always in the know. Did he?"

"Obviously, I am woefully behind, because I knew nothing about this." But I was sure going to find out.

Shelley raised her chin as though she was looking at something behind me. "Ask your grandmother. I'll be right over with coffee."

I turned around. Oma and Gustav were taking

seats at a table. I wasn't sure whether I should join them or not, but Oma waved me over.

Before I could sit down, Gustav greeted me with an unenthusiastic *good morning,* and Oma asked, "Do you have my Gingersnap?"

"She's fine. The dogs had another party in the pantry last night. They're all sleeping it off in the private kitchen."

"I don't understand. How could she have left my apartment?"

I wasn't about to embarrass her in front of Gustav. Not to mention that he might have been the one who let Gingersnap slip out. "I don't know." It was the truth. I really *didn't* know.

"Can you pick up more kibble after breakfast?" asked Oma.

"I already have a list."

Shelley set a basket of breakfast breads on the table and poured coffee for everyone. "Did you ask about Bob Lane?"

Oma looked at her. "News goes around this town far too fast. Dave just called to tell me that he will be questioning Bob."

Shelley's eyebrows raised. "I always thought he was such a nice guy. You can't trust anybody!"

Poor Gustav. He hadn't managed to get a word in other than *good morning.*

"What's for breakfast, Shelley?"

"Specials today are ham steak with fried eggs and hash browns, Belgian waffles with mixed local berries and cream, and three-egg omelets with mushrooms."

After we ordered and Shelley was gone, Oma asked Gustav, "How do you feel?"

"I have been better."

"Is something wrong?" I asked.

"The hospital only gave Gustav a few pain pills when they released him. Maybe you could get his prescriptions filled when you pick up the dog food?"

"I would be happy to. Do you have the prescriptions with you, Gustav?"

He pulled two of them out of his pocket and handed me cash. "This is very nice of you, Holly. When I was younger, I would have told myself to work through the pain, but when one is my age, being slammed to the ground takes a toll. I am very stiff and so grateful that your grandmother has loaned me a golf cart to get around. I love to hike, but I'm not sure I can do it without the pills to help my achy bones."

"Gustav, perhaps we should cancel our hiking plans."

"No, no, no. After I take the pills, I will be fine."

When Shelley brought our food, I ate my mushroom omelet quickly. It was still early, but Heal!, the local drugstore, would be open.

I excused myself and dashed upstairs to brush my teeth and grab my purse. On my way out, I stopped by Oma's private kitchen and poked my head in. "Anybody want to go for a ride?"

Trixie and Gingersnap jumped to their feet. Huey did, too. Duchess and Lulu were already gone, so I assumed Sky and Nessie had found them.

I took a golf cart to transport the heavy bags of kibble to the inn. All four of us sat on the front bench. The dogs lifted their noses into the wind. I wondered what interesting scents they were picking up.

It was a gorgeous, crisp summer morning. Not a cloud marred the stunning blue sky. The electric golf cart made so little sound that I could hear birds chirping in the trees.

I turned the golf cart right on the street where Zelda lived. A few people sat on their front porches with mugs that I assumed contained coffee. They waved at me as we drove by.

And then, without any warning whatsoever, Trixie, who had ridden in the cart like a champ, barked in her frantic tone, scrambled past Gingersnap, leaped off the moving golf cart, and ran like crazy.

Gingersnap and Huey bounded out after her.

The day hadn't started well—and now this. I could see them running through front yards on the right side of the street. I gunned the golf cart, but the dogs dodged behind a house and disappeared.

I pulled over in front of Zelda's place.

Trixie barked like a crazed dog in the tone that I dreaded so much. It meant something was horribly wrong.

NINETEEN

I ran through Zelda's side yard, screaming, "Zelda!" The grass was still wet with dew, causing my sandals to slip and slide.

Trixie continued to bark, and Gingersnap let out a long sad howl that set off other dogs nearby.

And then I saw a hand on the ground.

"Zelda!" Her name rose from my throat involuntarily. *Not Zelda!*

As I neared, my breath came nosily. The hand lay palm down. Surely Zelda's hand wasn't that large. It looked like a man's hand to me.

Trixie, Huey, and Gingersnap sniffed around the base of a pine tree, the large branches hanging over their backs. I fell to my knees. My gaze followed the blood-spattered hand to an arm clad in a short-sleeved black T-shirt.

I pulled aside a low-hanging branch and peered in the shadows beneath the tree.

He lay on his stomach, his face turned toward me. There was no doubting the bloody mess that was Hank's neck. His eyes were wide-open, his expression one of surprise. I didn't think there was any point in CPR, but I felt his wrist for a pulse out of an abundance of caution.

It was cold.

Shuddering, I pulled away from the grisly scene

and, for the first time, noted blood on the grass.

"Trixie? Holly, is that you?"

I looked over my shoulder to see Zelda stumbling toward me. Her long blonde hair was mussed, as though she had just rolled out of bed. She wore an oversized T-shirt long enough to cover her rear. "Holly, what are you doing?"

She screamed when she saw the hand. "Who . . . who is it?" she whispered.

"I'm sorry, Zelda. It's Hank."

"What?" She must not have believed me because she knelt on the grass and looked under the tree branches. She pulled out fast, a trembling hand covering her mouth. "He was massacred!"

That was a good word for what had happened to him. Zelda was so pale that I feared she was in shock. I took her arm and helped her to a lawn chair.

"Trixie! Gingersnap! Huey! Come!" I pulled out my cell phone and called 911.

I described Trixie, Gingersnap, and Huey finding Hank's body and told the dispatcher that I thought he was probably dead given the amount of blood I saw.

That brought on a torrent of tears from Zelda. I hung up the phone and stroked her hair, hoping like crazy that she didn't have anything to do with it. I hated that the thought even crossed my mind, but they had been married, and he had been a royal nuisance to her.

Dave was the first person on the scene. He strode into Zelda's backyard, taking in every little detail.

I left Zelda, motioned to Dave, and walked over to the trees where Hank lay.

Dave kept his calm. "When did you get here?"

"Maybe five minutes before I called nine-one-one."

"You see anyone?"

"No. Only Zelda. She looked like she had just rolled out of bed."

"What were you doing back here?"

"Trixie jumped off the golf cart, and other dogs followed her. They found him."

He nodded. "Figures. Can you wait with Zelda, please?" Dave pulled out a camera and photographed Hank's hand and the grass.

I hadn't taken two steps when he said, "Holly? I changed my mind."

I turned back.

"Hold up the branches so I can get some shots of him before he's moved?"

I lifted the branches and got a much better look at poor Hank. Murder was never pleasant, but someone had whacked him in the worst way. I couldn't imagine how anyone could have inflicted the bloody wounds on his neck and back. "You don't think it could have been a bear, do you?"

"Bears are not in the habit of hiding their kill. A bear wouldn't have pulled him under the tree like this."

"How do you know that's what happened?"

"Holly! Look how dense the trees are. If he had rolled under them to protect himself, he might have lived. The tree limbs aren't hacked up. I'll bet the autopsy shows that somebody clobbered him from behind and then kept at it when he fell to the ground."

When the rescue squad arrived, I hustled Zelda and the dogs into her house. Her cats—I counted seven—were appalled and scrambled away, with the notable exception of Leo, who was convinced he was the king of Wagtail. I had never seen him run from a dog.

I put the kettle on for tea and watched the goings-on in the backyard through the window. "You'd better get dressed, Zelda."

Without a word, she left the kitchen. I could hear the stairs creaking as she walked up them. I used her wall phone to call Ben's cell phone.

He sounded groggy.

"Are you up yet?"

"No."

"I think Zelda's going to need a lawyer."

"Why?"

"Because I just found her ex-husband dead in her backyard."

Ben wrote down Zelda's address and promised he was on his way.

Zelda's kitchen was as sunny and cheerful as Zelda herself. The cabinets had been painted a soft green. There were no upper cabinets, only shelves that hung over white wallpaper dotted by old-fashioned cream medallions. Neatly arranged dishes, mugs, platters, and spices occupied the shelves. A Victorian-style lamp hung over the country kitchen sink. Herbs grew in little mismatched pots on the windowsill behind the sink.

Watching Dave through the diamond-paned glass made it all seem even more surreal. It was almost as though no one had brutally murdered Hank, and I was watching a film.

I grabbed a mug off a shelf. It said *There's always room for one more cat.* Zelda certainly lived by that motto. I searched for black tea to calm her nerves. She had a collection of herbal teas, some which I had never heard of before.

I finally found a box of organic black tea. I was pouring water into the cup when Zelda returned. She had changed into a blue sundress with a cabbage rose print.

"They're going to think that I murdered Hank. I can't pay a lawyer. Whoever did it is going to get away scot-free, and I'll end up in jail. I wish I had never met Hank."

I poured milk into her tea and added a spoonful of sugar. "We'll work something out. Don't you worry about that. Oma and I will stand by you. I called Ben."

I poured a second cup of tea and leaned against

the sink sideways so I could keep an eye on what was happening in the yard. "*Did* you kill him?" I tried to sound ever so casual about it.

"No!"

Out of the corner of my eye, I spied Ben in the backyard, speaking with Dave.

Ben walked toward the kitchen door. I opened it for him.

Zelda dabbed at her eyes with a tissue. "Thank you for coming, Ben." She sniffled. "I don't know why I'm crying. I guess because I loved Hank once."

Ben sat down at the table, and to my complete surprise, he took her hand and said, "It's okay to cry. You've had a big shock."

I made tea for Ben and handed the mug to him. He sat with Zelda quietly while she composed herself. What happened to the insensitive, geeky guy I knew?

"Tell me what you did last night," he said to Zelda.

"I was at Tequila Mockingbird with Axel Turner."

"What time did you leave?"

"I don't know. When they closed. Around two, I guess?"

"And then?"

"I walked Axel to the Wagtail Springs Hotel, where he's staying, and then came home and went to bed."

"Did you hear or see anything during the night?"

"Nope. We might have had a little too much to drink. I fell asleep and didn't wake until I heard barking this morning. Then I heard someone yell my name."

"Who?"

Zelda looked at me. "I guess it was Holly. When I came downstairs, she was in the backyard."

"Okay. I know I asked this before, but I want you to think back very carefully. Did you hear anything last night? Did you notice anything at all out of the norm?"

Zelda's forehead crinkled with worry. "No. Nothing. Really."

"When did you last see Hank?"

"When Holly lured him away last night."

Ben set his tea down on the table so hard that it splashed out of the mug.

I grabbed a dish towel and wiped it up.

"You want to explain that?" he asked.

"It's nothing. Hank was lurking around Zelda's house. He had been a pill the night before when she was out on a date, and then he followed them out on the lake! Zelda asked me to distract him so she could get away and meet her date without being followed. I pretended to be Zelda and left by the front door while she sneaked out the back way. No big deal."

Ben covered his face with his palms. "So you're the last one who saw him?"

"Well, I don't know about *that*. When I got to Hot Hog, I stepped inside to see if he would walk by, but I never saw him."

Ben swallowed hard. "And then where did you go?"

"I'm not a suspect. Quit acting like I am. I went to Tequila Mockingbird to see if Zelda had made it there without Hank."

"Great. Very good. So people saw you there?"

"Sure. I talked with Macon and Nessie . . ." My voice trailed off.

"Who's Nessie?"

"She's staying at the inn. Lots of jewelry, has a little dog named Lulu."

"Oh yeah. I thought she was going to propose to me when she heard I was a lawyer."

"She was showing us a picture of her daughter, Celeste, and the doctor she met here. But the guy wasn't a doctor at all. It was Hank."

"You told her that?" Ben asked.

Zelda finally perked up. "Yes! She brought a picture on her phone over to me to verify that it was Hank. She couldn't believe he had conned them."

"And then?" asked Ben.

"Then Nessie and Sky left in a big hurry."

My phone rang, and all three of us jumped at the sound. Oma wanted to know what was taking me so long with Gustav's pain meds. I promised to get them right away. "I have to run."

"You can't leave," said Ben.

"Of course I can. You take care of Zelda." I gave her a hug before Trixie, Gingersnap, and I left via the front door. I had my doubts about leaving Huey with Ben, but Zelda would watch out for him.

I drove the golf cart the remaining blocks to the green. We all hopped out and walked across the grass to Heal! on the other side. Trixie and Gingersnap roamed with their noses to the ground.

When we reached the sidewalk on the other side, Trixie dodged to the right and ran a little farther than she should have. My heart sank when I saw where she went.

TWENTY

Trixie wagged in delight and touched noses with Cooper. A few feet away, John was having breakfast with Laura.

Maybe Laura Pisani was the reason John had decided against having dinner with me. If that were the case, Ben and I were both out of luck. It surprised me that I felt disappointed. I barely knew John. But he'd been nice. I sucked in a deep breath of air. It clearly wasn't meant to be. Holding my chin high, maybe too high in compensation for my hurt feelings, I called Trixie and walked into Heal!

Bob Lane smiled at me. "Morning, Holly."

I handed Gustav's prescriptions to the lanky man with the high cheekbones and facial structure worthy of magazine covers.

"This will take a few minutes, if you want to shop around."

"Thanks. Gustav is in pain, so I'll wait for it."

Trixie and Gingersnap had made their way back to the dog and cat treat section. The two of them sniffed all the displays.

I eyed the old-fashioned soda fountain. There wasn't a single empty seat. In fact, the drugstore was packed. The son of the owner was busy filling breakfast orders.

Pssst.

I looked around.

Pssst. Someone tapped my shoulder, and I turned.

Oh no. My Aunt Birdie. I loved her because she was my aunt, but the woman complained more than anyone I had ever known. She was bossy, opinionated, and demanding. In the old days, they would have called her a handsome woman. Gaunt enough to be bony, she was impeccably dressed in a black wrap-front knit dress. A white border ran up the left side like a stripe. It went around the neckline and was accented with a black button, as though it held the wrapped side in place. "Hello, Aunt Birdie."

She pecked me on the cheek and slid her cool hand into mine. "We need to talk."

She pulled me toward the front of the store. I had learned the hard way that there was no point in fighting her.

"Trixie! Gingersnap!" I called.

Birdie pushed the door open and hustled me out onto the sidewalk. I held the door for the dogs.

"Holly, dear, I don't want you getting any prescriptions filled at Heal! You drive down the mountain and over to a drugstore in Snowball if you need anything." She frowned at me. "What are you getting a prescription for, anyway? Are you sick?" She felt my forehead. "Does your mother know about this? Honestly, child, I have to do everything for you."

"The prescriptions are for a guest of the inn."
I wasn't about to tell her he was a new friend of
Oma's. Aunt Birdie and Oma didn't care for each
other much. Birdie would surely turn information
about Gustav into dreadful gossip.

"Thank heaven for that."

"Does this have anything to do with a rumor
about Bob?" I asked.

"So you do know."

"Actually, I don't." But I felt certain that she
would tell me.

"You know the man who was murdered over in
the Shire?"

"Randall Donovan."

"Yes, that's the one. Bob murdered him."

"And you know this because . . . ?"

"Holly, it's all over Wagtail. Bob hushed
everything up, but you know how small towns
are. The truth always comes out. Back about four
years ago, Bob filled a prescription written by
one Dr. Randall Donovan for a girl with anorexia
nervosa. Her parents were vacationing here, so
her mother had the prescription filled right here
at Heal! Well, don't you know, it caused that poor
girl's heart to stop, and her parents sued Bob Lane
for causing her death."

"Wouldn't Randall Donovan have been the one
at fault for prescribing the medicine?"

"That's the point, Holly. But Bob was sued too,
and that's a fact. So I don't want you letting him

fill any prescriptions for you. You hear me?"

But Bob didn't do anything wrong. In a way it was sweet of her to be so concerned about me. But I feared that she was just repeating a rumor and there was either no truth to it at all or more to the story.

"Don't you see the connection?" Aunt Birdie scowled at me. "You're usually much sharper than this. Are you getting enough sleep? Bob blamed Randall for the lawsuit, and murdered him because he was so upset that the girl died from the medicine he dispensed."

Assuming the story was true, I could see that Bob might have had reason to be very upset with Randall and distressed over the girl's death. I would have to find out more about it, but from a reliable source. I tried to wrap up the conversation. "Thank you for your concern about my well-being, Aunt Birdie."

She bestowed a smile upon me and reached out to touch my hair. "But there isn't a reason in the world you can't get a trim of this beautiful long hair of yours. Stop by the beauty parlor. A decent manicure with a nice ladylike pink polish is in order, too. I don't want your mother to think I'm not looking after you."

Thank heaven from inside Heal! Bob knocked on a window and waved a white bag at me.

"I need to dash back with that, Aunt Birdie. Excuse me."

I left her standing on the sidewalk while I paid for Gustav's prescriptions.

"Did Birdie tell you I murdered Randall?" asked Bob.

He'd caught me completely off guard. How do you answer a question like that? Or was it a statement of guilt? "You know the rumor mill in Wagtail."

Bob looked me straight in the eyes. "I didn't kill him. But I sure would have liked to. I slugged him pretty good, though. When Dave figures out who ended the life of that miserable scum, I'm going to shake his hand."

He was usually so even-tempered and friendly! I hoped he hadn't said that to Dave. Feeling just a little bit shaken by his anger, I abruptly turned to leave, and hurried out of the store with the dogs.

Thankfully, I didn't see Birdie anywhere. But John and Laura were still gabbing and laughing.

No matter, I told myself. I barely knew the guy. Maybe he had nice eyes and seemed sincere, and his dog, Cooper, was a sweetheart, but I would manage just fine without them.

Trixie and Gingersnap ran ahead across the green, and I followed. We hopped into the golf cart and rolled by Zelda's home. I slowed down and observed police busily coming and going through her side yard. I hoped she was holding up okay.

In a matter of minutes I parked at the inn and jogged to the sliding glass doors of the reception lobby. I heard voices in the office, and Huey bounded out to meet us.

I skirted behind the reception desk and held up the medicine bag as I entered the office. "I'm sorry it took so long. I was . . . detained."

Oma and Zelda sat on the sofa with coffee and pastries on the coffee table in front of them. Gingersnap trotted straight to them and laid her head in Zelda's lap. Not to be left out, Trixie jumped on the sofa, barely wedging in next to Zelda. It was as though they knew instantly that Zelda was in crisis.

Gustav held a coffee cup and saucer on his lap. At the sight of me, he placed them on the table. He gladly took the bag, tore it open, and immediately swallowed two capsules. I could see that he moved with stiffness. "Thank you, Holly."

"I'm sorry for the delay." I handed him his change.

"One can never anticipate murder."

"The Ben brought Zelda to be with us." Oma patted Zelda's hand.

Zelda's eyes were huge with terror. "They already have a search warrant for my house! Ben's there taking care of everything. He thought dogs would be in the way, so he left Huey here. I'm sorry, Holly. I never was very fond of Ben, but I'm so glad that he's helping me now."

"Me, too. Has anyone seen Nessie?"

Oma gasped. "Holly! I do not believe that

Nessie murdered Hank. She is a lovely woman."

"Then who?" I asked.

Zelda gazed around at us. "Half of Wagtail! He probably owed money that I didn't even know about. There's no telling what underhanded things he did to people."

"That casts a rather broad net." Gustav helped himself to a cinnamon bun. "Do they know how he was killed?"

"He was so bloody!" Zelda buried her face in her hands.

I nodded in confirmation.

"I don't know why I can't stop crying. I hated him," Zelda blurted. "Hated! He could be so sweet, but he left me with mounds of debt that I haven't been able to pay off yet. Maybe I never will! I've been furious with him for a long time, and now I'm crying because he's dead!"

In a very gentle tone, Oma said, "Perhaps you never wished him such a terrible end."

Zelda sniffled. "Don't be so sure about that. When I was struggling and angry I wished some pretty awful things on him." Her face contorted with sorrow. "But you're right, Oma. No matter what ugly things I said about Hank, I never would have wanted this."

Gustav watched Zelda, showing no emotion. "What about the young man with whom you went out yesterday evening? Maybe he encountered your Hank and a fight ensued."

"That would be awful! I hope that's not what happened."

"Dave has the name of your young man?" asked Oma.

"Yes. I don't think he killed Hank, though."

"Too nice?" asked Gustav.

"He is very nice, but I never told him where I live. You know, as a precaution. He was a stranger."

Part of me longed to hang around the inn and have a cup of tea. But I still had to pick up the dog and cat kibble before someone pitched a fuss because it wasn't available. "I'm off to get the pet food now. Is there anything else I should pick up while I'm out?"

"Hurry back, *liebling*," Oma said. "We will eat lunch here in the privacy of the office. Or maybe on the terrace just outside. It's such a beautiful summer day."

I called Trixie and Gingersnap. Trixie jumped to the floor and ran out the door ahead of me. Gingersnap didn't budge from Zelda's side. She gave me a look, though, and I understood. It was Gingersnap's mission in life to comfort everyone.

Trixie and I took the golf cart back to the green. But this time, I avoided Zelda's street. Mostly because the next street over was closer to the store and it would make loading the kibble bags easier. But also because it was a little creepy. I hoped Zelda wouldn't feel that she had to move.

She loved that house, and it suited her personality so well, with its old-fashioned cottage feel.

I parked, and we walked to the store. Her nose to the ground, Trixie sped inside.

I ambled toward the owner and handed him my list. "Another raid on the pantry last night."

He laughed. "I need to teach more dogs to do that. I'd sell twice as much food." He hurried to the back, clutching my list.

I knew why Trixie had been eager to enter the store when Cooper loped toward me. *Oh no.* It wasn't like I could dash out now to avoid John. I patted Cooper and stroked his soft ears.

John was carrying a bag of kibble when he spotted me. "Holly." He sucked in a breath so large that his chest heaved.

I tried to be cheerful. "Hi, John."

"I'm just picking up some food for Cooper." He edged away, keeping his eyes on me.

I nodded. I had no idea what to say. "So, how's the thriller coming?" There, that was neutral and harmless.

"Look, Holly, I'm going to be in town a couple more months, so I'm just going to come right out and ask you to stop this."

TWENTY-ONE

I honestly didn't have a clue what John meant. "Stop what?"

"Please don't make this difficult."

"Mmm, okay." I shrugged.

Clearly annoyed with me, he set his bag of kibble on the checkout counter. "I guess I should be flattered, but it's kind of creepy."

I blinked at him. Hank's death was creepy, but I couldn't imagine why he would be flattered. "I have no idea what you're talking about."

"This. Exactly what you just did by following me into this store."

I was speechless and wishing I could think of a stinging retort when the store owner wheeled out a cart loaded with bags of dog and cat food and said, "If you'll give me a second to help this gentleman, I can load these on the golf cart for you."

His timing was perfect. I was just a little bit satisfied by the burn of embarrassment on John's face.

"Thanks, but I can handle it." I didn't want to wait one second longer with John in the store. "Send the bill to the inn?"

"Sure thing, Holly."

Feeling vindicated and just a little bit smug, I

pushed the flat cart toward the door. It was heavier than I expected, but there was no way I was going to let them know that I was straining. I had *some* pride, after all. I lifted my chin and pushed like crazy, nearly slamming into a woman who was entering the store. Happily, I missed her and was out on the sidewalk, where I could breathe easier knowing John wasn't watching me anymore. The nerve of him to imagine that I was following him around. I glanced down at Trixie. "This is your fault. And Oma's. And Macon's. I knew I should stay out of this matchmaking stuff, but the three of you had to go and introduce me to John."

Trixie cocked her head at me.

"It's okay. Cooper is very sweet. I can see how that might have been misleading."

It took a few minutes to load the golf cart. Trixie roamed around while I fit everything in. I was just finishing when the store owner showed up to help. I handed over the empty cart, thanked him, and was off.

The temperature had crept up, but it was perfect weather for lunch outside in the shade of an umbrella. Along the street, lush red and pink roses bloomed against white picket fences. Masses of daisies stood out in the green grass, and geraniums in pots brightened porches.

A scream shattered my pleasant thoughts. It was followed by a series of short shrieks.

Trixie leaped off the moving golf cart.

Not again!

I pulled over in front of my Aunt Birdie's house and ran after Trixie, who was a better judge than I of where the scream came from.

She yelped a few times before I made it into the backyard. I stopped short.

Aunt Birdie held her hands at shoulder height, her fingers splayed. Red smears marred her long-sleeved white shirt. She stared at something on the ground.

"Aunt Birdie? Are you all right?" I approached her with my eye on the grass in case there was a snake.

She held her hands out to me. "I don't think this is paint."

"Are you bleeding? What happened?" I looked for a cut on her hands.

"I went to the shed for birdseed to fill the feeder, but the hoe was in the way."

My gaze followed hers down to a two-pronged garden hoe. An uneven film of dark red covered parts of the wood handle. Heavier red coated the two sharp prongs.

"It wasn't where it was supposed to be. I *always* hang it on the wall, but it was propped up between the birdseed bag and the lawn mower."

I pulled out my cell phone and called Dave. "Go wash that off, Aunt Birdie."

"Do you think it's blood?" she whispered.

I nodded. "Zelda's ex-husband was murdered in her backyard last night."

Aunt Birdie's hands flew to cover her nose and mouth. It took only a second for her to realize she had spread blood on her face. Her expression turned to horror. "Ick. Ugh. Ugh!" She rushed to the house.

A scant three minutes later, Dave ran into Aunt Birdie's backyard.

I pointed at the hoe. "Aunt Birdie found it in her shed."

"Did she touch it?"

"Oh yeah. It's still tacky. It smeared on her hands and shirt."

Dave took a look in Aunt Birdie's shed. He backed up and stared at me without speaking. "Is that your dog food out there on the golf cart?"

"Yes. I was on my way back to the inn when Aunt Birdie screamed."

His mouth twisted to the side. He lowered his head and rubbed the back of his neck before looking up at me. "I want you to go back to the inn and stay there. Understand?"

I didn't understand at all. "Are you saying someone dangerous is on the loose?"

I had known Dave for a while now and had never seen him quite so uncomfortable.

"I don't know. Things are developing pretty fast. Just stay there, okay?"

"Should I take Aunt Birdie with me?"

He thought for a moment. "No. I need to talk with her."

"Dave, what's going on?" He had confided in me before. He had even asked me for help.

He shook his head and looked very disturbed. "Go home. I have work to do. I'll see you later at the inn."

Trixie must have picked up on my mood, because she no longer ran and sniffed with joy. She hopped into the golf cart and snuggled close to me. I drove back with one arm draped around her.

Our handyman spied me parking the golf cart, and walked over to unload it. I was thanking him when Trixie barked and ran to the front of the inn. I followed her.

A crowd had gathered outside. Everyone gazed upward. There were cries of *Get a net* and *Can't someone do something?*

It only took a minute to see what they were looking at. Marmalade was climbing the stone wall of the inn. How could he do that? Granted, the stones were roughly hewn and uneven, but I had never seen a cat climb like that. He appeared to be headed to my balcony.

Laura startled me when she seized my arm. "Holly! Call the fire department! They must have a tall ladder. Marmalade will fall!"

"Has he ever done this before?"

"Not that I know of." She frowned. "He has jumped from my balcony to my neighbor's a few times. She insists that he comes over to visit them a lot, but I thought she was exaggerating. Now I wonder if he gets out when I'm not home."

"Wait here." I dashed inside and up the stairs to a housekeeping closet, where I located an old fitted sheet on a bottom shelf. A box of disposable housekeeping gloves had landed on the floor under the shelf. When I set it where it belonged, I found what appeared to be a newly opened box. Hurriedly, I stacked them and rushed out and down the stairs. On my way through the lobby, I grabbed the handyman.

Outside, volunteers lined up to help hold the sheet to catch Marmalade in case he fell.

I ran back into the lobby and up the grand staircase to my apartment, Trixie on my heels. Panting heavily, I fumbled with my key, but finally swung the door open. I hurried through the apartment to my bedroom, where I discovered Twinkletoes locked out on the balcony. She stood on her hind legs, scratching desperately on the glass of the French doors to be let in. I flung open the doors and picked her up. I peered over the railing. Marmalade mewed at us but kept climbing.

Twinkletoes tensed in my arms and hissed at her friend.

The crowd below began to cheer. My heart pounded because I was terrified that Marmalade would fall. Fortunately, the roof of the porch would break his fall, so I hoped he would be okay. I had read somewhere that cats righted themselves and landed on their feet when falling a long distance. They didn't have time to flip in shorter distances. But how long a distance did it have to be?

I set Twinkletoes down and knelt on the deck, ready to grab Marmalade.

To my complete astonishment, his front paws appeared over the edge, and he tried to pull himself through the bars of the wrought-iron railing. I grabbed him under his arms and helped him.

I didn't know what he did to insult Twinkletoes, but instead of acting like Juliet greeting her Romeo, she was annoyed and spat at him. She clearly did not appreciate his courageous efforts to visit her.

I tried to stroke both of them, but Twinkletoes hissed and arrogantly stalked inside.

I picked up Marmalade. "Sorry, pal. I guess we've both been dumped."

I was boiling mad that someone, most likely Ben, had locked Twinkletoes on the balcony. The poor baby must have been stuck there all morning.

"You are quite the friend to climb all the way up here to be with Twinkletoes," I told Marmalade.

"Holly?" called a female voice.

"I bet that's your mom. She's very worried about you."

He purred his acknowledgement.

I walked inside and made sure the French doors were locked so Marmalade wouldn't get any crazy ideas about leaving the way he had arrived.

We met Laura in my living room, and I handed her baby over to her.

"Thank heaven he's all right! I can't imagine what possessed him to do that." Laura switched to baby talk. "What was Marmi thinking? I don't know what I would do without my wittle Marmi." She looked up at me, let out a deep breath, and shook her head. "Thank you so much, Holly. Sorry to create such a big scene. From now on, Marmalade will stay in our room or be on his leash."

I watched them go, closed the door, and turned around. Twinkletoes, the damsel in distress who had spurned her daring rescuer, jumped to her favorite armchair and nestled into it for a nap.

I spooned some Tunalicious cat food into her bowl in case she wanted a snack when she woke.

Trixie looked on with envy. Her ears perked, and she yipped.

"Not to worry, Trixie. I'm sure there's something equally delicious waiting for us downstairs."

I wasn't sure she believed me, but she raced to the door, which made me think of Randall. Trixie knew exactly what I had said.

From the landing of the grand staircase, I saw a young lady looking around. She held a newspaper in her hand, and her little dog looked like a white Wookiee peering from a fancy bag on her shoulder.

"May I help you?" I asked.

"Yes. Can you tell me what room Nessie Jamieson is in?"

Aha. The beautiful Celeste. Unlike her mother, she was slender, but I could see the resemblance.

Shelley was busy serving, but she turned long enough to say, "Holly!" and point at the terrace.

I led Celeste to the terrace and over to the table where Nessie and Sky were seated.

Paige from WAG was eating lunch with friends. She waved at me and smiled.

"Mom!" Celeste slapped the newspaper next to her mother's plate. "Did you see this?"

I couldn't help myself. I slowed my departure to a crawl, pretending to tend to a potted hibiscus. Craning my neck, I could see that she had the Snowball newspaper. Had they put out a special edition about Hank's murder?

"Isn't this your friend?" Celeste asked Nessie.

"No. Don't be silly. Do you want some lunch?" Nessie looked up at her daughter.

Celeste pulled out a chair and joined them. "Hi, you must be Sky. Mom told me about the Sugar Maple Inn and her roommate last night after she embarassed me to death by dragging me out of a restaurant like a naughty child." She shot her mother an annoyed look. "Mom, I'm sure it's him. We met him at your class reunion. It looks just like him. I remember his name, too—Randall Donovan."

TWENTY-TWO

I accidentally broke a little twig. When I glanced back at their table, Sky's eyes met mine. Had Sky been rooming with Randall's killer?

Randall was Sky's brother-in-law. If Nessie had known him, wouldn't she have told Sky? One of those it's-a-small-world-type things? A shiver crawled across my neck. Could Nessie have killed Randall? That would have been an excellent reason not to disclose the fact that she knew him.

I itched to hear more. Grabbing the pitcher of ice water, I lingered near them, refilling glasses.

"What have you been doing this morning?" Nessie asked her daughter.

Rats! Nessie was deftly changing the topic.

"Mom, remember the sorority sister I told you about?"

"Sweetheart, I have told you before that we do not need a private plane."

"Not that one. The one who had an affair with the professor! He's here!"

"Well, don't *you* get mixed up with that man. You hear me? I swear I'm beginning to understand why the parents pick spouses for their children in some cultures."

Sky excused herself and cocked her head at me ever so slightly.

I followed her into the inn. She headed straight for the library.

In the smallest whisper, Sky asked, "Do you think Nessie could have killed Randall? No. No, that's ridiculous. No one is a good enough actress to have pulled that off and faced me every day."

I liked Nessie. The last thing in the world that I wanted to imagine was that she could be a murderer. But if, and that was still a big *if,* she knew Randall, was it possible that she had killed him, and Hank, too?

"Where did you go last night when you left Tequila Mockingbird?" I asked Sky.

"Nessie was beside herself. She was headed for the restaurant where Celeste and Hank were in the photo."

"Did you go with her?"

"No. That whole mix-up with Hank was Nessie's fault. She's the one who changed the guy Macon picked for Celeste. Remember how pleased she was to set up Celeste with a doctor? I probably shouldn't have pointed that out to her."

"She got mad at you?"

"She was a little huffy. More at Hank than at me. So I made an excuse about my feet hurting because of tight shoes and came back to the inn."

"When did Nessie return?"

"I don't know. I fell asleep before she got back."

"That must be how Duchess got out."

"Maybe. Nessie came back briefly, but when I

211

woke in the middle of the night neither she nor Lulu was there." Sky scowled at me. "Why are you asking where she was last night?"

The news about Hank clearly hadn't made it far yet. "Hank is dead."

Sky's eyes widened in shock. "No! What happened?"

"Looks like he was murdered."

She staggered backward and collapsed into a chair. "It's just a coincidence. It has to be. Nessie is headstrong and controlling, but it's unimaginable that she would go to those lengths."

Sky covered her eyes with her palms and dragged her hands down her face. "He was a liar and a con man, but he didn't deserve that."

She looked away, shaking her head. "Holly, I'm going to check out today. Maddie and I need to go to my sister's anyway. Given this development, I think that's best. Would you get my bill ready, please?"

"Of course." I couldn't blame her. Who would want to hang around when two men had been murdered? "I'll have it waiting for you at the desk."

Sky left at a good clip. I walked to the office to finalize her bill.

Oma, Gustav, and Zelda were having lunch on Oma's private terrace just outside the office. I took a minute to tell them what had happened before I sat down at the desk inside to work on Sky's account.

I printed the bill out and carried it to the desk in the reception lobby. I was placing it in the drawer when Dave walked in.

He didn't smile at me. "I need to talk with you."

"Sure. What's going on?"

"Can we speak in the office?"

I nodded. "Come on back."

He walked around the counter and followed me into the office. Dave stopped short when he spotted Oma, Gustav, and Zelda outside. He closed the French doors and motioned for me to sit down.

I perched on the sofa, beginning to worry that someone else might have been killed.

Dave sat on a chair, winced, and rubbed his eyes before he spoke. "Tell me what you did last night."

"Me?" I grinned. "You think I had something to do with Hank's death?"

"Just answer the question, Holly."

I explained about distracting Hank so Zelda could get away from him. Last night, when Hank was alive and being annoying, it had seemed sort of logical and funny. Now that he had been brutally murdered, it didn't sound quite as amusing. I took the coat, life vest, and wig out of the closet and showed them to him.

"Why did you take them off in Hot Hog?"

"I was watching for Hank and thought it best if he didn't get a good look at me in the wig. If he did, he might realize that we had tricked him. Plus, they were very warm and uncomfortable."

"Then you came back to the inn?"

I relayed what had happened at Tequila Mockingbird. "Nessie was outraged that she and her daughter had been conned by Hank. She stormed out."

"What did you do?"

"I came back to the inn and went to bed."

"Did anyone see you?" Dave asked.

"Casey. He would remember too, because the cats were ripping up something, and I asked why he didn't stop them."

"How about later on?"

"If you're asking whether I spent the night with anyone, the answer is no. Ben was there, but he slept in the guest room."

"Did you talk to him during the night?"

"No. He was sleeping when I came in. I woke him around six, because the dogs and cats were gone and the door to my apartment was open."

Dave's eyes narrowed and his head tilted ever so slightly. "How did that happen?"

"I have no idea. The dogs and cats have had a pantry party two nights in a row. I suspect that Ben isn't closing the door all the way, but that doesn't explain how the other dogs have gotten out. Unless . . ."

"Unless what?"

"I don't want to point fingers, but I think a few

people might be slipping out at night to meet up with"—I searched for the right word—"love interests. And maybe the dogs and cats manage to sneak out with them? You should know that Sky says Nessie was out last night."

Dave studied me. After a moment he said, "Do you want to rethink anything you've told me?"

What was he talking about? I thought back. Had I omitted something? "No. I don't understand. The important thing is that I never saw Hank once I reached the restaurants. There were huge crowds on the sidewalks, so I might have missed him, but I don't think he followed me all the way there. So I don't know where he went or who he saw after that."

Dave's mouth twitched to the side. "Holly, I have at least ten witnesses who saw you at Hot Hog last night."

"That's not surprising. The place was packed."

He stared at me. "I'll need the coat, life vest, and wig as evidence."

"You have to be kidding. You think *I* murdered Hank? Have you lost your mind?"

"I believe I'm the one who should be asking that question."

"I tried to fool him, okay? This is silly. You know me. Do you really think I could murder someone?"

Dave sighed. "Under the right circumstances, people do things I would never expect of them.

215

Don't you realize how suspicious you looked stripping off this costume at Hot Hog?"

"Don't *you* think I would have been smart enough to shed them in the ladies' room or in an alley if I was concerned about people seeing me? I didn't give it any thought because I hadn't murdered anyone. Last I knew, it wasn't against the law to trick a stalker."

Dave looked me in the eyes. "Holly, I have someone who can place you in Zelda's backyard last night around the time of the murder."

TWENTY-THREE

I felt like Dave had just hit me with a bat. Shudders ran though me and goose bumps prickled my arms. For a long moment I was too stunned to speak. That person was simply wrong. I knew I hadn't been there in the middle of the night. He or she must be mistaken. "Who? Who saw me there?"

"I really can't say."

If I had been a dog, my hackles would have risen, because I was furious. "Then you had better take a really close look at the person who made that claim, because it's a lie. In fact, I would bet that he or she is trying to throw suspicion on me to deflect attention from him- or herself."

"Listen, Holly. I have to ask you to stick around Wagtail. Don't leave town, okay?"

If I were a dog, I would have bitten him. Okay, maybe I would have only tugged on his pant leg, but still, as a human I couldn't lash out the way I'd have liked. I was more than a little snarky when I responded with, "Listen, Dave. You have told me that request is unenforceable, so I believe I'll go wherever I like."

He recoiled like I had bitten him.

I hated to admit that I got a little satisfaction out of his reaction.

"Do you think I murdered Randall, too?"

"*I* don't."

He put such emphasis on the word *I* that it prompted me to ask what he was implying. "Are you saying someone else thinks I murdered Randall?"

He didn't answer, which meant the affirmative to me.

Fortunately, someone knocked on the door. I jumped to my feet, ready to end this aggravation. Dave was a friend, and to be honest, I found it offensive for him to turn on me and suspect me of murder. It was his job, and I appreciated that he was thorough and conscientious, but he knew me well enough to flip the tables on whoever it was that had tried to point the finger of blame at me.

When I opened the door, Ben waited outside. "You're late," I grumbled.

Ben walked in and addressed Dave. "You know you can't interview my client without me present."

Dave flashed me an annoyed look. "I did not interview Zelda."

"He thinks *I* murdered Hank," I clarified.

"Oh no." Ben sank onto the sofa. "I can't represent both of you."

"That's fine with me." I looked straight at Dave. "Because I haven't murdered anyone." I scooped up Trixie, stalked out, and closed the door behind me.

I set Trixie on the floor and took some deep breaths. Who would have been roaming around Zelda's backyard? Clearly, the murderer was there. If he'd noticed me in the raincoat and wig earlier, he might have taken advantage of that and lied about seeing me in the middle of the night. That made the most sense to me. Maybe Ben could get Dave to tell him the name of the person who put me at the scene of the crime.

There were other possibilities, too—Zelda's date for starters. He knew about our little prank on Hank. And he might even have murdered Hank for Zelda. I loved her, but I wouldn't have killed Hank for Zelda or anyone else. Still, she had been attracted to slimy Hank in the first place. Maybe the new guy wasn't exactly a Boy Scout either.

I had told Macon, Nessie, and Sky about misleading Hank. If each of them passed that information along to other people, then it could be just about anyone.

But as I thought about it, I realized that Macon and Sky had something in common—each of them had known Randall, the first victim. And Nessie might have, too.

I heard footsteps tapping along the hallway and took a deep breath when Sky showed up with Duchess. I opened the drawer and removed her bill.

Sky spoke softly. "Holly, I hope I didn't put you to a lot of trouble. My plans are changing again. My sister is on her way here. I know you were booked a couple of days ago. Nothing has opened up, has it?"

"I'm afraid not."

Sky nodded. "Nessie didn't sleep in her own bed most of last night. If I knew she was going to continue sleeping elsewhere, I would move my sister in with me." Sky wrinkled her nose at me. "But that's not really the sort of thing one asks of someone. Well, if anyone checks out, would you let me know? If not, could you fit another bed in our room?"

"Of course. You're not worried that Nessie might be the killer?"

"I think I was overreacting. Everyone is on edge. I tried asking her if she knew Randall, but she changed the subject so fast that I felt the wind blow through the room. I'll let you know if I can coax information out of her."

She and Duchess left quickly.

Now that it appeared Nessie had known both of the murder victims, I wasn't sure I would want to be sharing a room with her. Then again, Sky had spent a lot more time with Nessie. Maybe Sky trusted Nessie? But where had Nessie been last night?

Trixie growled at me. Not a vicious growl, more of an attention getter. When I looked down at her, she barked and ran toward the hallway like she was following Sky.

I stuck Sky's bill away and hurried after Trixie. I found her in the dining area, begging Shelley for lunch.

"One of the other dogs must have told her we have roast chicken for dogs today. It's very popular."

"Okay. Let's have one of those. What are the specials for people?"

"Cheeseburgers and chicken Caesar salad, but I recommend the shrimp pasta with asparagus."

"I think I'll go with the shrimp today, Shelley, and hot tea, please? I need to calm my nerves. Don't worry about serving us. I'll pick up the dishes when they're ready."

I walked over to the corner table and settled in, still obsessed by the horrendous notion that Dave considered me a murder suspect.

The service window opened, and my hot tea slid out. I collected it and was sitting down again just about the time Macon spotted me.

He waddled over and joined me, his face flushed. "I'm madder than a wet hen. What's *wrong* with people?"

"What happened?" I asked.

"It's that Nessie Jamieson. To start with, she stole my computer and changed my selection for her daughter. Now that *Nessie's* selection of that con artist, Hank, has bombed, she's running around bad-mouthing me. Honestly! It's like that awful Randall all over again. Don't people understand that they're harming my livelihood? This isn't a hobby. It's my job! What ever happened to common civility and politeness? There are things I don't much care for, but I don't make it my business to disparage the people behind them. Do they think I'm some kind of machine without feelings? If she keeps it up, she'll ruin my reputation!"

"I guess some people don't take matchmaking seriously. I'm sorry about Nessie's behavior."

"It's odd that people view it as a game or some kind of carnival ride when it's the single biggest choice that they make in their lives," he said. "Can you imagine marrying Randall or Hank? It's the equivalent of signing up for years of torture. Yet women did it so readily. Sky told me Randall was as much a jerk toward his wife as he was to everyone else." Macon leaned toward me and lowered his voice. "Just between us, I believe I heard a huge sigh of relief echo through the world when Randall died. Sky and her family are probably comforted to know that the years of Randall's tyranny have come to an end."

The serving window slid open again. Trixie yelped and jumped like a pogo stick was wired into her legs.

"Excuse me. I think that's our lunch. Could I order something for you?"

"Lunch? I ate hours ago. Gracious! Look at the time. I'm off to rematch."

"Rematch?"

"Dahlin', when it comes to love, even *I* am not one hundred percent perfect. They think they're comin' to fill out new forms, which they are, and hopefully they'll have learned not to lie about themselves this time, but they're supposed to bring their dogs and cats, and I expect those cute little furry friends will do most of the matchmaking for me."

Macon chuckled and rose to leave. He turned, though, and looked back at me. "I wasn't wrong about you and a certain Mr. John Adele, though."

I fetched our lunches and set Trixie's on the floor, along with a bowl of fresh water.

Lulu appeared suddenly, racing toward Trixie's bowl. She had the decency and wisdom not to vie with Trixie for the food, but that didn't stop her from looking on and barking while Trixie ate.

Nessie arrived a couple of minutes later. She scooped up Lulu and scolded her. "You already ate lunch. Honestly, I think your pantry raid friends have been a bad influence on you."

Still clutching Lulu, Nessie sat down at my table.

"Could I order some lunch for you?" I asked her.

"No, thank you. I'm so upset that I couldn't eat a bite."

"Upset?" I chose my words carefully. "You heard about Hank?"

"I never want to hear that man's name again. Can you imagine, Macon had the audacity to tell Celeste that *I* set her up with Hank, and now she's not speaking to me—her own mother!"

Nessie *had* interfered with her daughter's plans.

I was willing to bet that happened on a fairly regular basis. "I'm sure she'll come around."

"She's determined to do the exact opposite of what I advise. She's out at some kind of rematch thing right now. I swear, if she ends up with that musician, I'll strangle Macon with my own two hands."

I had pretended to be interested in the savory shrimp but looked up at her, wondering if she had done that to Randall. Trying to sound very casual, I said, "I hear Randall was a friend of yours."

Nessie eyed me and set Lulu on the floor. She was silent for a minute, as though she was thinking things through. "Celeste outed me, didn't she? I didn't want Sky to know because I had such a low opinion of her brother-in-law. Randall was *not* my friend. *Acquaintance* would be more apt. I barely knew the man at all."

"But Celeste knew him?"

Nessie frowned at me. "We attended the same university and were in the same graduating class. I barely remember him."

"Celeste was born while you were in school?"

"Good heavens, no." Nessie sucked in a deep breath. "We took Celeste to a reunion once. I'm amazed that she remembered him."

I kept feigning interest in my pasta, but had a growing feeling that there was more to Nessie's relationship with Randall. I tried to bait her. "I only met him once for a few minutes, but he was very opinionated."

"A zebra's stripes never change. And I hear they're pretty mean animals. Even when we were young, that man thought he was superior to everyone else. He loved putting people down and was always telling everyone what to think. And he did it in the worst way, by ridiculing people. Frankly, I never thought he was that bright. He just had an attitude about him that convinced people that he was brilliant when he was really a horse's patoot."

It sounded to me like she knew him better than she claimed. "He was your husband's friend?"

"He certainly wasn't *my* friend. Have you heard of Jamieson Mills and Iron Works?"

"I'm afraid not. The family business?"

"My granddaddy started a lumber mill and expanded to include an iron works. My daddy grew the businesses, and by the time I came long, the family was very well-to-do. Seems like a lot of girls have huge weddings these days, but mine was something special, with five hundred guests. My husband wanted Randall to be in the wedding party as an usher. I loathed Randall so much that I banned him from the wedding altogether. I was not having him there, not even as a guest. I wasn't going to have my one special day spoiled by that man. He had already ruined enough for me."

I finished my pasta and shoved it aside. "What did he do to you?"

The corners of Nessie's mouth pulled back. "Randall destroyed my one chance at true love."

TWENTY-FOUR

That was the last thing I expected to hear, but it was hardly a motive for murder. Or was it? "But you married Celeste's father, didn't you?" Nessie had been married three times. That seemed like a lot of true love to me.

"I was madly in love with someone else. Unfortunately, he was Randall's roommate and best friend. But Randall didn't like me. Probably because I knew he was a pompous blowhard, and I didn't hesitate to say so. Randall convinced my perfect man that I was the wrong girl. Randall lied to him, and he believed Randall instead of me. We had such a terribly melodramatic breakup. My parents wanted me to change schools so I wouldn't have to see him again. But I stuck it out and met Celeste's father."

"So it all worked out," I said cheerily.

"No, it didn't. I wouldn't trade Celeste for anything, of course. But the marriage didn't work out because I settled. He was never the big love of my life. Macon says there's something in our brains that helps us overlook faults and flaws in the people whom we truly love. I've never met anybody else I could do that with."

That hit a little bit too close to home for me. I had turned down Ben's proposals because I didn't want to settle. I didn't want to marry someone if I wasn't special to him.

Nessie smiled at me. "You know what I'm talking about. Have you ever known anyone like Randall? Someone so self-confident that he imposes himself and his views on everyone and is convinced that he's right? He was like a Svengali. I'm surprised he didn't become a cult leader. I feel so sorry for his psychiatric patients. I doubt that he was very empathetic or helpful. Anyway, I have *never* forgiven Randall. My *entire* life might have been different if he had butted out. So you can see why I wasn't going to have him at my wedding. I couldn't take the chance that he would talk my fiancé out of marrying me!"

"Did you see him here in Wagtail?"

Her eyes shifted to the left, and I wondered if she was looking for an answer. "No. He looks much older in the picture in the newspaper. Sky would have recognized him. Unless, of course, she didn't want anyone to know about their connection."

"I'm glad things worked out between you and Sky."

"She's a lovely woman. Very kind and thoughtful. It's obvious that she's on her last dime with that sad old leather bag she carries. Not to mention the way she dresses. She hasn't got a single good piece of jewelry. It's all costume."

Nessie glanced around. "But the way she talks about Randall! I know it's all true because I know what an absolutist he was. It would not surprise me one bit if she and her sister cooked up a way to get rid of Randall. I mean, seriously, what would a married man be doing in Wagtail by himself during a matchmaking event?" She waggled her finger. "There's something suspicious about that. You just watch. Randall was a miscreant. When they figure out what happened to him, I guarantee it will turn out to have been his own fault."

Nessie glanced at her watch. "Look at the time! Do you think it's too early for me to spy on Celeste at the rematch?"

It wasn't my place to interfere, but I said what I was thinking anyway. "Do you really want to do that when she's not speaking with you as it is?"

Nessie thought for a moment. "Yes! I do. It was nice talking with you, Holly. We'll have to do it again sometime."

If my mother had been as overbearing as Nessie, it would have driven me nuts. I liked her, though. Nessie had spunk and character to spare. But that didn't erase the fact that she had hated both Randall and Hank. Could she have strangled one and slaughtered the other with a garden hoe? She was clearly clever enough to have enticed them to places where she wouldn't be seen. I feared she could have killed them if she'd wanted to.

Nessie had also had the opportunity to murder them. Her first night here, she'd been looking for Sky when John and I had returned from finding

Randall's body. Which also begged the question—where had Sky been?

"C'mon, Trixie, we're going to take a walk."

At the mere mention of the *W* word, Trixie jumped to her feet and danced in an excited circle.

"Let's make sure Oma doesn't need us. Okay?"

We found Oma enjoying the beautiful day on the front porch of the inn. Gustav sat on a rocking chair next to Oma, and Gingersnap lay at their feet.

"Do you need me for anything? I thought I would take a little *W-A-L-K*." This time I spelled it out, but that didn't stop Gingersnap from understanding the word and pricking her ears.

"Where is your young man?" asked Oma.

"I think he has found someone else."

Oma tsked. "If he is so silly, then he does not deserve you."

It was sweet of her to say.

"You go right ahead." She glanced at Gustav. "We're not going anywhere."

It looked to me like Gustav was on the verge of a nap. I pointed at Oma and made a little walking motion with my forefinger and middle finger.

Oma winked at me and shook her head. "But I think Gingersnap would like to go."

"Walkies?" I whispered to the dogs. They were down the porch steps before I hit the top one.

I walked across the plaza and along a small residential street. The car-accessible road on the east side of Wagtail dead-ended at the Wagtail Animal Guardians facility.

Happily, WAG provided a new start to many dogs and cats. Located on an old farm, the facility had space for cows and horses as well as smaller animals. I opened the door of the main building and stepped inside to a chorus of high-pitched barking.

That was odd. Hadn't they told Ben that they were out of small dogs? I strolled along a line of empty kennels until I spied two Chihuahuas and a Pekingese.

"Hi, Holly!" Paige, the woman who had handed Huey over to me, came running. She adjusted the lightweight blue scarf dotted with paw prints that she wore.

"We don't need a bell on the door around here," she joked.

"Cute scarf," I said.

"Thanks. It was a gift. I'm so glad to see you. I've been wanting to talk with you about Ben."

Aha. She had realized her mistake in pairing Ben with Huey. "He's not right for Huey," I said.

"Ben?" She knelt to greet Gingersnap and Trixie. Standing again, she wiped outgrown bangs to the side of her face. "Actually, he's adorable with Huey. We went for a walk and Ben did great. But the one who is truly amazing is my cat. I've never seen him gravitate to anyone like he does to Ben. It's incredible."

Ben was friendly with a cat? I didn't want to disappoint her, but I found that hard to believe.

"So are you okay with this?" Paige asked. "I would never want to do anything to hurt you."

"I appreciate that, I'm sure. But I don't know what you're talking about."

"Ben didn't tell you?"

"I don't think so. But I have to admit that I haven't seen much of him in the last couple of days."

"He didn't tell you that we were matched by Macon?"

"I had no idea."

"Oh gosh. I'm sorry. I didn't mean to step on your toes."

"It's fine," I said. "Ben and I are friends, and to be honest, I would be very happy if he found someone special."

"That's so nice of you. And very mature."

She didn't need to know the details. It was only fair to let her get to know Ben on her own terms. Besides, the things that bothered me might not irritate her. I was still confused, though. This seemed to be a new Ben—one who liked dogs and cats? I wondered if she knew he was also seeing Laura. I opted for the safest course and changed the subject. "Actually, I wanted to ask you about Duchess."

"Is there a problem? I thought she was the perfect match for Sky. They're both so elegant.

And I know Sky would give her a great home. Talk about a lucky dog."

"They seem to be getting along very well. I wanted to ask you about matching them. Did Sky call ahead about participating in the If the Dog Fits program?"

"No. I'm a little bit embarrassed to admit this, but like most of the other single people in this town"—her tone dipped showing her disapproval—"and a few married ones, I went out the first night of Animal Attraction. You understand. I wanted to check it out and see if there were any men I might find interesting. When I was at Hair of the Dog, I happened to strike up a conversation with Sky."

I was shocked. WAG was well-known for its thorough investigation of potential adopters. I should have chosen my words better. "You met someone in a bar and handed over a dog? How did you know she would take care of it?"

"She came up here the next morning to fill out all the forms. I don't know why you're making such a fuss."

I didn't know a nice way to ask and blurted, "Are you in the habit of turning dogs over to just anyone?"

"Of course not! But she's not just anyone. She's Sky Stevens."

"That's a relief. So you knew her? That's different."

"I had never actually met her before. I just knew

232

about her. She's in a lot of the society rags, and when she said her name was Sky I recognized her."

I used to work in fund-raising, but I had never heard her name before. "Who is she?"

"Oh, Holly!" Paige chuckled at me. "Stevens Leather? Really? I thought everyone knew about them. Sky's great-grandfather started out making halters and saddles for horses. Then they branched into luggage, and now they make some of the most expensive purses. They're so beautiful. I have one that I bought secondhand. No one does leather better."

I had met unbelievably wealthy women like Sky who chose to live simply. They didn't fuss with their hair or appearance, and usually drove old cars or trucks that had seen better days. I hadn't had a clue.

"I have to admit that I'm partial to Duchess," Paige said. "And when I realized who Sky was, I couldn't help doing some doggy matchmaking of my own. I've seen magazine spreads of her home. She lives in a historic family mansion not far from Charlottesville. It's on a sprawling farm that you would not believe."

Things clicked into place. That was what Sky's daughter, Maddie, must have meant when she said she didn't want her Animal Attraction match to know who she was. The wealthy always seemed to have it so good, but money presented a whole new set of problems for people, like friends who were only interested in their money. "So Sky has an alibi," I murmured.

"Alibi? You mean for Randall's murder? I'm sure you're way off suspecting her. Sky is high society."

I didn't think that disqualified anyone from murder. But there was one bigger issue. "It doesn't sound like she would have had enough time to knock him off if she was at Hair of the Dog that night."

"I don't know exactly what time he died, but I met Sky in the bar around ten, and then we came up here to get Duchess," Paige said. "The Shire is close by, but"—her brow wrinkled, and she shook her head in the negative—"I don't see how she could have done it unless she had everything arranged very precisely ahead of time."

"She could have planned the murder and suggested that they meet there."

"But she couldn't have planned on meeting me. And she took the time to come up here to see Duchess."

"I guess it's too far-fetched to think she might have been looking for something to do so she would have an alibi."

"I don't know why you think she could be a murderer anyway. She lives such a glamorous life. Why would she murder him?"

"He was her brother-in-law," I told her.

"Ohh. I know all about that kind of problem. There are times when I wouldn't mind knocking off my brother-in-law. He went to Dr. Donovan for depression and wound up hooked on horrible drugs, which has made my sister's life a nightmare. She's always worried about him, he doesn't come home for days, and he steals money from everyone they know. It's awful. I wouldn't wish anyone an awful death like Randall's, but he brought pain and misery to a lot of people. I never went to him as a doctor, but what he did to my brother-in-law impacted my entire family." She motioned to me with her forefinger. "Come outside with me."

I followed her out the door, and the dogs tagged along.

She pointed to the east side of the street. "The river runs through this farm. It's not very far to where the body was found."

"Did you walk back to the bar with her?"

"No. I live in the house right behind the kennel. There didn't seem to be any point in going back."

I thanked her and walked down the empty road, reeling from Paige's words. She had uttered them so innocently. But I couldn't help wondering if she'd sought out someone who might be interested in Duchess so *she* would have an alibi. No one would have noticed her slipping quietly back to her house behind the shelter in the dark of night.

What if Paige was the person Randall had been looking for? It was possible.

Two things seemed to be key. Randall had been looking for someone when Oma and I met him. He had come to Wagtail to meet somebody. And the spot where he was murdered was sufficiently isolated that his killer must have followed him there, or talked him into going there.

Whistling for the dogs, I crossed back into historic Wagtail. I paused at Hair of the Dog, the pub located on the corner of the road and a residential street. The entrance to the Shire was within sight. Someone could have been sitting at one of the outdoor tables that night, watching people cross over to the Shire. But it may have been such a zoo that no one paid any attention to the Shire.

I made a mental note to bring Zelda or Ben with me at night for a test. I bet the lack of lighting made it impossible to see much more than the shadowy outlines of people. But it was worth checking out.

Deep in thought, I turned back toward Hair of the Dog when the creepy sensation of someone watching me caused me to take a look at the people seated outside.

TWENTY-FIVE

John Adele stared at me.

I couldn't tell if he was scared or sad or some combination of the two. Either way, it appeared to be an odd reaction at seeing me there. Was he going to accuse me of following him again? Marmalade's mom, Laura, sat at the table with him and appeared to be flirting.

Trixie, who evidently had not received the message that we had been dumped, ran over to John and placed her paws on his thigh. Cooper and Gingersnap wagged their tails and politely sniffed each other.

It was way too late to pretend I hadn't seen them. There was nothing I could do but give a gracious wave, lift my chin, and walk by on the sidewalk, ever so conscious of their presence. I whistled for Trixie and fervently hoped she would *not* make me go get her.

A few steps past the outdoor dining tables, Trixie and Gingersnap caught up to me. I breathed a sigh of relief and slipped each one of them a mini-treat as a reward. But a third nose wanted one, too. Cooper! I fed him one and stroked his broad head.

When I continued on my way, Cooper loped along with the other dogs. He also hadn't gotten the message that John wasn't interested in us. I heard John call him, but I didn't look back or stop.

I could hear footsteps hitting the sidewalk behind me.

John caught up to me and called Cooper. "Sorry about that, Holly."

I faced him. Why did he have to be so cute? "John, this is silly. You're going to be in town awhile longer, and we're going to run into each other. Let's just get over the awkwardness and be friends. Okay?" I held out my hand to shake in a gesture of peace.

He took my hand and said, "You'll quit stalking me now?"

I could feel my face and ears getting hot. I yanked my hand out of his. "I have never stalked you!"

There was nothing to do but turn and walk away as fast as I possibly could. After all, I had *some* dignity left. To my amusement, though, Cooper continued to walk with me. I couldn't help grinning and slipped him another treat as we walked. It was bad of me, of course.

John called his dog, and I noted a pause in Cooper's stride, but he stayed with me.

"Holly!" John jogged up to us and snagged Cooper's collar.

"Bye-bye, Cooper," I said. And then I added, "I couldn't be stalking you because Cooper would have given me away." With that, I continued on my way.

John shouted after me, "It wasn't Cooper who gave you away."

I kept going. The last thing I wanted to do was have a shouting match on the sidewalk. I turned left as soon as I hit the green and walked down to Heal! for a soothing calorie-rich treat. I deserved it. I hadn't murdered anyone, or stalked anyone. Why were people accusing me of things?

The drugstore bustled with customers, but I found empty seats at the end of the soda counter and jumped up on the last one.

Bob wiped the counter in front of me. "I hear it's hot out there today."

"It is. Could I have a bowl of water for the dogs, please?" I looked down at them. "They'll pick out their own biscuits. And I need an indulgence because nothing is going my way."

"How about my special? It's guaranteed to make you feel better about whatever ails you."

"Okay. Surprise me."

While he worked, I watched Gingersnap choose a hard beef-flavored cookie that would take her a while to eat and would probably be good for her teeth. Little Trixie, on the other hand, opted for an iced cookie in the shape of a squirrel. The drugstore had placed cookies near the floor, where dogs could choose their own. The clear bins had lift-up lids that Gingersnap and Trixie had learned to open with their noses. I kept an eye on them so they wouldn't be piggy and help themselves to more.

John brought me a chocolate milk shake. The icy concoction cooled me right away. "Mmm. This is delicious!"

"One of our bestsellers. Once people try it, they forget about their troubles."

"Looks like business is good."

"Animal Attraction has been phenomenal. We've had a lot of people come in and get to know one another over ice cream, milk shakes, and just plain old coffee. The merchants are talking about making this an annual event. You know, I think we might even see one or two marriages come out of it."

"Really! That's hard to imagine. But maybe so. Macon said we make up our minds about people in minutes."

With his sculptured good looks, I imagined Bob had had more than his share of admirers over the years. "How about you? Did you participate?"

He pointed at his graying hair. "Those days have passed me by. No one is interested in an old coot who has been single all his life. I'm a nightmare," he laughed.

"Never wanted to get married?"

Bob rubbed the back of his head. "There were a few ladies along the way who interested me. But one of them spoiled me for the others. I connected with her in a way that I never did with anyone else. It was a little weird, actually. Like we were synced up. We would order the same dishes in restaurants. We read the same books. Liked the same movies. Just little things, but we meshed. Never met anyone who could compare."

"What happened to her?"

"I thought I was too young to marry at the time, and I wanted to go to pharmacy school. She married someone else." He swiped his hand through the air. "Ah, but that was all years ago. I've been alone too long to change my ways. But that's okay. Louis and I manage just fine." He gazed lovingly at his papillon. "Hey, Holly." He leaned toward me and lowered his voice. "I heard about Hank. You're usually in the know about these things. Have they got any suspects?"

"Yeah. Me. Did you know Hank?"

Bob snorted. "I know Dave's got problems if he's accusing you. Unfortunately, I had some encounters with Hank. I was working here by myself one day when five hundred dollars went missing. I thought I'd be fired for sure. The owner was pretty nice about it, but I paid him back every single cent. It was on my watch, and I felt responsible. Not a week later, I caught Hank with his hand in the cash register. I told him he owed me five hundred bucks. Do you know that worm laughed in my face? I think every merchant in Wagtail was glad to see Hank leave town. We were always on the lookout for him in here. When he came in the store, I followed him around to make sure he didn't help himself to anything.

There are a lot of people in Wagtail who would have liked to punch Hank in the nose or worse. Dave can't seriously think *you* killed him."

"Afraid so. Some idiot claims he saw me in Zelda's backyard last night."

Bob stood up straight and eyed me. "And of course, we single people have no alibi for the middle of the night."

"Exactly. Ben has been staying in the guest room, but that doesn't help, because I didn't wake him up every five minutes to prove that I was there."

"Must have been a neighbor who claimed he saw you."

"A neighbor!" Of course. That made perfect sense. "I was thinking the murderer might have tried to pin it on me."

"Dave ought to listen to you. It's been quite a week around here. At least Dave had the decency to interview me at home and not here."

I tried to sound casual. "So what was the deal with you and Randall?"

"I'm sure Birdie got the gist of it right. There's a drug that isn't meant for anorexia, but one of the side effects is weight gain, so some doctors prescribe it for that. Unfortunately, it caused heart issues in this sweet young woman, and she died. Her parents' lawyer did what they call *suing up and down the line,* meaning they sue everyone who was involved from A to Z. I filled the prescription, so they sued me, too."

"But you didn't do anything wrong. Right?"

"Exactly. Ultimately, Randall's insurance company settled with the girl's parents, but I was out the money for a lawyer to defend me. You have to respond and do all kinds of stuff when you're sued. It cost me a lot of money and damaged my reputation. Not to mention that he killed that poor girl by prescribing a questionable medicine."

"That's why you'd like to shake the hand of the person who murdered him?" I asked.

Bob grinned. "That may have been a little harsh. But you know, around here all anyone remembers is that I was sued. They don't think about the fact that I was cleared. I could have lost my license. And, more important, an innocent child lost her life because of that man."

"I'm beginning to think he brought misery to everyone he met."

Bob leaned against the counter. "Hey, Holly? Who lives in the house across from Birdie? The one that backs up to Zelda's property?"

"I don't know. But I bet Birdie does." I tilted my straw to slurp out the last of the delicious puddle at the bottom of the tall glass, a little embarrassed that I had managed to consume the whole thing. I paid my check, thanked Bob, called the dogs, and walked out the door.

We ambled leisurely across the green. Trixie and Gingersnap met friends and sniffed the messages left by other dogs along the way. When we reached the west side of town, we walked straight to Birdie's house.

She was outside, holding a steaming kettle in her hand.

"Aunt Birdie? What are you doing?"

"Boiling dandelions."

"Don't you have to pick the greens first and boil them in a pot?"

"Law, child! What kind of heathen do you think I am? I'm not going to eat them. I'm killing them. They blow into my yard because others don't bother to keep their yards neat."

I was glad I wasn't Aunt Birdie's neighbor. I was certain they couldn't make her happy no matter what they did. "Speaking of which, who lives in the house across the way?"

Aunt Birdie groaned. "Albert Hemplewhite bought it to use as an unhosted bed-and-breakfast. It drives me completely mad. The worst idea in the world."

"Unhosted? I've never heard of that."

"It's the lazy man's bed-and-breakfast! He has a woman come to clean and change sheets. She leaves some staples like milk, bread, and eggs in the kitchen, and that's it. The *guests,* and I use that word lightly, because if you ask me, they're really very brief tenants, pick up the key from one of the real estate companies in town, then they come and go as they please. There's no host to monitor them. This week, to my complete horror, they rented it by the bedroom, which I suspect may be illegal. A bunch of women who are strangers to one another are staying there. And let me tell you, they have come down this street singing at the top of their lungs, drunk as sailors, in the wee hours of the morning. I've seen them running around in their nighties. A couple of the girls have stood in the middle of the street smooching with young men. It's disgraceful. I've half a mind to move over to the Shire, where rentals are banned. I don't care for this at all, and trust me—I plan to bring this issue up next week at the town council meeting."

Uh-oh. That might be quite a meeting. "Did you see anyone last night?"

"You are not on the ball today, Holly. If I had seen someone, I would know who left that bloody mess in my garden shed."

"What did Dave have to say about that?"

"Not to touch anything. How am I supposed to tend to my prizewinning gladioli?" She pointed toward the rainbow of tall blooms along the side of her house. "All my tools and plant food are in the shed. I can't even go in there to clean it yet." Her mouth pulled back and she shuddered.

"That's not very helpful."

"He tried to reassure me that I am not likely to be the next victim, but I don't think he can possibly know that. Two men have been murdered, and from what I understand, that Dr. Randall Donovan was quite upstanding and a prominent psychiatrist.

You can't compare him with someone like Hank, a lowlife who sneaks into unoccupied houses to sleep."

"How do you know he did that?"

Aunt Birdie blinked at me. "I saw him with my own eyes. Just yesterday morning I caught him coming out of Randolph Hall. Must have been nigh on to noon. I guess he had just stepped out of the shower, because his hair was all wet. He looked like a shaggy dog. I loathe that day's-growth-of-beard look. It makes every man look like a criminal."

"That place hasn't sold yet?"

"The *for sale* sign is still on the front lawn. It will be a while, I imagine. Not many people want to take care of a mansion with eleven bedrooms."

"Hank walked out of the front door?"

"Indeed he did. Like he owned the place."

I tried not to show my amusement. Aunt Birdie took note of everything. Too bad she hadn't seen anyone last night.

"Thank you, Aunt Birdie. I believe I'll poke my nose in the yard of Albert's unhosted bed-and-breakfast."

"If you happen upon any of those girls, you tell them I do not want to see them engaged in carnal relations out on the street anymore."

I called the dogs and waved at Birdie as I crossed the street. No one sat on the porch. I hoped no one was home, and cut through the side yard, taking the same route I had the night before but walking slowly this time.

The white clapboard house was larger than it seemed from the front. The side revealed multiple additions in various styles. One room boasted the same diamond-glass windows as Zelda's house. The rest of it was a ramshackle farmhouse, as far as I could tell.

The property was well shielded from Zelda's land by shrubs and pine trees, much like the ones in Zelda's backyard. It would have been possible for one of the guests to have seen me racing through here to Zelda's. It seemed unlikely, though. She would have had to be looking out at exactly the right time. But with the yellow wig, would I have been recognizable on such a brief glance? Especially to someone who didn't know me?

I turned to examine the back of the house. Upstairs, framed by a sizable window, Nessie and Celeste were engaged in a heated argument.

TWENTY-SIX

Their agitated voices floated down to me. Celeste must be one of the girls staying there. I couldn't make out what they were saying, but their motions and faces left no doubt in my mind that they were steaming mad with each other. I thought I heard one of them say *Hank,* but wasn't sure.

"Trixie, Gingersnap!" I hissed their names under my breath and ducked behind shrubs and into the dense pine trees that separated the lots. Thankfully, Trixie and Gingersnap seemed to think the trees were more interesting than the lawn and gladly bounded in behind me.

I forged through the trees, the branches slapping at me. On the other side, I could see the scene of the crime. Not a soul was in Zelda's backyard. Crime scene tape ran around the other side of the grass, but no one had bothered to mark off the back, where I stood.

It wasn't a problem, though. I had no intention of stepping into the crime scene and messing anything up. Zelda had neighbors to the left and to the right. They could have seen me, too. Or thought they had.

I didn't want to emerge in the backyard, where Nessie and Celeste might see me. What with John claiming I was stalking him, I didn't want them thinking I was spying on them, too. I made my way through the trees to the east side of Zelda's place. I could see the bungalow next to her house very well.

My blood ran cold when I realized that someone in that house was watching me with binoculars. I turned quickly and thrashed my way through the brush into the yard of the house next to the one where Celeste must have been staying.

I ran through the side yard to the street as fast as I could. Trixie and Gingersnap must have thought it was a game, because they passed me and reached the street before I did.

Aunt Birdie watched as I bent over to catch my breath. "Is someone chasing you?"

"No," I muttered. "Aunt Birdie, did you tell Officer Dave about Hank staying at Randolph Hall?"

"I did *not*." She said it crisply, as though she took some satisfaction in not having told him.

"Why not?"

Her attitude softened. "To be perfectly frank, I was more than a little discombobulated from having Hank's blood on my hands this morning. It didn't occur to me when Dave was here. Besides, Hank is dead now. What difference would it make that he broke into Randolph Hall and trespassed? It's not like Dave can arrest him."

I didn't bother pointing out that the site might contain clues to the identity of his killer. "Thank you, Aunt Birdie. Do you know anything else about Hank or Randall?"

"Holly?"

"Yes, Aunt Birdie?"

"Brush your hair. You look a mess. Do I have to make you an appointment at the beauty parlor myself?"

I reached up and felt a twig clutching my hair. I walked away, trying to dislodge it. Gingersnap and Trixie probably thought we were having a grand day of exploring, because we crossed the green again and headed for Randolph Hall.

The gigantic house had gone on the market half a year ago, when the owner was widowed. It was set up perfectly for a bed-and-breakfast and was remarkably lovely inside. I broke a large oak leaf off a tree as I walked up to the door. Using the leaf to avoid marring fingerprints, I pressed down on the door handle and the door swung open. I didn't dare step inside lest I mess up evidence of some kind. What if someone had been sleeping there with Hank? Could he have brought a woman to town with him? Surely not. But that con man Mick might be staying there. I'd better tell Dave about it. But I planned to use that little bit of information to my advantage.

I closed the door and walked around back. Sure enough, someone had broken the window in the back door. I didn't even have to open the door to the screened porch to see that. Hank had probably gotten in that way.

The *for sale* sign must have tipped Hank off that the house might not be occupied. No one had ever said he wasn't clever.

I trudged back to the inn. I had so many questions. Things that Dave probably knew but wouldn't share with me.

It seemed to me that whoever killed Hank had planned to murder him. Aunt Birdie's hoe hadn't walked over to Zelda's yard on its own. Someone had snooped around for a weapon. That meant the killer either knew that Hank was hanging around Zelda's house, or had arranged to meet him there. I didn't want to consider the former, because that limited the suspects considerably and pointed a finger at Zelda.

Zelda was one of my best friends. I loved her spirit and enthusiasm for life. I continued to be somewhat doubtful about her alleged ability to communicate with animals, but who was I to make that kind of determination? Just because *I* couldn't read their minds didn't mean that no one could.

Hank had been the worst thing that ever happened to her. She had thrown him out of the house and divorced him before I ever moved to Wagtail. If anyone had reason to murder him, it was undoubtedly Zelda. But Zelda wasn't stupid enough to kill him in her own backyard. She was bright enough to borrow a hoe from Aunt Birdie if she was going to knock him off, but I couldn't imagine that was the case.

She'd said she had walked her date to the Wagtail Springs Hotel and then went home. If she had seen Hank lurking around her house, she might have had an argument with him. But if that was what happened, she wouldn't have run over to Aunt Birdie's to find a weapon. Unless she was afraid and running away from Hank. But if he was chasing her, wouldn't Zelda have killed him in Aunt Birdie's yard and then called the police? That would have been self-defense.

Was it just wishful thinking on my part to imagine Zelda hadn't done anything so heinous? I didn't think so.

As I walked toward the reception entrance of the inn, I realized that I was surrounded by budding romances. Couples walked hand in hand down to the lake. Randall might have made fun of Macon, but something was happening. I supposed Randall would say that if you got enough singles together, some relationships were bound to result. Maybe so. But I had been to plenty of singles bars with girlfriends in the past, and none of us had met anyone we wanted to date.

The sliding glass doors opened for Gingersnap. The dogs rushed to the office. I could hear Oma cooing to them.

I peeked in at her. She appeared to be working. "Where's Gustav?"

She flipped her hand through the air. "He went

to take a nap. I never met such a tired man. Maybe he doesn't eat properly."

"Maybe he's still recovering from being attacked."

"Or maybe he is always this way. No matter, *liebchen.*"

"That's too bad. Any news on Hank?"

"Yes. I believe Dave is torn between keeping me apprised in my position as mayor and telling me things he does not wish you to know. But I am certain that deep in his heart, he realizes you are not Hank's killer."

"Gee, thanks. So what did he say?" I asked.

"That Randall Donovan's wallet was in Hank's back pocket."

TWENTY-SEVEN

"This means Hank murdered Randall. Don't you think so?" asked Oma.

The news took my breath away. "That seems like a reasonable assumption." I leaned against the doorway. "Wow. That changes everything."

"How so?"

"I think Dave was working on the assumption that Zelda or I murdered Hank. But now he has to consider why Hank would have killed Randall and whether that had something to do with Hank's death. It puts Hank's murder in a whole new light."

I needed to tell Dave about Hank sleeping at Randolph Hall. "Have you seen Dave?" I asked Oma.

"He interviewed Zelda a while ago, but I don't know where he went after that."

"Thanks, Oma. Are you having dinner with Gustav again?"

"I have invited Rose and some friends to join us. I don't want to see you alone. Would you like to come? Maybe Mr. Huckle could cover for us."

"I'll mind the fort. Frankly, I'm very happy to see you having a good time."

Gingersnap had settled at Oma's feet. But Trixie came with me when I headed to the main lobby.

Cocktail hour was approaching, and the dining area had cleared out.

I stopped by the private kitchen for a cup of tea. When I put on the kettle, Trixie whined at the door. I opened it for her and found Zelda and Ben encamped on the private patio overlooking the lake. Trixie stopped for a pat from Zelda, threw an annoyed look at Ben, and ran out to the grass, where Huey and Duchess lay watching the activities on the water.

"Hey! Where have you been?" asked Ben.

"Trying to figure out what's happening in this town. I had an interesting conversation with Paige McDonagh."

Ben opened his mouth and snapped it shut. His face flushed red.

"You're seeing two women?" I teased.

"No! I would not say that." He looked at Zelda and rubbed the back of his head. "Okay, maybe."

Zelda giggled. "Go ahead and tell her. I think it's sweet."

A long sigh shuddered from his mouth. "I'm just going to tell you the truth. Okay?"

"Always a good idea," I said.

"Not when one is engaging in games of romance."

Ben? Romance? I tried not to laugh. The kettle whistled inside. I asked if they needed anything, but they had an array of leftovers in front of them.

After pouring my tea, I took a moment to phone

Dave. His voice mail picked up, so I left a message telling him where I was and that I had some information about Hank. I was back on the patio with my tea in a minute. "So what's going on?"

"I read about Animal Attraction in the newspaper," Ben said. "I thought it might be a great way to get back together with you. I called WAG and asked for a dog through the If the Dog Fits program. I've never had a dog or a cat, and yours hate me, so I thought, perhaps incorrectly, that I should try to understand what it is that you like about dogs."

I glanced at Zelda, who nodded.

"I filled out one of Macon's matching forms online by giving answers that I thought would match me to you."

"So you lied."

"I prefer to think of it as fudging. Like *Where does your dog sleep?* I don't have a dog, so it's not a lie to say that my dog sleeps on my bed. I knew that was how you would answer the question. But Macon matched me to Paige. And the night I arrived, I happened to meet Laura at Hair of the Dog."

Ben rubbed both his hands up his face. "This has never happened to me before. I have never met a girl at a bar. They usually avoid making eye contact with me."

"You're making it sound like you never went out with anyone. You dated your boss's daughter."

"Do you think she would have been interested if her parents hadn't pushed us together?"

"Yes. I dated you!"

"Ben," said Zelda, "I think you don't have enough self-confidence. A lot of women like nerdy guys."

"Really? Given a choice between Hank and me, which one would you have chosen?" He didn't give her an opportunity to respond. "Hank, of course! It's hard enough to find a girl, but to have two that like me at the same time? Wow. My plan to cozy up to you backfired in every way possible. I got the wrong dog, and I was matched to the wrong woman. But Huey gave us something to talk about. There was never that awkward painful silence when nobody knows what to say. I thought for sure I would be matched to you, Holly. But, by golly, they actually like me! I'm worn out from running between the two of them, but also kind of jazzed because this has been a lot of fun."

"And you have Huey to thank for it." Zelda smiled at him.

"In a way, I guess you're right. He broke the ice and made me more comfortable."

I pondered whether it was worth pointing out that the women liked someone he was pretending to be. But maybe I was wrong.

"I hope you like Paige better than Laura," I said.

"Why? Do you have something against Laura?" Ben frowned at me.

"Not at all. But I've seen her a couple of times with John Adele, and they looked pretty friendly."

"You misinterpreted that. They worked together years ago and are old friends. She says he's a nice guy but got into some trouble and had to leave the university. I'm sorry, Holly. I could tell you liked him, but it sounds like he comes with some serious baggage."

"Did she say what happened?"

"Not exactly, but I can't imagine it's anything good if he had to leave his job."

Ben bit into a mini–ham croissant. "What did you find out in your nosy wanderings?"

I filled them in about everything except where Hank had been staying. Something told me I might need that nugget to coax information out of Dave. He was usually pretty forthcoming with me, but he probably wouldn't tell me much as long as he thought I was a suspect.

Zelda sagged in her chair. "I wish I had never met Hank. That Randall sounds like an awful guy, but that's no reason to murder someone."

"Zelda," I said gently, "was Hank ever violent? Is it possible that he killed Randall?"

"I don't think so. He was too doggone lazy. I swear the man was a couch potato. It drove me nuts that he couldn't hold a job. I think there's actually a dent in the sofa from him lying there watching TV and eating potato chips. He was home all day, but do you think he could have washed a dish or cleaned the cat litter?" Zelda's eyes opened wide. "I'm speaking ill of the dead! I didn't mean it. What I meant to say was he never lifted a hand against me. Ever."

"It's okay, Zelda," said Ben. "It's not like lightning will strike you for telling the truth. I think we can agree that Hank was a jerk, and he probably conned plenty of people. But I don't know why you suspect anyone else, Holly. It seems clear to me that Mick the small-time crook probably killed both of them for money."

Someone cleared his throat in the doorway to the kitchen. Dave walked toward us, a glass of ice water in his hand. "May I join you or is this a private conference?"

"You can join us," said Zelda, "as long as you agree that I did not kill Hank."

"Just doing my job, Zelda. We always look at wives and husbands first."

"I haven't been married to him for a couple of years."

"Exes are equally suspect. I've heard you complain about Hank."

Ben asked eagerly, "What about my theory that it was Mick?"

"I appreciate your speculation, Ben. I had the same thought," Dave said. "But it wasn't Mick who killed Hank. Couldn't have been."

TWENTY-EIGHT

"For starters, we found Randall's wallet in Hank's pocket. There was a large amount of money in it, which indicates to me that Hank wasn't murdered for money," Dave said.

"Maybe there was more and Mick left part of it?" Ben suggested.

Dave snorted. "I don't think so. If you're killing someone for money, you're not going to leave over a thousand dollars behind."

"Why would Randall have been carrying that kind of money in cash?" I asked.

Dave picked up one of the ham biscuits. "Your guess is as good as mine. Some guys like to carry cash. His wife is due in town today. That's something I would like to ask her."

"Her sister, Sky, said his wife didn't even know Randall was coming here. I hardly think he would have told her what he needed a thousand bucks for." I popped a red raspberry in my mouth and savored the sweetness.

"It still could have been Mick who murdered Hank," argued Ben. "Maybe Hank murdered Randall, pocketed his money, and had an argument with Mick. Mick might not have known the money was on Hank."

"I might buy that, except for one thing," said

Dave. "Zelda, you might be happy to know that in the last hours of his life, Hank did something very noble. Mick was trying to snatch Celeste Jamieson's purse. Hank punched him in the nose and held Mick in the restaurant until I could get over there to arrest him. He spent the night in the slammer over on Snowball Mountain. I'm afraid Mick has the best alibi of anyone for Hank's murder."

"I heard about that." Zelda looked like she might cry again. "Hank wasn't without a few redeeming qualities. Of course, he had lied to that poor girl and told her he was a doctor. Classic Hank. First he lies to you, then he defends you."

"Dave, do you think that could have been a setup between Mick and Hank?" I asked. "Maybe they planned it to make Hank look good?"

Dave's eyebrows raised ever so slightly. "Possible. But even if it was a setup, Mick was still in police custody when Hank was killed."

"What about Randall? Do you think Mick murdered *him?*" asked Ben.

"We have eyewitnesses who place Mick all over town around the time of the murder, including the two of you." He pointed at Ben and Zelda. "Holly and John found Randall shortly after he was killed, so we have a pretty narrow time frame. We're putting together a map of his movements, but at this point, it seems unlikely. Ironically, Mick confessed to mugging Gustav Vogel."

"I guess that's not terribly surprising since you found his fingerprints on the letter from Oma to Gustav. But how does he explain the letter being in Randall's pocket?" I asked.

"I had the same question," said Dave. "Mick insists he doesn't know anything about a letter."

"Hold everything," I said as the implications sank in. "If Mick confessed to mugging Gustav, then the letter ties him directly to Randall's murder."

"It seems like that would be the case. But the bartender at Hair of the Dog remembers Mick very well. He's not the only one. Not to mention that his alibi for Hank's murder is ironclad. I would have liked to think this mayhem was the fault of a lowlife who graduated to bigger crimes, but clearly that's not the case."

I was surprised that Dave was speaking openly with me present. I sat back and quietly sipped my tea, afraid he would realize his mistake at any moment and clam up.

It seemed to me that the letter and the wallet made everything pretty clear. Mick stole the letter from Gustav when he mugged him and planted it on Randall. How else could Randall have gotten the letter? I didn't know why he would do that, but it was the only reasonable explanation.

And when Mick murdered Randall, he must have stolen Randall's wallet. He planted it on Hank to make it look like Hank had killed Randall. But if

Mick was in custody, he couldn't have murdered Hank, which meant Mick didn't have Randall's wallet. Someone else did. I groaned aloud. What had Oma said? *Something is not right.*

Ben glanced my way. "It's hard to come by an alibi for the wee hours of the night, when everyone is in bed."

I glared at him. Unfortunately, Dave looked straight at me when he said, "I understand that."

"Then I'm no longer a suspect?" I barely breathed in anticipation of his answer.

"That's not what I said."

"Casey!" blurted Ben. "Casey would have seen Holly if she'd left the inn."

In a dull voice, Dave said, "Ben, I know about the hidden staircase. Holly could have left the inn through the door right behind us with Casey none the wiser."

I didn't think it was the right time to point out that Casey often napped at night as well. "Look, Dave. Can't you please tell me who allegedly saw me? I might be able to straighten things out."

"How?"

I had no idea. I couldn't prove that I wasn't someplace unless I could show where I really was at that time. That's what I got for sleeping with Trixie and Twinkletoes. This was one time I wished they wouldn't keep my secrets.

"Okay, then," I said, "you leave me no option but to prove that someone else did it."

"Like who?"

"May I ask you some questions?"

"Sure. I can't promise I'll give you answers, though."

"Fair enough. Have you fingerprinted Randall's wallet and Aunt Birdie's hoe?" I asked.

Dave's mouth twitched, and I knew he had that information. I waited patiently.

"Preliminary tests suggest the wallet was wiped clean. There may be some partial smudges. The only clear fingerprints belonged to Hank."

"Hank?" Zelda sat up straight. "Of course. They would have to be on it if the wallet was in his pocket. Hank was pestering me for money when he arrived in Wagtail. I figured he'd come here broke and wondered how he was wining and dining Celeste."

"Wait a minute. How did you know it was Randall's wallet? If I had murdered someone"—I hastily added—"which I haven't, I would have removed all the identification from the wallet."

Ben frowned. "I'd have gone further than that. I would have taken the money and thrown out the wallet."

Dave mashed his lips together. "You'd think a killer would have done that, wouldn't you?"

"Maybe he was planning to pass himself off as Randall?" suggested Ben. "Or maybe he planned to use Randall's credit cards. Hank was pretending to be a doctor. He could have claimed that his real name, Randall, sounded formal, so he uses his nickname—Hank. But I still would have gotten rid of the original wallet."

That made sense to me. "What about the hoe?"

Dave seemed reluctant to tell us but finally said, "It was a bloody mess. But unless your Aunt Birdie was out there in the middle of the night hacking at Hank, it's a dead end. It appears the perpetrator wore gloves."

That was disappointing. We sat in silence until Dave said, "We haven't found the item used to strangle Randall yet. There were some fibers on his neck, but we haven't been able to link them to anything."

"Hi, Ben!" Laura waved at him from the lawn and headed our way.

Ben dashed to the kitchen and returned with an extra glass. He invited Laura to join us and introduced her to Dave.

"Where's Marmalade?" I asked.

"He was exhausted from his escapade." Laura relayed the story of Marmalade climbing the wall to get to Twinkletoes.

Even Dave smiled and laughed. I didn't tell them about Twinkletoes spurning poor Marmalade after that heroic effort. Nor did I yell at Ben for locking her out on the balcony. That would have been cruel to do in front of one of his new flames.

Dave sat forward, and I thought he was planning to depart. "So, what did you call about, Holly?"

He'd been open and honest even though I was present. The least I could do was tell him what little I knew. "You might find something at Randolph Hall. Aunt Birdie saw Hank leaving through the front door. The window in the back door is broken. I imagine that's how he got in."

"He was sleeping there?" asked Zelda.

"That was Aunt Birdie's assumption."

Dave scrambled to his feet so fast he nearly toppled the wine bottle. He paused for just a moment, though. "How long were you going to keep that from me?"

"You don't need to sound so miffed. I called you. Zelda and I are the ones being accused of murder. I don't think you'd like that any better than we do."

"Holly Miller, I am tired. I'm grumpy, and I need a shower. You better not withhold information from me." Dave strode into the house.

Laura watched him with big eyes.

"Laura," said Ben. "Tell Holly about John."

"We go way back. I hadn't seen him for years."

"Tell her what he did," Ben prodded.

"He had an affair with a student. It was stupid of him. She was in one of my classes. So pretty and a good student, but she was hopelessly naïve. It wasn't fair of him to take advantage of her like that. He was in a position of authority! And then he made matters worse by dumping her. One day they were having an affair, and the next day he

266

wasn't interested anymore. I don't think she ever recovered from it. You know how young girls can be when they're infatuated. Plus, he threatened to flunk her if she told anyone. Really, he couldn't have made it worse!"

That sounded familiar to me. One minute he was eager to have dinner, and a couple of hours later he wasn't interested in me anymore. "You seem to like him."

"He's not a totally bad guy. Plus, we have mutual friends, and we used to hang out together when we taught, but I sure wouldn't date him."

Zelda pulled out her phone and poked at it. "Which university was it?"

"Douthier?" said Ben. "That's where Laura works now."

"Uh-oh. I'd say he had trouble. You'd better have a look at this, Holly." Zelda handed me the phone.

The page showed a picture of a younger John. I read aloud.

Professor Loses Tenure
Over Sexual Allegations
Dr. John Adele, professor of history at prestigious Douthier University, lost his bid for tenure following the well-publicized claims that he engaged in a sexual relationship with a female student. Suspended for inappropriate conduct with

a student, Adele is no longer teaching, pending the outcome of the investigation into the student's allegations. According to a knowledgeable source, the university acted quickly to deny tenure to Dr. Adele, a move that effectively guarantees termination of his association with the school.

I handed the phone back to her.

Ben shot me a pained look. "Ouch. I wonder how the investigation turned out."

"I'd guess it didn't go well. He edits history books and is writing a thriller."

"I'm sorry, Holly." Ben sounded sincere.

"It's okay. I wasn't looking to be matched up anyway," I said.

Zelda shot me a look of commiseration. "Don't feel bad. Look at me—I married Hank! But to tell the truth, even though some of the evidence points toward Hank murdering Randall, I truly don't believe he could have killed anyone. There's a difference between being a murderer and being a jerk. He took advantage of people, including me, but it takes more than that to knock somebody off. And I saw Hank's body. I don't know much about murder, but if you ask me, somebody was plenty mad at him."

TWENTY-NINE

I didn't know if that was wishful thinking on Zelda's part or if I should rely on her assessment of Hank's personality. After all, she knew him better than most people.

Ben picked up a pen and notepad that I hadn't noticed on the table. "I think Holly has the right idea. The way to clear the two of you is to figure out who the real killer is. Besides Hank and Mick, who had a motive to murder Randall?"

"Apparently everyone who ever met him," I said. "Start with Sky Stevens and her sister. Dave just said they always begin with the spouse."

Ben made a note.

"Her sister?" asked Laura.

"Sky's sister was married to Randall."

Laura looked at Ben. "You didn't tell me that."

"And then there's Nessie," I said. "I'm not completely convinced that I have the whole story, but apparently she disliked Randall intensely."

"And Bob Lane the pharmacist," added Zelda. "Half the people in town think he did it for revenge over that lawsuit."

I didn't want to criticize Paige in front of Laura, but Ben had to know. "You can add Paige, too."

Ben stopped writing and gazed at me in surprise. "She blames him for getting her brother-in-law hooked on drugs. Why don't you make a second list of people with a reason to knock off Hank? Maybe they'll intersect somewhere. Probably at Nessie," I said.

Zelda groaned. "That paper isn't long enough. You could include most of the people who live in Wagtail."

"Start with Nessie. She was furious with him last night."

Laura peered at the list. "Nessie knew both of the men?"

Ben wrote her name down. "I'm afraid so. I guess that goes for her daughter, too. What's her name?"

"Celeste. And jot down Bob Lane," I added. "It's kind of a long shot, I think, but the killer isn't going to come right out and admit to it."

Ben looked up. "That's actually a very short list. How about Sky?"

"She left Tequila Mockingbird with Nessie last night. But Sky claimed they had a spat when Sky criticized Nessie. I believe Sky returned to the inn. But she said Nessie left their room during the night and didn't return until morning."

"I don't like to point a finger at her," said Zelda, "but you were at Tequila Mockingbird, Holly. You saw how upset Nessie was. She's one mad mama when somebody messes with her baby."

"Did you tell Nessie that Hank was hanging out in your backyard?" I asked.

"No. But she could have followed him from somewhere."

"So could anyone else," I pointed out. "But that's a crazy notion anyway. What are the odds that she had gloves on her? Who carries gloves in the middle of the summer? No, I don't think it was a spur-of-the-moment thing. Someone thought about it and knew where to find Hank."

Zelda cringed. "Don't say that! It makes me the prime suspect."

"Other people have access to gloves," I said. "The housekeeping closet! I was in there a while ago and a box of disposable gloves lay on the floor. Nessie could have gotten gloves right here."

"What about her daughter?" asked Ben. "She's the one he humiliated by pretending to be someone else. Maybe we should find out where she was last night."

"She was having a whopper of an argument with her mom earlier today. Maybe I could drop by and have a chat with her. How about you, Zelda? Are you feeling any better?"

"I think I'd like to go home and snuggle with my cats."

I could understand that. Ben smiled and asked Laura if she felt like a walk. I left the three of them there, and headed to the store Lillian Elsner had bought. Best Friends carried everything a dog or dog person could dream of. Trixie ran inside like she thought she owned the place.

Lillian's Yorkie, GloryB, greeted us with joy. I knelt to pat her. "I think you like all the attention you get by being a store dog."

She waggled all over.

Lillian seemed almost as happy as her little dog. "We love it here."

"I need a trinket for a dog lover. Her mother is into bling, so I'm guessing she might be, too."

"Is this for Celeste Jamieson?"

"I gather she and her mom have been shopping here?"

"They have been a couple of my very best customers in the past few days." She showed me a selection of snap-on charms with dog themes. "I noticed her eyeing this cute little bone yesterday."

The silver tone charm was in the shape of a dog bone and encrusted with rhinestones.

"Perfect. What do people do with these?"

"Some women latch them onto their purses. One of my customers wears them on bracelets. But I think most people like to attach them to their dogs' collars."

It was exactly the kind of thing I needed. And even better because I knew it was something Celeste had admired. I thanked Lillian, patted sweet little GloryB again, and went to find Celeste.

Trixie romped ahead of me on the sidewalk, and as if she had known where we were going, she ran up to Celeste's little dog, who wore blue booties.

Celeste sat alone at a table on the sidewalk in front of Café Chat.

I paused beside her. "Celeste? I'm Holly Miller of the Sugar Maple Inn, where your mom is staying. We met briefly yesterday."

"Mom has mentioned you. Would you like to join me?"

"Just for a minute. I brought you a little something because you've had such a rotten time here in Wagtail." I handed her the box.

"You didn't have to do that!" She ripped it open and gushed. "It's just precious. I love it. Thank you so much." She clipped it onto her dog's collar.

"I'm sorry about Hank," I said.

"Ugh. The only thing worse than Hank turning out to be a worm is knowing that my own mother set me up with him. I don't know what she was thinking!"

"She wants the best for you. It's been interesting with your mom and Sky. Both of them want their daughters to avoid the heartaches they had."

"My mom's not doing a very good job of that." Celeste grimaced. "Then again, she didn't like my fiancé and warned me about him. She turned out to be so right that time. But Macon was very nice. He had coffee with me this morning, and it was like he knew Hank personally. Like he understood just how flattering and attentive Hank was. I think I attract the wrong kind of man."

Trixie and Celeste's dog had wandered over to a

medium-sized brown dog with a white blaze that ran from his nose to his forehead.

"I'm sure that's not the case. It was just a mistake. Your mom meant well. And Hank did save your purse from being snatched, so he wasn't all bad."

"That's true."

I wanted to ask questions about Hank, but she seemed so disheartened that I tried to tread carefully. "Is it true that Hank held the guy there until the police came?"

"Yes. Everyone applauded! It was really kind of amazing. Dinner was on the house. Hank and I had to wait for the cop. When the thief was finally hauled away it was late, but they brought us the most wonderful dinner, and then champagne with dessert. Wasn't that nice of them?"

"It was! Did Hank walk you home?"

She shot me an ugly look. "No. Because my mother arrived and ruined everything. Holly? Has your mother ever embarrassed you publicly?"

"It's not exactly the same, but my Aunt Birdie once set me up with a murderer."

Celeste's eyes grew large and round. "Okay, that's really bad. It's just that my mom doesn't seem to have any boundaries. It's as though she thinks I'm still twelve. I have never been so humiliated in my life. The way she carried on! Holly, the restaurant asked her to leave. I had no choice but to go with her just to get her out of there. I'll never find anyone. I think I might as well just be resolved to being alone. That will be my fate."

"Did your mom walk you home?"

Celeste's hand flopped in the air as she spoke. "My mom. Ugh. She was upset because she thought Hank was following us."

"Was he?"

Celeste shrugged. "I don't know. Wagtail isn't very big. There are only so many directions to go." She paused and looked up. "Although I think he said he was staying in a mansion on the east side of town, and I'm over that way on the other side. Maybe he *was* following us. I went in my room and locked the door to get away from my crazy mother. And then this morning, cops knocked on the door and told us someone had been killed. They wanted to know if we heard anything."

"Did you?"

She shook her head. "Not a thing."

"Celeste, I overheard you mention something to your mom about a sorority sister who had an affair with her professor. Was it John Adele?"

Celeste nodded. "I knew that was him! Eww. How gross to think that he's here, hoping to meet some poor woman."

Oh no. Wasn't that just my luck? "So what happened?" I asked.

"I never knew the girl, but she was legendary. It was years before I went to Douthier. Poor thing. It took a lot of guts to turn him in. And then he denied everything. I don't mean to sound like everyone at Douthier is wealthy, but most of my sorority sisters were from fairly well-heeled families. This girl was an outstanding athlete but didn't come from money. Suddenly, she turned up with designer clothes and pricey things, so they were pretty sure that he was paying her to change her story."

"Did she?"

"I don't think so, because they would have kicked her out for lying. She graduated and got a great job. About two years later, she died when she lost control of her car."

"How sad. That's terrible. She was so young."

Celeste looked exactly like Nessie when she shook her finger at me. "So steer clear of him."

"Are you telling me that he had a hand in her death?" I asked.

"That's what they say."

I was flabbergasted. John took revenge on her? I found it hard to imagine that the man with the sincere eyes could have done such horrible things. Could it be a different John Adele? Probably not, since Laura had worked with him there. Ugh. My stomach lurched at the thought. In that case, it was just as well that things hadn't worked out.

Upset as I was, it had not escaped my attention that the adorable owner of the brown dog with the white blaze had been looking our way. He was a good bit younger than me, so I was fairly sure he was interested in Celeste. I thanked her, apologized again for her lousy stay in Wagtail, called Trixie, and walked away to the green. But I paused and looked back to be sure Celeste's dog introduced her to the cute guy.

A Southern voice drawled behind me. "For a while there, I thought you were going to interfere with my carefully constructed plan, Miss Holly."

I gave an involuntary jerk and whipped around.

Macon leaned against a tree, one leg crossed over the other, his hands in his pants pockets. "She's very down in the dumps. I hope you cheered her up."

"It was nice of you to have coffee with her," I said.

"In spite of her mother's maniacal behavior, Celeste is a very sweet young lady. I should like to see her matched up properly to the gentleman I chose."

So much had happened that it seemed longer than a few hours ago that he'd seen Hank's photo. I felt certain Macon had recognized him. "Could I buy you a drink?"

Macon checked his watch. "Look at that. It's happy hour! Not that I have ever been one to let the time stand in my way when it comes to a lovely libation."

He escorted Trixie and me to Hot Hog, where he snagged an outdoor table while I bought two mango daiquiris.

I joined him at the table and Trixie settled at our feet.

"Thank you kindly, ma'am." Macon sipped the frosty drink. "Oh my. This is the ticket. It doesn't get quite as hot and humid up here in the mountains as it does in Georgia." He smiled at me. "Now, do I need to trick you and John Adele into kissin' and makin' up?"

"I'm sorry that we disappointed you. It obviously wasn't meant to be." I hurried to change the subject. "Am I correct in understanding that you arranged for Celeste and that young man to be at Café Chat at the same time?"

"You are."

"Is he the musician with whom she was originally matched by you?"

"He is, indeed. If I can keep Nessie away from them, we might have something there. I may have to invite Nessie to dinner somewhere just to keep her occupied."

I wanted to bring the conversation back to Hank. I went out on a limb. "Do you have any theories about who might have murdered Hank?"

A sly smile crept to his lips. "People think hate is at the root of murder. Perhaps it is. But love is probably the oldest reason of all for murder. It's often love or the loss of love that triggers the ugly reactions of hate and jealousy."

"I'm not sure I'm following you. Are you saying that you suspect Zelda?"

"Quite the contrary. Zelda was done with Hank. She was onto him and his wicked ways. But Hank returned to her. It's called frustration attraction when the spurned partner continues to pursue his love in an effort to figure out what happened."

"You don't think Hank knew why Zelda dumped him?"

"You overlook the obvious. Hank may have truly loved Zelda."

"What? You called him a con man."

"Oh, he was! But Zelda wasn't wealthy. He was attracted to her for other reasons."

"She smelled like his mother?" I teased.

"You're making fun of scientific fact now. It may have been something like that, though. Did you know that women are more attracted to men with immune systems that are different from their own? It's part of survival of the fittest. The women don't *know* that's why they're attracted. But deep down, on a more primal level, there's something about the smell of those men that lures them because it will make their offspring stronger and more likely to thrive."

I couldn't help giggling. I had serious doubts about that!

"Don't laugh, honey, this is scientifically proven. I'm not makin' it up! I'm not smart enough to do that. But I am smart enough to know that if Hank's relationship with Zelda was the reason for murder, Zelda would be the one pushin' up daisies, not Hank. It would have been a matter of jealousy. But Zelda had no reason other than self-defense to kill Hank. She had moved on."

"I'm under the impression that you knew Hank."

His eyes flicked to meet mine in alarm. "Well, it's not like we were close."

"But you called him a con artist."

Macon sighed. "In my line of work, I have met many hustlers. They gravitate to these match-making events in search of their victims. I find it fascinating that women of all ages succumb to the Hanks of the world. I always expect my mature clients to be too wise and sophisticated to be fooled by a hustler, but somehow, a kind word, a little flattery, and moonlight go a long way." He waved his forefinger at me. "You best watch out— Hank wasn't the only swindler in this crowd."

I didn't like that. "Are you telling me that there's another Hank amongst us?"

"No, ma'am. I'm just saying that appearances can be deceiving."

Did he keep changing the subject? I zeroed in with a precise question that I hoped wouldn't leave any wiggle room. "Did you meet Hank at a matchmaking event like this?"

"I wish I had." Macon drummed his fingers on the table before looking up at me. "My favorite cousin found herself in Hank's clutches. Her parents left her a considerable amount of money, but he ran through a good bit of it. She was on the verge of selling the family home in Charleston, South Carolina, when I met Hank and put an abrupt stop to his shenanigans. I called the locksmith myself." He paused and drained his glass. "While I'm not the kind to wish anyone ill, except perhaps the newly deceased Dr. Randall Donovan, I must say that I am not sorry that Hank's predatory days have come to an end. Now, if you would be so kind as to excuse me, Celeste isn't the only one who needs a push in the right direction." He winked at me and ambled away.

I wasn't sure what to make of him. Macon had reason to be furious with both Randall and Hank. Had that peculiar little guy knocked them both off?

Trixie and I strolled back to the inn. A few people sat on rocking chairs on the porch, but the main lobby was empty, except for Oma and Gustav.

"There you are!" Oma smiled at me. "Perfect timing. Are you sure you don't mind sticking around the inn? I could call Mr. Huckle."

I had nowhere to go. "Have a good time. Don't worry about a thing."

I walked up to my apartment to put away my wallet.

Ben met me at the door. "Zelda has a date tonight with that Axel guy. I'm going out, too. But I'll have my phone if you need me."

I didn't remind him about the lousy cell reception in Wagtail. "Who are you going out with tonight?"

Ben smiled and tucked his chin in bashfully. "Dinner with Paige. Laura has a date with some guy Macon matched her with." Ben leaned against a cushy armchair. "And then later, after we ditch our dates, Laura and I are meeting up."

"Ben!"

"I feel like I have more in common with Laura."

"Could that be because you lied on Macon's matching form? For heaven's sake, Paige rescues dogs and cats. She's like the ultimate dog and cat lover!"

He nodded. "And Laura is kind of cerebral, like me. She's not obsessed with animals. We've had some really interesting conversations."

"You better get dressed."

As he walked back to the guest room, I couldn't help thinking about what Macon had said. I had wondered why Ben visited me. Although he did silly things like fill out the matchmaking form in a way that he thought would match him to me, I had long ago come to the realization that we weren't right for each other.

Now I understood. Ben had come here out of frustration attraction. It wasn't because he loved me madly, it was because he didn't understand or couldn't accept that we had broken up. He was looking for closure, and now he had found it and could move on.

It probably should have been a melancholy moment for me, but the fact that it wasn't proved to me that I had been right. Ben wasn't the guy for me. I looked down at Trixie, whom Ben had wanted me to give away. "We're in it for the long haul, baby." She danced in a circle but stopped abruptly and barked once.

"Twinkletoes, too," I assured her. I gazed around. Where was Twinkletoes?

I checked the bedroom and the balcony. Surely she hadn't managed to get out there again. No sign of Twinkletoes.

"Ben?" I called. "Have you seen Twinkletoes?"

He emerged from his room. "Come to think of it, I haven't seen her since lunch. She usually hisses at me. I would have noticed that!"

THIRTY

It wasn't unusual for Twinkletoes to roam about the inn during the day. She had a favorite sunbeam spot in the Dogwood Room where she liked to stretch out.

I told Ben to have fun, called Trixie, and headed down the grand staircase. My first stop was the Dogwood Room. Twinkletoes wasn't there. I peeked in the private kitchen and the library. She wasn't on the front porch either. I was beginning to wish Trixie were a trained search dog.

"Find Twinkletoes."

Trixie put her nose to the floor and followed something that was invisible to me, but not surprisingly, it took her straight to the dog food pantry. For once, the door was firmly closed. I opened it. Neat and orderly, it contained no cats or other creatures.

I strolled down to the office. Still no sign of Twinkletoes. Trixie and I walked around the back of the inn. Maybe she was on one of the terraces enjoying the summer weather.

No such luck. Where had that sweet girl gone? Trixie and I returned through the terrace door and walked through the empty dining area.

I heard nails clicking on the floor before I saw Cooper. He sprang toward me joyously. "Hi, sweetie." If only John were as lovable as Cooper.

John walked in a moment later carrying Twinkletoes in his arms. He set her on the floor, and she rubbed her cheeks on his legs, winding between them.

"Twinkletoes!" I dashed over to him and picked her up. "Where have you been?"

John's mouth dropped. "You have to be kidding me. There's no use in pretending, Holly. I can't believe you brought your poor cat over to my house and made her scratch on my windows to come inside."

I looked down at Twinkletoes in my arms. "What a silly kitty. Why did you do that? I'm sorry, John. She has never done anything like this before."

"Sure she hasn't. Obviously you taught her to do it."

"How would a person teach a cat something like that?"

"Holly, I don't know. I'm sure there are ways. She didn't just wander over to my house on her own."

"Actually, she did. Because I don't even know where you're staying."

He smacked his forehead like he thought I was impossible. "I find it alarming that you have no compunction about lying right to my face. Do you really think you can convince me that you haven't been lurking around my house? For Pete's sake, Trixie came to my door the other night. If you're going to sneak around and spy on people, you should at least leave her at home. I'm done with you." He held his palms out like he was stopping traffic. "Don't send your cat or dog over anymore." He turned and walked out the door.

Of all the nerve!

In my arms, Twinkletoes purred. I nuzzled her head and the volume increased. What a relief to have her back.

Still holding her, I stepped out on the porch and yelled, "Hey, John!"

He paused and looked back.

"Thanks for bringing Twinkletoes home!"

He waved dismissively and continued on his way.

Zelda and her friend Axel approached from the other direction. "Hi. What brings you to the inn?"

"Would you mind if we hung out here tonight?" asked Zelda. "Everyone is staring at me and whispering like they think I'm the one who whacked Hank."

"Sure. You're welcome to check the magic fridge to see if there's something you'd like to eat."

They walked inside, but I settled into a rocking chair with Twinkletoes. I couldn't imagine what had possessed her to wander away from the inn.

I stroked her gently and looked out at the quiet plaza. The sun was setting on Wagtail. Lights inside stores and restaurants glowed in the twilight. People walked peacefully along the sidewalks. How could there have been two murders and an attempted purse-snatching in my beloved Wagtail?

I gasped aloud. How could I have overlooked something so obvious? There was a reason Hank hadn't followed me that night. The person lurking around Zelda's house hadn't been Hank!

THIRTY-ONE

Zelda had to know, immediately.

Apologizing to Twinkletoes, I set her on the floor of the porch and dashed inside. In the empty lobby, I took a minute to compose myself. Pretending to be calm, I poked my head into the private kitchen. Axel and Zelda were in a sweet embrace.

I cleared my throat. "Sorry to interrupt. Zelda, could I speak with you for a moment?"

"No," she said, not letting go of Axel.

Crooking my finger and wiggling it, I forced a smile and said, "I need to speak with you out here. Please?"

There was no mistaking her reluctance to release Axel. "I'll be right back." She glared at me and muttered, "This better be important."

When she emerged, I seized her hand and towed her over to the Dogwood Room in case Axel was listening at the door.

"Holly! What's going on?" Zelda looked at me with worried eyes.

"Remember when I went over to your house to distract Hank and lure him away?"

"It was last night, Holly. Of course I recall it."

"That wasn't Hank hanging around outside of your house."

She stared at me in silence for a moment. "Of course it was. I saw him."

"You saw someone. I did, too. But it wasn't Hank. A couple of hours earlier, Hank had stopped Mick from stealing Celeste's purse. *After* I tried to lure Hank away from your house, I went to Tequila Mockingbird. That's when Nessie found out Hank's real identity and left in an uproar. Celeste said her mother embarrassed her to death and walked her home. Hank walked separately but kind of followed them. That means it couldn't have been Hank outside of your house. He was with Celeste that entire time."

Zelda's right hand trembled as she covered her mouth. "Who was it, then? Why would anyone else be stalking me?"

I helped her to a seat, but she popped right back up and paced back and forth. Four steps away from me. Four steps back to me.

"Axel?" she whispered. "Is that who you think it was?"

"I don't know." I wanted to ask my next question kindly, but in the end, there wasn't a nice way to put it. "Have you been flirting with anyone else?"

Fortunately, she did not appear to be offended. "No. Well, maybe. You know what it's like. Somebody says something funny in a bar and you give him a retort."

There were hundreds of single men in town! "Zelda, I want you to concentrate. Think back. Did you notice anything about that person? Height, weight, was he carrying anything? Did you notice what he had on?"

Zelda shivered when she said, "He was a dark blob of a human in the night."

Unfortunately, I knew exactly what she meant. I had seen the same thing. A hunched-over person dodging through the yard.

Zelda seized the neckline of her top in her fist. "What do I do now? If it was Axel, he'll get angry if I try to ditch him."

I'd been thinking about that. We had to keep Zelda safe. "I think it's best if you stay here tonight. The more people around you, the better. Maybe when Ben comes home he can walk over to your place with us to get what you need for the night."

"Ben? He couldn't save me from an attacking wasp!"

She was right. I sucked in a deep breath. "I guess we have to tell Dave."

"What if he thinks we're making it up?"

"That's a chance we have to take," I said.

"Maybe we should talk to Ben first, so we don't do anything stupid. He told me not to say anything to Dave unless he was present."

I could understand that. "Ben's on two dates tonight."

"Two? Are you kidding?"

"Amazing, isn't it? Okay, here's what we'll do.

Oma and Gustav will be back soon. Meanwhile the three of us will stick together, and I'll try to get ahold of Ben."

"How do I explain to Axel that we can't be alone?"

That was a very good question. "Tell him you feel sorry for me because I had to stay here to work. Bring the food out to the dining area, and we'll be in full public view." My head was reeling, but another thought occurred to me. "Zelda, when did you first see Hank hanging around outside at night?"

"The first night he was in town. After he came to the inn looking for me. You know that."

"I wanted to be sure," I said.

Zelda looked like she might burst into tears. "Why is this happening to me? Who would want to stalk me?" She chewed on her lower lip. "Holly, I'm scared."

I gave her a big hug. And I took comfort in knowing that she was safe at the inn, and would soon be surrounded by a lot of people.

At that moment, Oma walked in with Gustav, followed by Sky and a woman who looked very much like her. Duchess bounded over to greet Trixie and Gingersnap while Sky introduced me to her sister, Cate.

"I'm so very sorry about your husband," I said.

"Thank you. It came as such a shock. Poor Randall. In spite of his tendency to be bullheaded and opinionated, I never imagined that anyone would murder him." She dabbed at her nose. "His last moments must have been horrific. I can't get them out of my head."

I wished I had something comforting to say, but I suspected she was right. "Do they have any leads?"

"If they do, they haven't told me. There's been such a fuss over his patient files. Our lawyer says the HIPAA laws permit them to be examined, but they're getting a court order first. Meanwhile, one of his patients could have killed him and fled the country by now!"

"Did he have dangerous patients?" I asked.

"Of course. He didn't talk about them, so I wouldn't know who to look for, but one of them made the news a few years ago when he took a knife and ran down a street trying to kill people. Randall was called to testify in that case."

Could Randall have been looking for a patient? My gaze strayed to our guests who were returning from dinner. Was one of his patients staying with us? It was impossible to know.

"Every place in Wagtail is still full up," said Sky. "Do you think you could put a roll-away bed in our room for my sister?"

"It will be tight, but we can do that. I assume it's okay with Nessie?"

"If she stays out like she did last night, she won't even notice."

"You're not worried about bunking with her anymore?"

Sky brushed off my question with a sheepish "No."

Behind me, Zelda said, "I'll help you, Holly!" I hadn't heard her join me. "We'll bring it up right away."

Sky and her sister thanked us and walked up the grand staircase.

Zelda elbowed me and hissed. "This is our chance to look around in their room."

"For what?"

"Anything suspicious or out of the ordinary."

"What about Axel?" I asked.

"I'll tell him something came up. Now that people are here, he wouldn't dare hurt me. Right?"

I hoped not.

Zelda hurried back to the kitchen and escorted Axel out within two minutes flat. When he tried to kiss her, she deftly turned her cheek.

Poor guy. He had to be wondering what he had done for her to go from not wanting to leave his arms to practically pushing him out the door.

"Come on. I need a bed, too," said Zelda.

In the basement, we loaded two folding beds onto the elevator. Twinkletoes jumped on top of one for the ride to the second floor.

I stopped by the housekeeping closet for sheets, blankets, towels, and pillows and stopped dead at the sight of the box of disposable gloves.

Zelda bumped into me. "What's wrong?"

"Nothing." Would Dave fingerprint boxes of gloves if I asked him to? But fingerprints on the boxes still wouldn't mean someone had murdered Hank. My fingerprints were on them, too. It wouldn't prove a connection at all.

Sky had left the door open. She and her sister had opened a bottle of wine and sat at the table by the window.

Zelda and I pushed the bed into the room. While I spread the bottom sheet over the corners, Zelda indiscreetly knelt on the floor.

What did she think she was doing? I tried to cover for her and finished making the bed. She popped up, smiling. I left the towels on the bed as well as an additional blanket in case the night was cool.

Sky thanked us profusely and promised to call if they needed anything else.

The second the door closed, I hissed at Zelda. "What was that about?"

She pulled a business card out of her pocket. It said *Randall Donovan, MD,* and gave a business address and phone number. On the reverse, someone had scribbled *SaurianPail@ selfdestructmail.com.* "What does that mean?" I asked.

She held it by the edges. "It means one of them met and talked with Randall before his death. How else would his business card have gotten into their room?"

"It was under Nessie's bed," I murmured. "Saurian Pail? What kind of name is that?"

"I don't know. But doesn't *saurian* sound familiar to you? Like something from a science-fiction movie?"

I nodded. "The Saurians. Like a group from another planet or something."

"Centurians, maybe? Who are they?" asked Zelda.

"Romans. I doubt there's any connection."

"Ben will know!" Zelda's eyes shone. "And in any event, it means one of them was in contact with Randall."

"His wife could have dropped it."

"Under the bed? I doubt it. She just arrived."

We took the elevator and the other bed up to the third floor and rolled it to the door of my apartment with Twinkletoes riding on top of it. I pushed it next to a wall in the living room, near the French doors. It had fit there well in the past.

Zelda disappeared into the kitchen. When she returned, Zelda scooped up Twinkletoes and cooed at her. I could hear Twinkletoes purring.

I phoned Ben but had to leave a voice mail message.

"I wrapped Randall's business card in plastic wrap so we wouldn't get any more fingerprints on it."

"We'd better hand it over to Dave."

"No way. I'm giving it to Ben. He can do it. I'm mad at Dave for treating us like suspects. Not to mention that he better find the guy who has been stalk . . ." Zelda paused before screaming, "My cats!"

THIRTY-TWO

I tried to be calm. "What about them?"

"They're at home all by themselves with no one to protect them. If someone is stalking me, how do I know he won't hurt my cats? What if he sets fire to my house? What if he breaks in? Didn't you see *Fatal Attraction*?"

As remote a possibility as that was, I understood completely. I would have been every bit as concerned about Trixie and Twinkletoes. "Let's go get them."

"Really?" Zelda's woe changed to hopefulness.

"Sure. We can take a golf cart. How many carriers do you have?"

"It's not far. Some of them can buddy up in carriers," said Zelda. "And Leo can ride in the golf cart like a dog."

I would have grabbed my white denim jacket, but I couldn't find it. Instead, I slipped on a lightweight teal sweater. I checked the time. Casey would be on his way soon. I called him and asked him to meet us at Zelda's house.

"Safety in numbers," I said.

I let Oma know where we were going in case anyone needed something at the inn, and we hurried out to the golf carts. Trixie tagged along. I hoped Twinkletoes wouldn't throw a hissy fit when she found she was having feline company for the night.

When we parked in front of Zelda's house, she started to step off the golf cart, but I nabbed her arm. "Wait."

We sat in the quiet night for a moment. Not a single light shone in Zelda's windows or in the house next to hers.

"What are we doing?" whispered Zelda.

"We're waiting for Casey and making sure the stalker isn't hanging around."

"Oh! Good idea. I don't see anyone, do you?"

"Not yet," I said.

"Boo!"

Zelda and I screamed. Trixie jumped out of the golf cart and ran to Casey, who had come up behind us.

"You scared us half to death." Zelda clasped a hand to her chest. "I thought you were the killer."

"Gosh, I'm sorry. How come you're so jumpy?"

While we walked to Zelda's front door, I explained the situation to Casey. Trixie scampered along, apparently unconcerned, which reassured me.

"You mean you called *me* to keep you safe from Zelda's stalker?"

Zelda unlocked the door and flicked on the lights.

I thought I saw Casey's chest puff up just a little. "Cool! Nobody has ever done that before."

Seven cats came running. I shut the door so they couldn't race outside.

Trixie yelped once. "Shh, Trixie," I said. "You're the guest here."

Zelda walked through the house with all the cats following her. Casey and I waited in the kitchen while she retrieved cat carriers.

She returned and said, "Everything looks okay."

We helped her coax unhappy cats into the carriers.

Zelda handed me a cat carrier. "Here, you take this one. Casey, would you carry the second one? I'll lock up and bring Leo and the other two cats."

I kept a watchful eye out for Zelda's stalker, but he didn't show up. I was glad that we didn't encounter him, but it made me wonder if the stalker knew Zelda was staying at the inn. Didn't that point a finger of guilt at Axel?

I didn't mention that to her. Zelda was already jittery, and I didn't think it would accomplish anything to tell her.

We were packed into the golf cart like the proverbial sardines that cats liked to eat. Zelda was right about Leo. He rode in the golf cart like a dog, sitting up and looking around.

At the inn, we piled into the elevator. Trixie had a fear of small, enclosed spaces and balked at riding the elevator. She waited until the doors were closing before taking off. She met us at the door to the apartment, wagging her tail.

Twinkletoes got along with Leo and appeared pleased to see her old pal. But the second she noticed the other cats, the fur on her back rose in panic. In one swift move, she turned and jumped to the fireplace mantel, where, with horrified round eyes, she watched six more cats enter her domain.

Ben hadn't returned from his dates yet. In the interest of a night without caterwauling, I gave Zelda and her kitties my bedroom and opted to sleep on the roll-away bed.

While she got them settled, I took Trixie and Twinkletoes down the back stairs to the kitchen for a very late dinner. Trixie dined on Country-Style Surf and Turf. I ate spinach salad with a honey mustard vinaigrette, but Twinkletoes turned her nose up at everything I offered.

We trudged up the stairs, and I tried calling Ben one more time. Still no answer. I gladly fell into bed.

In spite of my exhaustion, I tossed and turned that night, unable to think of anything other than the murders and Zelda's stalker. When I heard the sound of a key in the door around two thirty in the morning, I opened an eye. The light from the hallway illuminated Ben and Huey from behind.

I rolled out of bed, picked up Randall's plastic-wrapped business card, and followed Ben into the guest room. Huey wagged his tail in greeting.

Ben flicked on the light and when I spoke, he

let out a huge "*Gah!* You scared me. What are you doing up?"

"I cannot believe you're just getting in. And what's with your phone? Did you turn it off?"

"No." Ben sat on the bed and examined the phone. "Yes." He flicked it on. "Must have been accidental. What's so important that you waited up for me?"

I showed him the card. "What's a Saurian?"

"It's from a video game about dinosaurs and surviving in prehistoric times. But aside from the game, a saurian is a lizard. Why is it wrapped like this?"

"So we won't leave fingerprints on it. Lizard Pail? What does that mean?"

Ben shrugged. "Is there a definition of *pail* other than *bucket?*"

I borrowed his phone and looked it up. "Swell. A round container with a handle."

"Why are you obsessing about this?"

"It was in Nessie and Sky's room and had fallen under a bed. Zelda thinks it means one of them had contact with Randall."

"Did you call Dave?"

I told him about Zelda's stalker. "She thought it best for you to talk with Dave since we're under suspicion. But you were otherwise occupied."

"How do you get yourself into these things?" Ben yawned and stretched out on the bed. His head on the pillow, he closed his eyes and murmured, "I'll talk with Dave in the morning, okay?"

That was no help. "Brush your teeth," I said. Huey followed me out of Ben's bedroom, and I closed the door.

Now I was even more awake. Nevertheless, I crawled into bed. Twinkletoes jumped up to snuggle with me. I watched the time tick by on an illuminated clock. Two forty-five. Three o'clock.

The sound of dog claws tapped the floor ever so gently. Twinkletoes jumped off my bed.

I heard someone at the door. Somebody was trying to get in!

THIRTY-THREE

I was too scared to move. What should I do? Be still? Shout to wake Ben and Zelda? I lifted my head ever so slightly.

The light of the moon shone in through the French doors. I watched as Huey flipped the lock with his nose and pressed down the door handle with his paw. It swung open. Trixie and Twinkletoes paraded out behind him.

Those rascals! I rolled out of bed and tiptoed after them. So Huey was the ringleader. He knew how to unlock doors. It wouldn't be all that hard to unlatch the bolts by flipping them with a nose or dog paw. But most dogs didn't know how.

They followed Huey down the grand staircase. The inn was unbearably still. Not a single guest roamed the halls.

Huey walked straight to Sky and Nessie's room. He pawed the door handle. I could hear someone turning the lock inside the room. The door swung open, and Huey's tail wagged joyously when Duchess walked out.

The two dogs nuzzled each other. There was no sign of Lulu.

Huey led the parade to Oma's apartment. I tried to keep out of sight, but I had a feeling the dogs knew I was with them.

More pawing of the door handle, scratching sounds inside, and the click of the lock turning. Gingersnap joined the sneaky team.

They took the back stairs while I hurried to close the doors they had left open, then ran to the grand staircase and looked down. Sure enough, the whole gang ran through the main lobby on their way to the dog and cat food pantry. I scurried downstairs as fast as I could.

Happily, I caught Huey trying to open the door. The dogs had the grace to slink away and look ashamed. All except for Huey, who seemed happy to see me.

"All right. I can't sleep, either, so we might as well have a midnight snack. Come on." I headed for the private kitchen.

Casey was fast asleep with his head on the kitchen table. A book was open in front of him and a coffee mug sat near his right hand. He had fallen asleep with his glasses on.

I poured water into the kettle for a cup of hibiscus and rose hip tea. The fridge contained leftovers of meals the inn had served to dogs and cats the previous day. I found bowls and spooned Summer Supper into bowls for the dogs, and Feisty Feline Fantasy, which looked like salmon and beef, into a bowl for Twinkletoes. Was this why she hadn't eaten earlier? She had looked forward to the pantry raid?

I helped myself to a banana cupcake with chocolate frosting.

Casey's head jerked up. "Holly! Is it morning?"

"Only the wee hours."

He removed his wire-rimmed glasses and rubbed his eyes. "Don't tell your grandmother you caught me sleeping, okay? She gave me a lecture when I came in tonight."

When I picked up the dog dishes, I noticed a small backpack by one of the easy chairs. Casey hadn't had a backpack with him earlier. What a fake he was. He'd thought if he pretended to be asleep I would go away. Two could play this game.

The dogs all watched me innocently. Casey chewed his upper lip and avoided my eyes.

I poured hot water into my mug. "You know, I feel like a cookie. Casey, would you like a cookie?"

At the mention of the *C* word, the dogs followed me like baby ducks when I walked across the kitchen to the pantry. But Casey stiffened.

I was having way too much fun playing with him. "Maybe not. I can't sleep. What are you reading? Maybe I'll stick around here for a while and read, too. Is it any good?"

"Uh, yeah. You're going to be tired tomorrow if you stay up all night, though."

"You're so right," I said.

He sagged with relief.

"A cookie it is." I jerked open the door to the walk-in pantry.

A truly beautiful, petite girl with long brown hair and big brown eyes handed me a box of cookies. "Chocolate chip?"

I liked her instantly and couldn't help laughing. "Get out of there. Who are you?"

"Allie."

"I don't think I've met you. Did you come for the matchmaking event?"

"Gosh, no. You might know my uncle. Bob Lane? My mom and I moved into his guesthouse a couple of months ago, when my dad left us."

"We go to the community college together," said Casey.

Allie couldn't have been a day over nineteen. "I see. Isn't your mom worried about you? It's the middle of the night."

"She's a nurse. She works the midnight shift at the hospital in Snowball."

"Allie, I don't want to scare you, but two people have been murdered in Wagtail recently."

"That's why she's here," said Casey. "She feels safer. There are so many people in the inn that someone would hear us if we needed help."

I figured it was a convenient excuse to hang out together, but it also made some sense. No wonder Casey had missed so much that was going on. Instead of being at the desk in the lobby, he'd been cozying up with Allie in the kitchen. "Casey, what would you think of an e-mail name that was *Saurian Pail*?"

"I'd think it was somebody who was into dinosaurs."

"Have you ever heard of selfdestructmail.com?"

"Yeah. Their big deal is privacy. There's some kind of double layer of security for anonymity. Your e-mails vanish from their server and don't show up on your computer history."

"Is that possible?"

He shrugged. "I've never used it."

"So you'd use that address if you wanted to hide something?"

"I guess. Some people probably think it's cool."

"But if the recipient keeps the e-mail, it's still out there," I said. "It's not like it vanishes from the recipient's computer, right?"

"Yeah. I'm not really sure how it works. Maybe like if I wanted to keep something from my mom?" Casey suggested.

I sipped my tea. Or maybe if a psychiatrist wanted to keep a secret. But from whom? And why? "Did you see Nessie Jamieson tonight?"

"Nope. The guy staying in Fetch came in late. He met some lady he likes. And Laura Pisani came in really late, too. She said if I apply to Douthier University, she'll put in a good word for me."

"That was nice of her."

"I thought so. It's pretty expensive, though. I don't know if I could afford it."

"Maybe you could get a scholarship," I said.

"I couldn't work here anymore. It would be too far away."

Casey was like a little brother to me. As much as I liked having him around, I would never do anything to stop him from having a great future. "It wouldn't be the same without you. But maybe you should apply and see what happens."

Allie looked none too happy about that. "What was that e-mail name again?"

"Saurian Pail."

She wrote it out and showed it to me. "Is this right?"

"That's it!"

"It could be an anagram."

"I don't think so," said Casey. "A saurian is a thing. We just need to figure out what other meaning *pail* could have."

"That's silly," Allie said. "*Pail* doesn't mean anything else. *Lizard bucket* is stupid. Who would call himself Lizard Bucket?"

Their argument continued and my eyelids grew heavy. "I'm going to bed. Let me know if you come up with anything. All dogs and Twinkletoes, come!"

I opened the hidden door in the bookcase and they filed past me, evidently equally tired. Back in my dining room, I latched it securely. With a wink at Huey, who watched me very carefully, I tilted a dining chair and propped the back under the door handle of the front door to the apartment. If Huey tried to open it again, he would have to knock the chair over first, hopefully making enough noise to wake me.

I woke at eight o'clock, when Huey knocked the chair over to admit Mr. Huckle. I hadn't slept that late in ages.

The commotion woke Zelda and Ben, who rushed to see what was happening.

Mr. Huckle righted the chair. "I understand Mr. Huey is something of a Houdini. Casey suggested you might want to sleep in. I'm terribly sorry to have awakened everyone."

"I'm glad you did." I gratefully took the steaming mug of tea he offered me.

"You get room service every day?" Zelda helped herself to a chocolate croissant. "I'm moving in."

Ben thanked Mr. Huckle for his coffee and slouched in one of the large armchairs, half-awake.

Mr. Huckle opened the French doors. Cool morning air wafted in. "It's a beautiful day. And no one was murdered last night."

"I wouldn't be so sure," Ben muttered. "Trixie hasn't been out yet this morning."

Zelda's cats emerged slowly from the bedroom. Twinkletoes watched them from the fireplace hearth.

Two of them jumped on Ben and rubbed their heads on his T-shirt and chin.

"Will you look at that?" Zelda watched with astonishment. "They're saying they like the way you smell."

Ben smiled. "I have a way with cats. Except for that one." He pointed at Twinkletoes.

"Perhaps they know that you are assisting Miss Zelda," opined Mr. Huckle. "Have you identified your stalker yet, Miss Zelda?"

"Nooo," she wailed.

"Do you know something?" I asked.

"Nothing important, I'm sure. Although when I walked to work yesterday morning, I encountered Miss Nessie in your neighborhood, walking back to the inn. I must say she looked exhausted."

Two more of Zelda's cats crawled into Ben's lap.

"It's like you're the cat whisperer." I noted that he was tentative about stroking them, but that didn't stop them from marking him by pressing the sides of their faces along his chest.

Excusing myself, I hurried through a shower and dressed in a white short-sleeved, scoop-neck top and a long pale green skirt that fell in gentle folds a couple of inches below my knees. A turquoise necklace and simple gold hoop earrings, and I was done. My hair would dry fast in the summer weather. I pinned it back loosely, so I would look somewhat pulled together.

I shoved my feet into white sandals, waved at Zelda and Ben, who were still lounging, and took all the dogs with me.

Mr. Huckle had been correct. It was a beautiful summer day. If only the murders didn't cast a shadow over Wagtail. I escorted the dogs out to do their business.

In the distance, Macon scurried off somewhere, and Gustav walked slowly toward the inn.

I watched Huey, suspecting that the escape artist might be one of the smartest dogs I had known. He had been with us only a few days, but he seemed to stay with me, even off leash.

When we entered the main lobby, Sky called Duchess. "I wasn't worried this morning when she was gone. Did they have another party?"

I told her who the ringleader was and what I had witnessed. "I wouldn't have believed it if I hadn't seen it with my own eyes."

Sky lowered her voice. "Nessie didn't sleep in our room again last night."

"I suspected that when Lulu didn't join the midnight raid."

Sky and her sister selected a table in the dining area, and I settled down with Oma and Gustav. I noticed that Trixie and Gingersnap stayed with us, but Huey followed Sky.

After I ordered buttermilk pancakes with fresh raspberries for Trixie and me, I told Oma and Gustav who had been letting the dogs out.

Gustav looked doubtful, as though he didn't believe me.

"I have heard of this," said Oma. "How interesting that Gingersnap and Duchess caught on so quickly." Oma cast a fond glance at Gingersnap.

"I have always known my little one was very smart."

Oma folded her napkin and placed it on the table. "Normally, Zelda would work today, but she needs time to recuperate, *ja*?"

"I can fill in for her."

"*Danke, liebling.* Perhaps you take the morning, and I can relieve you around three in the afternoon?"

"That works for me."

Ben and Zelda sauntered in just as Oma rose to leave. After a polite exchange of morning greetings, they slid into the chairs vacated by Oma and Gustav.

Shelley delivered our pancakes and poured coffee for them. "I wish I could sit down with you. I'm dying to know what's going on." She hurried away to pour more coffee for Sky.

I poured raspberry syrup over the pancakes and dug in. If summertime had a flavor, it had to be fresh, juicy raspberries.

"I called Dave this morning." Ben added cream to his coffee. "I don't like being out of the loop like this. He's usually so forthcoming with information, but this time I think he's afraid to share what he knows."

"I feel the same way. We're going in circles," I complained. "There has to be something that we've overlooked."

Laura ambled over to our table with Marmalade

on a leash. "Is this a private confab or can we join you?"

Marmalade seemed put out and yowled.

"What's wrong with him?" asked Ben.

"I've been keeping him cooped up in our room and on a leash when we go out. He's not happy about that."

"I guess he liked roaming during his first days here."

"You could take him to the cat park." Zelda sipped her coffee. "It's loads of fun for them. Or how about the cat agility center? Leo loves to go there."

"I'm a little bit embarrassed. I've had such a great time here that I haven't taken Marmalade to play at the cat places."

I polished off my last bite of the fluffy pancakes and excused myself. Leaving them to their breakfasts, I dashed upstairs to brush my teeth in the company of Zelda's cats, and hurried down to the registration lobby to work.

It was a fairly ordinary day at the Sugar Maple Inn. The housekeeper came to clean rooms. The handyman arrived to clean the doggy poop areas and take care of the outdoors. I fielded a couple of phone calls about hosting weddings at the inn. Trixie napped in the office, and Twinkletoes napped in the sun. But through it all, the ugly shadow of the murders hung over me.

At three o'clock in the afternoon, Ben made an appearance.

"Holly," he said, "I thought I'd packed a green T-shirt. Have you seen it anywhere?"

I had completely forgotten about it. I jumped to my feet instead of ratting out the animals and telling him they had destroyed his T-shirt. "I have to buy a few things. Why don't I pick up a new one for you?" I whistled for Trixie and sped upstairs to fetch my wallet before he could question me. If Ben was warming up to cats, I didn't want to discourage his progress by telling him the cats had ruined his clothes.

In spite of the murders, the sidewalks of Wagtail buzzed with people, dogs, and cats. I suspected most of the Animal Attraction participants knew nothing about the two deaths. I strolled to a casual clothing store called Petunia. Their merchandise leaned toward clothes with dog and cat themes, but I thought I could probably find a green T-shirt that would be acceptable to Ben.

I pushed open the door and headed straight to men's T-shirts. In an instant, I found just the right thing. I looked down at Trixie. "I hope you had nothing to do with that misbehavior. No shredding clothes."

Her tail wagged, which I took to mean she wasn't involved. I had suspected the cats all along.

I spied a blue scarf with white paw prints like the one Twinkletoes and Marmalade had been playing with. Someone would be looking for it, so I might as well buy it too, and be prepared to replace it. I added it to the T-shirt that I carried and took my items to the front of the store.

"Hi, Holly! It's nice to see a familiar face." The owner of the store took the clothes and rang them up. "Not that I'm complaining. I've been open early and late to accommodate all the gift-giving people are doing." She held up the scarf as she folded it. "These have flown out of the store this weekend. This is the last one. Would you like it wrapped as a gift?"

"No, thanks. I'm replacing one that some cats got hold of."

She glanced around and lowered her voice. "You know the doctor who was killed? He bought one of these scarves."

THIRTY-FOUR

"Dr. Randall Donovan?" I asked, just to be sure she didn't think Hank was a doctor.

"Yes. Wasn't his death just awful? But between the two of us, he was kind of a jerk. You'd think he would have realized how proud I am of my store, but he made fun of the merchandise. I was a little bit offended. Who does that?" She chuckled. "But despite all that pompous superiority, I got the last laugh because he bought something!"

"Did he ask you to wrap it?"

"Nope."

"He didn't happen to mention who it was for?"

"Are you kidding? He couldn't stop putting people down long enough to talk about anything else."

Too bad. He could very well have bought it as a gift for his wife.

"Was anyone with him?" I asked.

She stopped and stared at me in alarm. "I see what you're getting at. The person who killed him could have been with him." Her gaze dropped to the items in her hands, which she slid into a bag. "No. I don't think so. I can't imagine who would have wanted to spend more than two minutes with the man. Don't get me wrong. It's never right to murder anyone. Not even if he was a total nincompoop. But he was so obnoxiously pretentious, I just about wanted to strangle him myself."

I thanked her and left the store with Trixie. The scarf had not been on Randall when we'd found him. That meant he had left it wherever he was staying or he had already given it to someone as a gift. Or the killer had taken it with him. Where *had* Randall planned to stay? Maybe Dave knew. Not that that would help, since he wasn't sharing much with me about the murders.

Just to stretch our legs and enjoy the weather, Trixie and I took the long way back. We rambled along the lakefront near Tequila Mockingbird. Their outdoor bar was open and the place was packed. We walked on a little bit to a bench where Trixie chased ducks into the water, yapping and running after them.

I sat and was pondering the situation when Macon plopped down and handed me a drink.

"It's a watermelon lemonade slush. Reminds me of summer days in the deep South."

"Thank you."

"Any advances on the murder investigations?" he asked.

"If there have been, I don't know about them."

"I can't imagine that you're a serious suspect. Not with so many people despising Hank. It's funny that those two were linked in death."

"How so?" I asked.

"On the surface they appeared to be opposite ends of the spectrum. Hank was a lowlife at best and Randall was technically well educated and recognized as an authority of sorts. But the truth is that they had something in common. Neither one of them was what he appeared to be. They were both living a lie."

"Hank pretended to be a doctor."

"That's one example. Hank was a chameleon. He was whatever you wanted him to be, as long as it gained him access to your purse strings."

"You're not saying Randall did that, too?"

"No, but he was equally deceptive. He made a name for himself arguing against love. Claimin' it was a societal expectation. But he wasn't completely stupid, and I have no doubt that he had some familiarity with the workings of the human brain. He denied the existence of love, yet was married. There you have it, my dear. Randall was every bit as much a fraud as Hank."

I considered what he'd said.

He pointed toward a boat on the water. "Take Maddie Stevens out there on that boat, for instance. She's pretending she doesn't know how to sail. It's a good thing she had me around to match her up. I expect they'll have a bit of a falling-out when they discover that they're both pretending to be someone they're not. The irony is that their true identities are a good match."

In the boat next to Maddie's, a dog barked and

jumped into the water. He swam straight toward us.

"Is that Cooper?" I asked.

"From the panic on John's face, I'd say so."

On the boat, John leaned over the side, yelling Cooper's name. Laura was with him. I wondered if Ben knew about that.

I rushed to the water's edge. Trixie continued to bark.

Cooper swam steadily toward us. "Come on, Cooper!" I called.

John had come about in the sailboat, but the wind wasn't cooperating and he couldn't get close to Cooper.

I waded into the lake with my arms outstretched. "Come on, boy! You can do it!"

At last he reached me. I escorted him to shore, where he shook water out of his fur and then proceeded to greet Trixie.

"I guess they were borin' him," said Macon.

I waved at John and yelled, "He's okay! I'll take him to the inn."

Macon chuckled. "And Randall claimed there's no such thing as love."

"Did you know that John was accused of sexual misconduct with a student? And then she died two years later in a car accident?" I blurted.

"Really? I would imagine there's more to that story than meets the eye."

My drenched skirt wrapped around my legs, and

I had a feeling a little more of me was meeting the eyes of onlookers than *I* cared to imagine. I thanked Macon, called the dogs, and hurried back to the inn.

Even though I ducked in through the registration entrance, there was no avoiding all the odd glances. Trixie and Cooper ran up the stairs faster than I could go.

I barged into the apartment. Huey greeted us at the door.

Ben ambled out of the bedroom, his hair damp as though he had just showered. He raised an eyebrow. "That's quite a revealing outfit."

I grabbed a towel and wrapped it around me. "I have your T-shirt."

"Good timing." He removed it from the bag and held it up. "This is a different green."

Uh-oh.

"I think I like it better. What else did you buy?" He peered in the bag.

"Just a scarf." I took it out to show him. "Twinkletoes and Marmalade did a number on a similar one. I thought I'd better have it on hand when the owner of the other one realizes it's missing." I stashed the shredded one in the bag with it.

"Oh yeah. Paige has one like that."

"Ben, I just saw John sailing with Laura."

He scowled. "I guess I can't be too critical of her. After all, I'm going out with Paige again. Did you steal Cooper from him?"

"Cooper decided he would rather run with Trixie than sail with John."

"Dogs are weird," Ben said.

On that note, I hurried to the shower. When I emerged from the bathroom, Huey, Cooper, and Trixie waited for me. They were so cute. It brightened my day that they had waited for me outside the bathroom door.

Only then did it dawn on me that Zelda's cats were missing.

I pulled on jeans and a V-neck top. I couldn't help thinking how cute the paw-print scarf would be with it. Tempting as it was to wear it, I knew I had to reserve the new one for the guest who had lost the tattered scarf. I dug in the closet for my white Keds and jean jacket. I found the shoes immediately, but there was no sign of the jacket. Maybe I had left it downstairs.

"Ben?" I called. "Have you seen Zelda's cats?"

"They're all in my room."

"You're kidding."

"Nope. *I* am the cat whisperer."

Sure he was. I couldn't believe it. How could a person change so much that cats would suddenly be drawn to him?

We walked out together.

"Is Huey invited on your date tonight?" I asked.

"You bet. Paige really likes him."

No sooner had we hit the lobby than Oma waved me down.

"*Liebling*, Macon is looking for you." She turned and waved her hand. "Here she is!"

"Holly, darlin', could you give me a hand outside, please?" asked Macon.

"Sure. What do you need?"

"This way, sweetheart."

I followed Macon outside to a red-and-white checked cloth spread on the ground for a picnic. He handed me my apricot pashmina. I wanted to ask how he'd gotten it, but only managed to blurt, "What's this?"

"I need some publicity photos, honey. Your sweet Oma volunteered you. And Zelda gave me your lovely pashmina."

I was as good a sport as anyone, but publicity photos? Why hadn't anyone told me about this? "I'm not dressed for anything like that."

"You're fine. They should look very casual."

I capitulated. "What do you want me to do?"

"Just sit right down and pretend you're havin' a wonderful time."

I hoped I didn't need to tell him that I wasn't a professional model. Surely he could see that. "Maybe I should brush my hair?"

"Sweetheart, you're perfect just like that. Thank you so much for helpin' me out."

I was about to respond when I realized that he was talking to John. Where did he come from? *Oh no!* I smelled a big stinking Macon rat and jumped to my feet.

"Macon, thanks for the effort, but . . ." John leaned over and whispered something to Macon.

"I don't care what he says, I have not been following him," I protested.

I tugged Macon aside, and in the lowest whisper possible, I said, "I thought I told you that he may have murdered one of his students."

Macon patted my arm. "You two are so perfectly suited for each other. Now, don't embarrass me by making a fuss." He waved toward the inn. "The photographer and nigh on to two dozen people are watchin' you."

I sat down. "Let's get this over with."

John joined me on the checkered cloth. "I haven't had dinner. Was this your idea?"

"Obviously not. I thought I was done with you."

Macon deposited Twinkletoes by my side. She pawed at a basket. Cooper and Trixie looked on with interest. They must have smelled something wonderful.

John held up bowls with their names on them. "I assume we know who these are for. Let's see what's in the basket."

I peeked inside, which fascinated Twinkletoes and the dogs. "Looks like fried chicken."

"I haven't had that in years!" John handed me a plate before helping himself to a chicken thigh. He bit into it, swallowed and said, "Mmm. Macon knows his stuff. This tastes homemade."

Just to get his goat, I said, "I cooked it."

He choked and grabbed his throat with one hand.

"Now, how's that going to look in the pictures?"

He blinked. "You're joking? That's not funny."

"Look, neither one of us wants to be here. Macon clearly set us up. So let's just sit out here and be civil while you eat and then we never have to have anything to do with each other again."

"Sounds good to me. I'll be glad when you quit lurking in my trees."

"How many times do I have to tell you that I haven't been doing that?"

"I've seen you at my house," John insisted.

"Maybe there's someone who looks like me. Maybe I have a doppelgänger," I said sarcastically. "But it wasn't me!"

"Oh, right."

"The trees?" In my head, I could hear Aunt Birdie telling me I looked a mess. "John, where are you staying?"

His head fell forward like he couldn't believe I had asked such a stupid question, then he raised it to look at me. "Do you never give up?"

"Is it a bungalow? Next to the house where Hank was murdered?"

John laughed cynically. "How stupid do you think I am?"

"You're the one who looked at me with binoculars."

"And that's how I knew it was you."

"Ahh. That explains a lot. Zelda lives next door to you. I wasn't sneaking around your house. I was creeping around Zelda's house."

"I'm sure she's very happy about that." He clearly didn't believe me.

"You're afraid of me!" I laughed. "Cooper likes me." I said in my defense.

"He's also fond of rolling in cow pies."

"That's a nice comparison!" I pretended to be appalled.

John couldn't help smiling.

I sipped my wine, and while John ate potato salad, I launched into the tale of Zelda and Hank and how it was that I might have appeared to be sneaking around John's backyard, even though I was really in Zelda's backyard.

"You brought Trixie with you to lure Hank away?" he asked.

"Of course not. I left her in my apartment, but Ben must have stopped in and let her out. How did you know about that?"

"She's the one who gave you away. She came to my door."

"She caught up to me at Hot Hog."

"That's a peculiar story, complete with weird getup, but I have learned that life can be strange, so I'm willing to buy it. I suppose you have equally bizarre explanations for the other times?"

"Other times?"

"When I met Laura at Café Chat and when we

were at Hair of the Dog. You can't tell me you just happened to be there."

"Actually, I can. When you were at Café Chat, I was picking up medicine for Gustav at Heal! And when you saw me at Hair of the Dog, I was walking back from WAG where I went to talk with Paige about Sky. This is a small town. Just because you've been hiding in your house writing for a few weeks and you haven't met me before doesn't mean you'll never see me again."

"Not if you keep coming to my house to spy on me."

"If you mean when you saw me with the binoculars, that's very easy to explain. Some idiot told Officer Dave that I was in Zelda's yard when Hank was murdered, and now I'm a suspect. Isn't that ridiculous?"

He focused on the potato salad. He didn't look like he thought it was absurd at all.

"No!" The word blew out of my mouth. "It was you," I uttered as I began to put the pieces together. "That's why you're afraid of me? *You're* the one who thinks I killed Hank?"

Trixie nudged my hand in sympathy and received a bit of soft chicken breast without the fried part as thanks. Here I was, being nice to John. "I can't believe this. What would possess you to imagine such a crazy thing?"

"Why did you sneak back to the scene of the crime?"

I nearly blew up. "I was trying to figure out who could have reported seeing me there in the middle of the night! But now it all makes perfect sense. You know what? I think Cooper and Trixie, and Twinkletoes, and, oh my, especially Macon, were completely wrong about the two of us. You clearly have some kind of problem with women, given what happened at Douthier University and now this. I'm sorry. We—"

"How did you know about Douthier?"

"Laura mentioned something about it, so Zelda looked it up."

John had stopped eating. "I'm a little shocked to hear this attitude from *you*. Of all people, I thought you would understand."

"Me? Why?"

"You were fired from a job."

"That was entirely different. There were extenuating circumstances. My boss was doing something illegal, and I caught him at it."

"Then you should understand that there might be explanations and unusual situations when other people lose their jobs."

I ran my wineglass over my forehead, appreciating the coolness of the condensation on my hot head. "Okay. I'm listening. What excuse is there for sleeping with a student?"

"It never happened."

He had my attention.

"She was in one of my classes. Kind of an

average student, actually—I barely noticed her. One day she told the dean of students that we were having an affair and that I had threatened to flunk her if she mentioned it to anyone. Only it wasn't true. Not a single word of it."

"Were you able to disprove her allegations?"

"How? You can't prove a negative. Let me tell you, it was an eye-opener for me. When something like that happens, you find out who your true friends are. People who I thought were pals drew away and wanted nothing to do with me. I couldn't get another teaching job, of course. Her lie changed my entire life. Not to mention that I had been up for tenure." John snorted. "That was out of the question!"

He sounded convincing. Still, I had some doubts. "Why would she do that?"

John shrugged. "To this day I don't understand it. My parents thought it was some kind of misguided plea for attention. A couple of my friends thought the girl was angry because she had a crush on me and I was too stupid to notice. In the end, I was exonerated. But it was too late. All people remember is the allegation. They don't care that it never happened."

"Did you pay her off?"

John nearly snorted his wine. "Who gave you that idea?"

"A student."

"Really? No, I had my attorney's fees to pay

Trust me when I say there were no funds for paying anyone off."

I didn't want to come right out and accuse him of killing her. "I guess you know that she died."

He looked at me with such an open expression of shock that I thought it was the first he had heard of her death.

"A car accident," I said.

"I'm sorry to hear that. Truly sorry. She ruined my life, but she was way too young to die."

"I'm surprised no one told you."

"I haven't been in touch with many of them. A few friends and students from those days have found me on Facebook, which is kind of cool."

"How about Laura?" I asked.

"I hadn't seen her since I left Douthier. Funny, I thought I had reached the point where all that was behind me. Ten years later and it's still raising its ugly head. Remember when I went back to Macon to be matched to someone else? When he pegged me to Maddie Stevens, I nearly flipped out. Maddie is probably a very nice person, but she has to be at least sixteen years younger than me. I realized that night that those allegations have permanently changed me. There is no way I am ever going to be interested in anyone substantially younger than me. Ever. The minute I saw her, I knew there wasn't a chance."

"I guess Macon is right."

"Not about me and Maddie!" John said.

"He may have done that intentionally. I've noticed that Macon likes to play games to get people together like he's doing to us right now. I don't see a photographer, do you?"

"Nope. But how would it help to set me up with Maddie?"

"To send both of you scurrying back to your original matches."

"I get it. The wrong person makes the right person seem all that much better. What a sneaky guy. It might have worked if you hadn't been an ax murderer."

"You're going to have a tough time writing thrillers if you don't know the difference between an ax and a hoe."

John tried to suppress a grin.

Was he beginning to change his mind about me? "Macon can't know all our histories. I meant his assertion that we know within minutes or mere seconds whether a relationship is possible was correct." I ate a bite of creamy potato salad—nicely tangy, with pickles. "Hey, wait a minute. You did the same thing to me."

"I beg your pardon?"

"You told Dave you saw me when Hank was killed. But I was *not* there. Just like I jumped to conclusions about the allegations of sexual misconduct on your part, you somehow jumped to the conclusion that I was a murderer."

John set his plate down. Holding up his left

hand, he ticked items off on his fingers as he recited them. "One, you were sneaking around my yard in the dark in a disguise when you claim you were trying to distract Hank. Two, Trixie's arrival confirmed that you were there. Three, I saw you lurking in my backyard around three in the morning. Four, I caught you with my binoculars when you returned in the morning and hid among the trees. And five, you spied on Ben, thus setting a precedent for that kind of behavior."

I had just taken another bite of the potato salad and choked. "Ben? Why? Why would he say something like that?"

"I guess you did it to him, too."

"Never! How could I? That's not even physically possible. He lives in a condo on the fifth floor. He doesn't even have a balcony. Does he think I have a pole that extends five stories in the air with a camera attached to it?"

"That's odd. It does sound implausible."

"And why would you think, and worse, tell Dave, that I was in your backyard at three in the morning when that couldn't possibly have been the case?"

"You were wearing the same jacket you had on the night before. I saw you there."

He was so stubborn. "That wasn't me. You saw the murderer!"

THIRTY-FIVE

"Tell me exactly what happened," I said.

"Cooper woke me by barking. It wasn't like when he sees a squirrel and barks like a crazy dog. It was just a bark or two—more like an alert. It was around three in the morning. A large bedroom suite takes up the second floor of the house. There's a nook with cushions at a large window that overlooks the backyard, and Cooper had jumped up on it to look outside. So I got up and peered out, too. That was when I saw you. I considered going downstairs to yell at you, but thought better of it and went back to bed. Of course, at the time, it never occurred to me that it could be anything more than you snooping around. I wondered why you would bother, unless you were hanging around to see if a woman was staying over at my place."

"You never saw this person's face?"

"No," he said.

"You just assumed it was me?"

He blew air out of his mouth like a deflating balloon before he said, "I recognized the jacket you wore the night we found Randall's body. It's white, which, by the way, is not the best color to wear when you go out to murder someone at night."

I thought back to what I had worn the day before. "If you saw me earlier that night, then you knew I was wearing a dark coat over a life vest to bulk me up."

"Like you couldn't change clothes? Plus, I hear the killer used a garden hoe from your aunt's shed. You would have known where to find that."

"I suppose you think I murdered Randall, too?"

"No, I don't."

"I can't believe it! Why not pin that one on me?"

"I don't know exactly what time he was murdered, but you seemed to be pretty busy at the inn, and I seriously doubt that there would have been enough time for you to run over to the Shire, murder him, and get back to the dog play area before I saw you there," John said.

"Gee, thanks for letting me off the hook for that murder. Has it occurred to you that I might be too smart to wear a white jacket to clobber someone in the dark and that other people also own white jackets?"

"I'm feeling a little bit sheepish about that now. I really thought it was you. If it makes you feel any better, Dave found a button in the grass. There's a good chance it matches the jacket that was worn that night."

Now I wanted to run up to my closet and search for my white jacket.

"You've been turning up everywhere I go, and when I saw the jacket, I thought, *There she is again.* I didn't expect this, Holly, but I was a lot more comfortable when I thought you had murdered Hank. At least I knew who to watch out for. Now it could be anybody."

"Do you think you're the next target?"

"Not really. But I've been carrying pepper spray in my pocket, just in case."

"You bought pepper spray to protect yourself from me?"

"I bought it to protect Cooper and me from bears when we're out hiking on the mountain trails. But strange things have been happening in this town, so I've been carrying it around with me."

I couldn't help laughing. "That's why you were brave enough to sit out here with me. You have it on you right now?"

His eyes met mine. "I feel like a complete crumb. The thing is that since I met you, I've felt like I'm being watched. I've seen people lurking in the dark around my house. And you've turned up everywhere I go, so I thought it was you."

"Maybe you felt that way because Hank was hanging around Zelda's house and your backyards aren't separated by a fence. I saw him walking between your houses when I went over to lead him astray."

"You're probably right. I associated it with you because it didn't happen to me before I met you. But Hank arrived in town just about that time, didn't he?"

"I don't know when he arrived, but he came to the inn a couple of hours before you did."

"So if you didn't murder him, who did?" asked John.

"Ben, Zelda, and I discussed this. I think we can eliminate Sky Stevens. She's Randall's sister-in-law, but I don't think she had time to kill Randall."

"You're assuming the same person murdered Randall and Hank?"

I looked at him in surprise. "Randall's wallet, containing a large amount of cash, was in Hank's pocket."

"Whoa!" John exclaimed so loud that the dogs jumped up. "That puts everything in a new light."

I nodded. "Nessie Jamieson appears to have known them both. She was steaming angry at Hank the night he died. As far as I can tell, she had the opportunity to knock both of them off. I guess her daughter could have, too. And then there's Bob Lane, one of the pharmacists at Heal! Have you met him yet?"

"Is that the good-looking guy, around forty-five or fifty?"

"That's him," I confirmed.

"I don't know him, but he has always been nice when I've gone in to buy something. And he makes a great old-fashioned milk shake. I didn't think anyone made those anymore."

I told him about the lawsuit against Bob and

how Hank had stolen from the drugstore. "That's really all we've got in terms of suspects."

"You left a few people out. I know she's your friend, but you have to consider Zelda—"

"No way! I've seen Zelda catch spiders and bees. She takes them outside and releases them. I know Hank was a pain in her neck, but she wouldn't have killed him unless it was in self-defense. But don't forget Macon." *And you,* I thought. I immediately hated myself for even thinking such a thing. After all, I had no reason to imagine that he had known Randall or Hank. Nevertheless, I glanced back at the inn and took comfort in the murmuring I could hear only a few yards away, where Oma, Gustav, and Zelda talked on Oma's patio.

If I'd truly thought John had killed someone, I would have left already. I looked at his face. Even in the fading light of day, he had honest eyes. I didn't want to run away. I wanted to kiss him. Surely I wouldn't want to kiss a killer!

Was I doing what Macon had described? Was something in my brain overriding the fact that John had turned me in as a killer? I should be too furious to speak with him. But I wasn't. Drat that Macon. Would I be questioning my reactions in relationships the rest of my life?

I decided to go with my gut feeling. After all, Trixie liked him. Dogs were known to be excellent judges of character.

"Macon. Randall said such awful things about him." I glanced up the hill toward the inn. "Seems unkind to talk about him that way when he set up this picnic for us."

"Holly, I haven't met many people in Wagtail who haven't been nice. To me that means someone who seems terrific is really evil to the core." He lowered his voice. "And Macon certainly had the opportunity. I've seen him all over town. I seriously doubt that he had an event scheduled in the middle of the night, when Hank was killed, or Thursday evening when Randall was done in. But I don't know why he would have murdered Hank unless it was because he lied about being a doctor."

"You heard about that, huh?"

"Everybody heard about it. I think it made a lot of people reconsider their matches. I know Laura had second thoughts about Ben."

"They weren't matched to begin with. They just met in a bar. But Macon had a big reason to loathe Hank. Seems Hank took financial advantage of Macon's favorite cousin. Macon interfered in the nick of time, but I gather quite a bit of money went to Hank."

"Macon. Who would have thought it? Should we tell Dave what we know?" John asked.

"You should certainly tell him that you have changed your mind about seeing me there at the time of the murder!"

The sun had almost set and the moon glowed in the sky. We would need lanterns soon. Cooper and Trixie played along the edge of the lake. Cooper jumped in and out, and Trixie sniffed along the shore.

I was feeling much better. John would clear me with Dave, and I wouldn't be a suspect anymore. And I was convinced that he was telling me the truth about the terrible allegations against him at Douthier.

We had made it to the chocolate-dipped strawberries when Trixie started barking. I bit into a strawberry and turned my head to see what Trixie was fussing about.

Cooper appeared to flounder in water that was over his head.

THIRTY-SIX

The two of us leaped to our feet and dashed toward the lake. We splashed into the water, headed for Cooper.

John threw his arms around Cooper's chest and tried to help him to shore. I saw the problem immediately. Cooper wasn't drowning. He had grabbed hold of a waterlogged branch and refused to release it.

"He's dragging a branch," I yelled over the sound of thrashing water.

"Cooper, drop it!" John shouted.

But Cooper was stubborn. He'd found that branch and didn't intend to let go of his prize.

I did my best to grasp it. When I pulled, whatever it had been stuck on finally gave way.

Cooper jerked it away from me, and I fell backward into the water. I scrambled to my feet.

Trixie continued to bark.

John struggled toward the shore holding Cooper, who still clenched the large branch in his mouth. As soon as they were in shallow water, John let go and Cooper bounded out, dragging the surprisingly large tree branch. A rag hung off it.

John waded in my direction. "Are you okay?"

By that time, Oma, Gustav, Macon, Zelda, and

half a dozen other guests had heard the commotion and waited for us on the shore.

"I'm fine. I'm just glad Cooper is okay." Weighed down by wet jeans, I trudged toward Cooper, who still held on to his branch, even though Trixie tugged at it. Gingersnap joined in the fun.

John reached toward me for my hand. We were both drenched.

A lone person on the shore stepped away from everyone else and walked over to the dogs. He ignored their playful growling and lifted the fabric off the branch.

As we drew closer, I realized it was Dave, and he was looking straight at me.

"Hi!" In spite of my wet clothes, I was eager to be off the hook. "John has some news."

Dave held up the cloth in gloved hands. "Does this look familiar?"

I walked up to him to examine it. What I had thought was a rag turned out to be a whitish denim jacket. Probably *formerly* white, before it spent time in the lake. In the moonlight, I couldn't make out too much more, except that it had stains on it and it looked an awful lot like my jacket.

"That is *not* mine." Blood pounded in my ears so loud that I was afraid everyone could hear it. I hadn't been able to put my hands on my white denim jacket a couple of hours ago, but I hadn't taken the time to look for it carefully. Surely I had left it in the office or in the private kitchen.

"How can you tell?" asked Dave.

I desperately wanted to say the cut or the buttons weren't the same. But they were. "Mine wasn't stained. And I'm sure it's not in the lake."

Dave nodded. "That's a relief. Let's go up to the inn and have a look at your jacket."

We started up the hill to the inn.

It wasn't cold out. And the lake water had been a pleasant temperature, but I shivered as though a cold wind had blown through. What if I couldn't find my jacket? What if Hank's killer had disposed of the white jacket he wore in the lake and it wound up near the inn? How could I prove it wasn't mine?

I could hear Zelda, Macon, and Laura assuring John that they would pack up the picnic items.

John caught up to me. "Are you all right? I can stick around."

It was kind of him to offer. But there wasn't a thing he could do to help, and he was as wet as I was. "Go on home and change into dry clothes. I'm sure everything will be fine here." I said it with fake confidence. I wasn't sure at all.

As we walked toward the inn, I hoped the jacket in the lake was the wrong size. It was fairly unlikely that it would be too small for me. But maybe it was very large. I could hope! Would Dave even allow me to try it on when it dried? I didn't think so. Certainly not if he thought it could be tied to Hank's death.

I headed straight for Oma's office. Dave followed me with the jacket.

I offered him a white trash bag for it, but he hesitated before placing the jacket in it.

"Something wrong?"

"Plastic isn't good for preserving evidence."

I wanted to say, *You could leave it outside,* but it might sound sassy, and that was something I couldn't afford at the moment. I simply pointed out, "It's dripping."

"I guess I don't have much choice. Hurry up. Where's your jacket?"

I wondered if any old white jacket would satisfy him. I glanced around the office and poked my head in the closet. My hands trembled, and I was so nervous that I could barely focus. I took a deep breath and went through the hangers one by one. It wasn't there.

I debated telling him the truth—that I couldn't find it. But that would be like admitting that the jacket in the lake was mine. If I said that, would he have enough evidence to put me in jail? To charge me with the murder?

I was panicking. I needed to calm down and think logically. Taking another deep breath, I turned around. "It must be upstairs in my apartment."

Dave didn't smile. He didn't nod. He wore a stony expression that made my panic level rise even more. I wanted to reason with him. To tell him again that the jacket wasn't mine, and that

I hadn't been there, and I had nothing to do with Hank's murder. Yet somehow it seemed if I said it all again, I would be pleading with him and admitting that the jacket he held belonged to me.

We walked up the stairs and through the second-floor hallway to the grand staircase. One more floor and we were at my door. I unlocked it and fled to my closet.

The jacket had to be there somewhere. It had to! I wished I were a more organized person who kept everything in very precise order. I wasn't a mess, but I did toss clothes on chairs sometimes. And I didn't always run up to my apartment to put away a jacket. It wasn't at all unusual for me to leave it in the private kitchen or the lobby.

Before I opened my walk-in closet door, I paused. What was I so afraid of? If I didn't find the jacket, it didn't mean I had killed Hank. It only meant I couldn't put my hands on my jacket. Nothing more.

"Got it?" Dave yelled.

Anxiety ratcheted up inside me again. I opened the door and surveyed the contents for anything white. White shirts and blouses, white sneakers, white purse, white tops. No sign of a white jacket. This wasn't working. I started at one end and was flipping through hangers when Dave spoke behind me.

"Holly, what's this?"

I looked over my shoulder. He held the blue

scarf adorned with paw prints that the cats had shredded. "It's a scarf. Twinkletoes and another cat were playing with it one night. It must belong to a guest."

He held out the new one.

"I bought a replacement. No one has claimed the scarf yet, but someone will notice it missing when they're packing to check out. They're very popular. I was lucky to get the last one the store had."

"I gather you bought it at Petunia, since their logo is on this bag?"

"Yes. Why all the questions? It's just a scarf."

Dave ran a rough hand over his eyes before he answered. "The coroner found tiny blue and white fibers on Randall's neck."

THIRTY-SEVEN

The implication hit home right away. "I didn't see any fibers on his neck!"

"They're microscopic. No one would have noticed with the bare eye."

"Am I correct in deducing that you now think I strangled Randall because I happen to have these scarves?"

"Holly—"

I stepped toward him. "Don't you *Holly* me. You know me, Dave! You *know* me. I didn't murder anyone. This is ridiculous."

"I don't like this any better than you do."

"Then find the real killers. For starters, there are probably half a dozen women in this town who own that scarf. In fact . . ." I stopped talking.

"What? Tell me!"

"The owner of Petunia said that Randall Donovan bought the exact same scarf."

Dave's jaw tensed. "I need to get these to the lab."

My hopes crashed.

It must have shown in my expression, because Dave said angrily, "Find the doggone jacket, will you? I don't want to have to arrest you when Hank's blood turns up on this one."

He left, and I locked the door behind him,

hurried to the bathroom, and stripped off my wet clothes. When I stepped out of the shower, I reflected on my situation. I had washed enough clothes to know how hard it was to get blood out. The lake water had been cold, but I feared that the lab would still be able to identify the stains on it as Hank's blood.

I returned to my closet, pulled on a skort and a sleeveless top, and then searched the entire closet methodically from end to end but found no sign of my jacket. There were no other choices. I had to figure out who'd killed Randall and Hank. If that was my jacket in Dave's possession, and they found Hank's DNA on it, along with mine or with my fingerprints, then they would lock me up for sure.

The thought drained me. How could I feel so unenergetic just when I needed to be on my toes and thinking? I needed to focus. A hot drink wouldn't hurt either.

But I didn't want to run into a bunch of people and have to explain myself. At that moment, I was immensely grateful that Oma had installed the secret stairway from my apartment to the kitchen. Trixie and I hurried down the stairs.

I found Oma and Zelda seated at the table, picking at a lemon meringue pie still in the pie plate.

Oma handed me a fork. "We have put on tea. Zelda thought we could all use something to calm our nerves."

I poured myself a mug and stirred in sugar and milk. I settled at the table with them and sipped the hot tea. Surprisingly, it did make me calmer.

I told them about the jacket and the scarf. "I'm scared to death that the jacket is going to turn out to be mine."

"Does it look like yours?" asked Zelda.

"Unfortunately, yes. But don't all denim jackets look a lot alike?"

They agreed so fast that I suspected they were trying to console me. "We have to identify the killer before the lab connects me to the murders." I tried to keep my voice level. In spite of my efforts, I squeaked a bit.

Zelda gazed at me with pity. "I've been over and over this with anyone who would listen. All we've got is a bunch of people who disliked Hank and Randall. There's nothing concrete tying anyone to the murders."

"Gee, thanks. No wonder Dave is so excited about the scarf and jacket."

"Let us consider this from a different angle," suggested Oma. "Who would have had the opportunity to take your jacket?"

"Anyone," I groaned. "I was wearing it when John and I found Randall. We came straight back here. I could have left it here in the kitchen, or outside on the patio, or I could have taken it upstairs with me and hung it in my closet."

"Aha! It blew from the patio into the lake. You

wait and see. It will be yours, but it will not tie you to Hank's murder." Oma smiled at me.

"Then what were those brownish stains on it?"

Oma ignored my question. "The cats were playing with the scarf? This would indicate it belongs to one of our guests."

"That was my assumption."

"Then we can narrow down the suspects, no?"

"Assuming they didn't drag it in from outside or that the killer didn't happen to drop it while having lunch here."

Zelda gasped. Waving her fork in the air, she said, "Or plant it here so Holly would be the suspect. Think about it! It's the perfect setup. The killer has lunch here and accidentally drops the scarf he used to strangle Randall. He looks for it but can't find it because the cats have made off with it. So he steals someone's jacket—in this case it happens to be Holly's—and then after he kills Hank, he throws it off the dock in the middle of the night. That way, the police find both items in or near the inn and think the killer is staying here, but really, it's—"

"Paige!" I pointed my fork toward Zelda. "She had one of those scarves. You're so right. Someone could have planted both of those items."

Oma shook her head. "But I have seen our darling stinker Twinkletoes in guest rooms pulling items out of their luggage."

"And out of drawers," I added.

"So we're back at square one," Zelda griped.

"We're going at this all wrong." I sat back with the warm mug in my hands. "We have to start with Randall. He came here looking for someone who was participating in Animal Attraction."

"Probably a woman," said Oma.

"Nessie has said all along that a married man at Animal Attraction was up to no good. So maybe he had a girlfriend?" I suggested.

"Now we have something." Oma sipped her tea. "Because she used his gift to strangle him."

"What would have made her that angry?" asked Zelda.

"He wanted to break off their relationship?" I got up and poured more tea for all of us.

"Why come to Wagtail to do that?" asked Zelda. "If she was here looking for a guy, then problem solved."

"Macon keeps talking about people who misrepresent themselves. Maybe he was going to give her away for who she really is. Maybe he was going to ruin her plans?" I brought the sugar and milk to the table.

"One of his patients, perhaps?" Oma asked. "Maybe he wanted to prevent a patient from doing harm to someone else?"

I shook my head and sat down. "Now we're getting into speculation again. I do think the killer was a woman, though. Not many men would have used the scarf to strangle him."

"Then we can eliminate Macon and Bob. Where's the bag?" asked Zelda. "Wouldn't he have carried it in a bag?"

"Great point!" We toasted with our mugs.

I took a bite of the lemon meringue pie and started to feel better. Maybe we *could* figure this out.

"Paige!" I almost shouted her name. "She said someone gave her the scarf as a gift."

"Eww. And she was wearing it after strangling him? That's just gross." Zelda grimaced.

"The thing is," I said, "I really don't see how Paige or Sky could have had the time to kill him. They didn't plan on Sky picking up Duchess."

"Perhaps the murder was not planned," said Oma. "It could have been spontaneous. One of them ran into him, he gave her the scarf, they had words about some issue between them, and he was strangled. It could have taken less than fifteen minutes."

"She took his wallet but didn't keep the money," I pointed out.

"*Ja!*" Oma exclaimed. "This is significant. Why? If I had killed someone, I would have disposed of the wallet."

"That's where it all falls apart. Why murder Hank? Why place the money on him and make it obvious that there's a connection to Randall?"

"To mislead." Oma gave Zelda a sad look. "Your Hank was not an honest man. Perhaps he entered into a shady deal with her. She wanted to make it appear that Hank had murdered Randall."

"Hank's killer was very angry with him." Zelda gulped hard. "Like the people who stab someone one hundred fifty times. I think she kept hitting him and hitting him."

"Then why didn't your stalker see her?" I asked.

"Maybe he did. We don't know who he is," Zelda whined.

"Or maybe," I said, "she was the person we thought was Hank."

"I have a woman stalker?" Zelda said.

I sat up straight. "She was waiting for Hank to show up!"

THIRTY-EIGHT

Oma and Zelda gazed at me like I had lost my mind.

"Don't you see? I thought the person lurking around didn't follow me because he wasn't Hank. But what if that person was waiting for Hank?"

Oma said, "Sky and Nessie were at Tequila Mockingbird, *ja*? And if it was a woman, then we can count out Macon and Bob. Who does that leave?"

Zelda and I spoke simultaneously. "Paige."

"I will call Dave to inform him," said Oma.

"Ben!" I shouted his name.

"Ach. The Ben. What can he do?" asked Oma.

"He's with Paige." I beat Oma to the phone and dialed his number. It rolled over to voice mail.

Reluctantly, I handed her the phone. "We have to warn Ben."

"Do you know where they went?" asked Oma.

"I bet they're at Hair of the Dog." Zelda jumped to her feet. "Grab a jacket and let's go."

Oma held out her hand. "Just a moment. It is not wise for the two of you to confront Paige. She has killed two men already."

"We won't do that. We'll make an excuse to get Ben away from her. We'll fabricate an emergency. Meanwhile, you will have reached Dave, and he'll show up and everything will be fine." I dashed up the hidden stairs to my quarters for a lightweight jacket.

An odd sound distracted me. What was that? I gazed around. No sign of Zelda's cats. I peeked in the guest room. Ben had left clothes in a mess on the bed. Zelda's kitties had stretched out on them and barely acknowledged my presence. It looked like a cat opium den.

The odd sound came from his duffel bag. It wiggled and shook. I used one finger to pull it open a bit. Twinkletoes gazed up at me with big eyes and a guilty look.

"Get out of there!" I picked her up. "What's this?" I looked more closely at the tiny flakes on her fur. Setting her on the floor, I took a better look inside of Ben's duffel bag. The smell was undeniable. Catnip.

That's why all the cats were attracted to Ben all of a sudden. He was wearing catnip-scented clothes! It was all so clear to me. No wonder Marmalade and Twinkletoes had shredded his T-shirt. There had probably been a kitty fight going on about it while I'd slept.

"Everyone out!"

Not a single cat moved. I carried each of them out of the guest room and closed the door. "No more catnip for you."

Trixie and I left the catnip-intoxicated cats and met Zelda in the lobby. "You won't believe what Ben did."

I told her how Ben had morphed into a cat whisperer.

Zelda laughed aloud. "You have to admit that it was a sweet gesture."

"I guess he was tired of Twinkletoes hissing at him."

"He can't fool her with catnip. Twinkletoes and Trixie knew Ben wanted you to give them up. Animals are very perceptive about these things. People are far easier to fool."

As we walked along the sidewalk, Zelda said, "I will be so relieved once Paige is arrested. The only downside to going home is no tea in my jammies first thing in the morning unless I get up and make it myself. What do you think Mr. Huckle would charge to bring tea and chocolate croissants to my house every morning?"

"That sounds like a great business. I wonder why no one does that? You should suggest it to one of the bakeries in town."

I took great comfort in the fact that the streets teemed with visitors. The outdoor dining tables were packed. Couples gazed into each other's eyes.

"I hope Axel is still speaking to me," Zelda said. "I'm pretty jealous of all these budding relationships."

"Focus, Zelda. What kind of excuse are we going to make for dragging Ben away?"

"That's easy. Preliminary results on the jacket

indicate that it's yours and it has Hank's blood on it. Dave is on his way to arrest you, so you need Ben's help."

"No way! Everyone will think I'm guilty. Besides, he can't represent both of us," I said.

"She probably doesn't know that. It's a small price to pay for rescuing Ben, don't you think?"

When she put it that way . . .

"Besides, it will feed into her plan. Don't you see? She'll feel safe knowing that her plan to make you look guilty succeeded."

I didn't like it, but it made sense to me. We approached Hair of the Dog. Music blared, even outside. Spotlights shone, illuminating the crowd. People mingled with drinks in hand all the way out to the sidewalk.

"Do you see them?" I asked.

"They're probably inside."

Afraid she might be stepped on, I picked up Trixie and carried her through the crowd. Someone sang karaoke off-key. I made my way to the bar, where I recognized the owner.

"Have you seen Ben tonight?" I shouted to her.

"Not tonight," she yelled.

Zelda came up behind me.

I spoke directly into her ear. "He hasn't been here."

"Should we try the Alley Cat?"

I motioned to her to follow me outside.

"Zelda! Zelda!" Axel broke through the crowd.

I hurried outside and waited for her.

Zelda towed Axel toward me and explained where we were going. "If I had wanted a romantic dinner, I would have gone to the Alley Cat," said Zelda.

I didn't relish the idea of going over there in the dark. But all the other options were on the west side of town. "Let's get this over with."

Dave had said they were putting out undercover officers around the Shire. I hoped they were still patrolling.

We crossed the street and picked up lanterns.

"You'd think they would have increased the lighting after Randall's death," said Zelda.

"I have a feeling Oma will hear about it at the next town meeting." I watched as Trixie trotted ahead, her nose to the ground, the moonlight shining on her white fur.

Zelda filled in Axel about Paige as we walked. He held her hand and listened.

"I'm sorry about Hank," he said.

"Don't be. I was the fool who married him."

"Macon said he might have actually loved you." I thought that might make her feel better.

"Then he had a funny way of showing it. The sad thing is that he could be really nice and fun to be with. But he had that sleazy side that drove me nuts."

We passed the spot where we had turned off to find Randall's body. I slowed and gazed in that direction. We heard voices and giggling, which was a little incongruous.

A sense of relief washed over me when Axel opened one of the double doors at the entrance of the Alley Cat. No one was dead. We hadn't encountered anything creepy. Under other circumstances, it would have been a lovely, calm evening walk.

I picked up Trixie again because there was such a huge crowd. But I did notice the expression of concern on the bartender's face when he spied Trixie in my arms.

Axel leaned over and shouted in my ear, "It's noisy in here. Is there a patio outside?"

I motioned for them to follow me. We wedged through the jolly crowd of flirters and out the back way onto the large patio.

"Much better," said Axel. "I feel like I can breathe out here."

I had to agree.

Zelda tugged at my arm and whispered, "There they are!"

Ben and Paige had snagged a table at the far end. A candle flickered between them as they ate.

Like in the rest of the Shire, the lighting on the terrace was discreet. Oma would have thought it too dark, but it was soothing and sort of magical. The partiers on the stone patio were much quieter. We heard occasional laughter, but overall, it was a very different crowd from the gang inside.

Beyond the patio, fields and hills lay silent in the dark. I had been there before during the day, so I knew a walking path wound around the Alley Cat far back in the distance. A few pasture fences were visible in daylight, but beyond those fields were woods with hiking trails.

I sucked in a deep breath. "Okay, let's do this."

Trixie ran ahead to her friend, Huey. Unfortunately, the three of us approached their table at the exact moment that Ben chose to feed Paige a spoonful of chocolate mousse. She was taking a little lick off his finger when they saw us.

In spite of the darkness, I could tell Paige was embarrassed. It bothered me that I felt for her. How could someone who spent her days rescuing animals possibly have murdered two men? It didn't make sense to me.

Zelda launched into a panicked recitation of my imminent arrest because of a preliminary match to Hank's blood type.

Ben listened to her, but I didn't think he was convinced. I let her babble.

"I can't represent both of you. What a mess. Excuse me, Paige." Ben rose from his seat. "Holly, could I have a word, please?"

He walked to the other end of the terrace and whispered, "Zelda is making no sense at all. What's up?"

"Paige is the killer."

Ben frowned at me. "On what basis did you come to that crazy conclusion?"

I told him our logic.

Ben placed his hand on my shoulder. "Go home. You've got nothing. Not a single shred of evidence tying Paige to the murders. So she has a scarf. You had two of them."

"I thought you liked Laura better."

"Can't a guy change his mind? Besides, Laura's out with some guy Macon picked for her. If you don't mind, I'm going to finish having dinner with Paige. We can discuss this in the morning."

I had been dismissed. He returned to his table. I had half a mind to stick around just to be on the safe side. But Dave would be there soon. And she wouldn't murder him in front of all these people.

Zelda and Axel couldn't believe that Ben refused to leave his date. There wasn't much we could do. I whistled for Trixie, and we left.

On the way back, when we neared Hair of the Dog and the karaoke blared, Zelda grinned. "Would you mind if Axel and I stayed here for a while?"

"Of course not. Have fun."

Trixie and I continued in the direction of the inn. I couldn't help thinking that I must be the only single person in town without a date. "What happened to John?" I asked Trixie.

She probably wondered where Cooper was.

"Yoo-hoo! Holly!" Macon waddled toward us

with his peculiar little walk. "Are you headed to the inn?"

"We are," I said.

"I'm glad you're still speaking to me after that little stunt I pulled on you today. You and John just needed a big fat push. Where is he?"

"I haven't seen him since then."

"Really? I thought for sure the picnic would bring you together."

"Macon, maybe it's time to admit defeat on the John and Holly project."

"I will not hear that kind of attitude."

"I heard you set up Laura on a date tonight."

"You heard wrong. Laura has never signed up to be matched. It's not a requirement, of course. And she's done fairly well for herself with Ben. I don't much care for her interest in John, though."

"They're old friends."

"Mmm-hmm. And she'd like them to be something more. That girl has had her eye on John since the day Animal Attraction began."

"She lied to Ben." I said my thought aloud.

"I imagine Ben isn't the first man she's ever lied to."

THIRTY-NINE

No sooner had we stepped inside the inn than the in-house phone rang.

Macon waddled off, cooing to Marmalade, who was playing kitty hockey with a stuffed mouse.

I recognized Nessie's voice immediately. "Sweetie, I know it's not on the room service menu, but do you think someone could make me some scrambled eggs and bring them up here? Maybe some for Lulu, too?"

"Certainly. Would you like something with that? Toast? Bacon? Coffee?"

"Toast sounds lovely. And aspirin. I don't want any caffeine. How about an herbal tea and some water?"

"I'll bring them up shortly."

I retrieved a room service cart and pushed it into the private kitchen, where I discovered Oma with John and Cooper.

John jumped to his feet. "Can I give you a hand with that?"

"Thanks, but I've got it. Nessie just ordered room service. I hope she's not sick."

Oma rose and prepared the cart while I started the eggs. "*Liebchen*, I'm so glad that you have returned. Dave said he cannot do anything without evidence. Did you find the Ben?"

"He was at the Alley Cat with Paige. I told him everything but he insisted on staying. They were being very romantic."

"That's odd," John mused. "I ran into Laura on the way over here and she told me that you were getting back together with Ben."

I stirred the eggs. "She lied to Ben too, and told him she was going out with someone Macon set her up with. But Macon says she never signed up to be matched."

The three of us looked at one another.

"I'll be right back," I said.

I pushed the cart through the doorway and rolled it to the elevator. Nessie's door was open when I arrived.

I knocked anyway.

"Thank you, darling. I just didn't have the strength to go out and get a bite."

"Do you feel ill?" I unloaded her food on the table.

"Oh no. Just exhausted. I've been sleeping on a desk chair in a tiny study in that house where Celeste is staying. And I'm worn-out. I had to give up my little secret early in the morning when a young man refused to leave the premises. He departed pretty darn fast once Mama Nessie showed him the door. *I* would have been appreciative. But, oh my, was there a *stink*. You'd think none of them had mothers. Celeste has all but disowned me. I give up. It's out of my hands if that child marries poorly."

"Maybe you should give Celeste some credit. She *is* her mama's daughter."

"You are sweet as honey. But the man she intended to marry made Hank look like a winner."

I was about to leave but thought I'd take a stab. I fudged a little. "We found a business card for Randall Donovan. Was that yours, by any chance?"

"Did it have the strangest e-mail address you ever saw scribbled on the back of it?"

"Yes, it did."

"It's mine."

So she had lied about not seeing him in Wagtail. "Who is Saurian Pail?" I asked.

"Isn't that peculiar? It's Randall's private e-mail address. He might have *been* a shrink, but I believe he needed to see one." Nessie frowned. "I suspect he gave me that address because he didn't want his wife to know if I emailed him."

"Why not?"

She sucked in a deep breath. "He was a slug. The man made a pass at me."

"Why didn't you say something sooner?"

"Someone murdered him. I didn't want anyone to think I did him in!"

I wished her a good night and closed the door. So Randall had been hiding e-mail. Probably from his wife. I hoped Ben was okay with Paige.

I took the elevator downstairs and stashed away the room service cart.

When I entered the kitchen, I could feel tension between Oma and John. "What's going on?"

"Your grandmother thinks it would be unethical to enter Laura's room for a quick look around."

"It would be," I agreed.

John's expression of hopefulness vanished.

"Unless, of course, we were turning down the bed and leaving a cookie on her pillow." I went to the pantry and found a box of wrapped sugar cookies. "Aha! Cat treats, too."

Oma sighed. "I don't approve of such sneakiness. But under the circumstances . . ."

John jumped to his feet.

We walked through the library to the cat wing. "Maybe you should hide in the library in case she's here," I whispered.

He nodded and retreated. I saw him peering around the corner.

Laura had hung a *do not disturb* sign on her door. That was a little dilemma. I whisked it off the door handle and hung it on the door behind me. I knocked on Laura's door. "Turndown service!" At my feet, Marmalade mewed. I knocked again. "Turndown service!"

I unlocked the door, my blood pounding in my head. The door swung open. "Laura? Laura!" I didn't see anyone except Marmalade, who strode inside.

John hustled down the hallway.

Laura was not the tidiest guest. Papers

and clothes littered the bed. She did indulge Marmalade, though. He had plenty of cat toys to play with.

The sheets on the bed were a mess. Laura must have used the *do not disturb* sign since she'd arrived, because it looked to me as though the bed had not been made for a few days.

Marmalade pounced on the bed, sending papers flying to the floor. I picked up flyers for Animal Attraction events, coupons for local services, and a letter. I placed them on the bed, where there were lozenges, a tube of lip gloss, car keys, receipts, and a small mirror. It looked like she had dumped the contents of a purse on the bed.

Marmalade wanted to play. He batted the letter to me. I flicked it back, and he jumped on it.

"Do you see anything interesting?" I whispered to John.

"I'm kind of disappointed. Just regular stuff like makeup and clothes."

Marmalade batted the letter to the floor again. This time I looked at it when I picked it up.

It was handwritten.

My dearest Vandoon,
Your continued blindness regarding this folly compels me to write. You cannot build a relationship on lies as they will eventually emerge and the foundation will crumble. You will live in fear of the day

when the truth will destroy everything for which you have yearned. You must reveal your transgressions to him, painful as it may be to do so. Only then can you begin again and find peace in your heart.

You know how distressing it is for me to give you this advice. I would much rather keep you for myself. My life will be desolate without you.

However, bear this in mind. I give you up freely in the interest of your happiness. But if you do not confess the evil you have wreaked upon him, then I will be forced to disclose your maliciousness.

In love,
Saurian Pail

Randall Donovan was a weird guy. I read the letter again. Laura had wronged someone. *Evil* was a pretty strong word. Yet even though he knew she had done something terrible to a man, Randall had been in love with her?

I tried not to snicker. This confession of love was written by the guy who said love didn't exist? What a phony. Macon had nailed him.

I gasped aloud. Randall had been looking for Laura, not Paige. It must have been Laura who'd killed Randall so he wouldn't divulge her secret.

And the only man she knew in Wagtail was John.

FORTY

"Quick," I hissed. "Let's go."

"I'm not done yet," John said.

"Yes, you are." I picked up Marmalade so Laura wouldn't notice immediately that we had entered her room. "Come on! Right now!"

John gave me a funny look but complied. I locked the door and raced to Oma's kitchen with John on my heels.

Macon had joined Oma. "Marmalade!" he cried.

I set Marmalade on the floor. He walked straight to Macon and wound around his legs.

"What did you find?" asked Oma.

John shrugged.

I didn't waste any time and dialed Dave's number.

He sounded aggravated when he answered. "I gather your grandmother didn't give you my message? I need evidence, not conjecture."

"Wait! I have evidence in my hand."

He groaned. "Holly, I have work to do. I'll make my way over to the inn as soon as I can." He hung up.

Macon's forehead wrinkled. "Who are Vandoon and Saurian Pail?"

"Saurian Pail is Randall, and I would have to guess that Vandoon is Laura," I said.

"What peculiar names," Macon observed as Marmalade jumped onto his lap.

"Vandoon is an anagram for *Donovan,*" John pointed out.

I took a sheet of paper and wrote *Laura Pisani* on it. Directly underneath I wrote *Saurian Pail.* I crossed matching letters off. "So is Saurian Pail. They were using each other's names in code. And he was using a superprivate e-mail account."

"And he was in love with her." Oma didn't hide her smile. "He was—how do you say it—a horse's patoot."

Macon roared. "Well said, Liesel."

"The letter is about you." I gazed at John. "What was her huge transgression?"

"I don't know. I can only think she must have known someone else in Wagtail."

"Do you have a history with her?" asked Macon.

"We dated ten years ago when I worked at Douthier. I broke it off after a few months and, well, you know the rest. I left town and never heard from her again."

I recalled Laura telling us about John breaking up with the student. Maybe she had been talking about herself. "Did you break it off abruptly?"

"I guess so. How do you break up otherwise?"

"Oh my!" Macon shook a finger at John. "You have to let the ladies down gently."

"I told her it wasn't working out, and then my

life fell apart. Laura was not uppermost on my mind."

"That girl was her student, too. Do you suppose Laura had anything to do with the accusations against you?" I asked.

John frowned at me. "I don't think so. How would that be possible?"

"By paying the student."

Oma's eyebrows raised. "So Laura paid the student to say you had an affair. Years later she confesses this to Randall?"

"He was a shrink. What do you bet she was his patient?" I said.

"This is so interesting," said Macon. "Laura came here looking for you"—he pointed at John—"and Randall came here looking for Laura."

"If you haven't seen her in ten years, how would she know where you are?" I asked.

John sheepishly said, "Facebook?"

"You have a public Facebook page?" I couldn't believe it.

"That's what they tell writers to do. I don't have many friends yet, but I'm working on it. Other than pictures of Cooper and some cartoons, I don't post very much. But I may have mentioned jokingly that I was going to Animal Attraction."

"She killed Randall so he wouldn't ruin her chances at getting you back," I said. "She was in full-fledged frustration attraction. She never understood why you broke up. First she wanted to hurt you, then when she never met anyone else who lived up to her expectations, she came running back."

"I don't know. I feel a little sick about all this. She killed two men!" John took a deep breath.

"Holly, *liebchen*, would you put on coffee and black tea?" Oma asked. "I fear it will be a long night."

"What's taking Dave so long?" I complained.

John stretched his legs out in front of him and rubbed his face. "Laura must have been my stalker all along. She was the one I saw in your jacket the night Hank was killed. I'm so sorry, Holly. I really thought it was you."

Ben pushed open the door, breathing heavily. "There you are! I lost Huey!"

That was all we needed at the moment. I dashed upstairs for my iPad, ran back down, and pulled up the tracking program. "Unit number four . . . Looks like he's at Aunt Birdie's house."

Oma's eyes grew large. She waved her forefinger in warning. "A dog in Birdie's garden? This is very bad. She will not be happy."

We had to go get him. There was simply no choice. I grabbed a flashlight. "Oma, you're in charge of coffee and tea. Macon and John, stay here with Oma and explain everything to Dave when he gets here?"

Ben, Trixie, and I ran through the lobby and out to the golf carts.

We hopped in. Ben drove, and I kept an eye on the iPad in case Huey roamed or changed direction. "He's still there. What happened?"

"Don't yell at me," he pleaded. "I had him on the leash. We were walking back to the inn when he jerked the leash out of my hand, tore down the street, and got away from me."

As we drove up, I heard a bark. Trixie took a flying leap off the golf cart. I'd have to train her not to do that. But I did the same thing before Ben parked.

Huey was in Aunt Birdie's backyard, standing on his hind legs and pawing at the latch on her garden shed. The crime scene tape lay on the ground. Huey managed to flip the clasp in the correct direction and nudge it open with his nose.

Behind me, Ben said, "I would never have believed it. What a smart dog."

I patted Huey and grabbed his leash so he wouldn't take off again. At least he wasn't lost. "Good boy."

I swung open the garden shed door, hoping I wouldn't see another bloody garden implement.

FORTY-ONE

The light of the moon cast just enough of a beam to see that a body lay on the floor of the shed, facedown. I flicked on my flashlight.

He groaned.

"Dave?"

Ben stepped inside and helped him sit up.

Dave rubbed the back of his head. He seemed woozy.

"Maybe I should call an ambulance."

"No!" Dave held his hand up to block the light from my flashlight. "Put that thing away. Man! She clobbered me."

"Who?" I asked.

"Laura. She said a kid was trapped in the shed."

Dave's phone rang. He pulled it out and glanced at it. "It's your Aunt Birdie."

"She's probably calling to report people in her yard."

I turned around. "Aunt Birdie? It's Holly!"

"You don't think she has a shotgun, do you?" asked Ben.

"I'm over here!" Birdie yelled.

Dave staggered to his feet with Ben's help.

"Head injuries can be serious," I said.

Dave cast a thoroughly annoyed look in my direction.

We walked around the side of the yard. Aunt Birdie stood over someone. She held a small black canister that appeared to be aimed at the hapless person huddled on the ground.

As we drew closer, I realized that it was Laura. She covered her face with her hands and moaned in agony.

"Put that away, Birdie," said Dave. "What is it, anyway?"

"Pepper spray. Nobody messes with my prize gladioli."

FORTY-TWO

While we waited for the ambulance, I brought Laura a cold, wet cloth. "This was all because of John?"

She didn't answer.

Ben skulked nearby, looking like someone had punched him in the gut. I walked over. "Are you okay?"

"She used me. What a fool I was. She always wanted to talk about the murders, and"—Ben gulped hard—"I thought she was just curious. Like you!"

I patted his arm. "It's all over now. Don't blame yourself."

I returned to Laura, hoping I could get her to talk. "So what was your big transgression against John that Randall died for?"

Still no answer.

"Did you arrange for that girl to report sexual misconduct by John?"

She dabbed her red face. Her eyes watered mercilessly.

"Did you murder her?" I pressed.

Laura finally spoke. "No. But she was a greedy little thing, always demanding more money from me. I would imagine she moved on to serious blackmail and discovered she wasn't ready to play in the big leagues."

"Why did you do that to John if you loved him?"

"Because he broke off our relationship. It was payback. Holly, you must understand. John was always the one. I tried to put him out of my head. I tried to date other guys. But they weren't John. Randall said it was just infatuation. That I had created a super-John in my memory. That the real John couldn't possibly live up to my dreams. But he did. I watched him on Facebook. Searched his name on Google constantly. I called him just to hear his voice on his answering machine."

"Then he knew you were trying to reach him."

"I'm not stupid. I blocked my number. He probably thought they were those annoying automated calls. You know what? Randall was wrong. Even after all these years, John is as adorable as I remember. And he liked spending time with me, too. I could tell. I just needed a chance, but everyone was determined to ruin it for me."

"Like Randall?"

"Randall! What an idiot. I was his patient, and he fell in love with me. Can you imagine? He would have said anything to keep me away from John."

"But you didn't love Randall."

"Of course not. He wasn't John. He said it would never work out with John. That I had to tell

John what I'd done to him. And that if I didn't tell him myself, he would. I couldn't let him do that. John would never get back together with me if he found out that I'd set up the sexual misconduct allegations at Douthier. Why is everyone intent on ruining my relationship with John?"

"Everyone?"

"Randall was going to tell him the truth. That would have ruined everything forever. John can never know! And that moron Hank threatened to tell John that I was spying on him. He had the nerve to demand money. I call that blackmail. What a scum bucket. But he got his comeuppance. He counted the money, stuck the wallet in his pocket, and the minute he turned I grabbed that hoe and slammed it on the back of his neck. It worked much better than I anticipated."

"He didn't notice that you were wearing gloves?"

She shrugged. "It was dark."

"Why didn't you take the wallet back?"

"Are you kidding? He'd put his fingerprints all over it. It was a perfect setup to make everyone think Hank killed Randall. Sort of like the letter from your grandmother to Gustav."

"How did you know about that?"

"Another stroke of luck. I thought I was very clever to plant that on Randall."

"But how did *you* get it?"

"On my way here, I stopped for lunch. I was

rounding a corner on a sidewalk when a guy smacked into me and knocked me down. He dropped the letter but ran off. When I read it and saw that he would be staying at the Sugar Maple Inn, I thought I would track him down and give him a piece of my mind when I got to Wagtail. But then I had to eliminate Randall, so I planted the letter on him to throw everyone off about his identity. It worked, too."

That must have been Mick, Gustav's mugger.

Anger distorted her face. "Look, Holly, you can have Ben. You don't need John."

She couldn't be serious. Even after all this, she thought she would win John's affections? "You took my denim jacket?"

"Child's play. Ben never noticed that I borrowed his keys. Your cat was hostile, though. I had to lock her out on the balcony."

On that note, I walked away and made sure the EMTs knew about Dave's head injury. He rode in the ambulance with Laura.

Before it pulled away, Laura looked at me with painfully red eyes. "Holly? Will you make sure Marmalade gets a good home?"

It was the least I could do. "Of course." I already had someone in mind.

Aunt Birdie, whom I had never seen without full makeup and perfect hair, was so excited that she had forgotten all about her appearance. She looked younger without makeup on. But the weird white wrap she wore on her head was something from the dark ages.

"You're a hero," I told her.

Aunt Birdie flapped a hand at me. "It was nothing. If that dog hadn't barked, I might not have known that girl was out here."

"Why don't you come to the inn for breakfast tomorrow morning?"

"I'd like that."

Ben drove Huey, Trixie, and me back to the inn, where we pronounced Huey a hero, too. It broke my heart that he would go back to WAG when Ben went home.

The next morning, Mr. Huckle appeared with our coffee and tea bright and early. Eight cats and two dogs greeted him at the door. He brought chocolate croissants for the people, apple barkscotties for the dogs, and crunchy dried salmon flakes for the kitties.

The adrenaline from the previous night must have still been in our systems, because everyone showed up early for breakfast at the inn. Most of the inn's guests still slept, except for Macon, who joined us with Marmalade.

"How did it go last night?" I asked Macon.

"He snuggled up to me like we'd been together for years. Do you think I can adopt him?"

"Absolutely."

We pushed tables together out on the terrace.

The sun shone on the lake, producing diamond sparkles that seemed to dance on the water.

John and I helped Mr. Huckle and Shelley serve strawberry cream cheese French toast to everyone so they could sit down and join us. We applauded Aunt Birdie, who took a bow and was delighted by all the attention. We applauded Huey too, who also took a bow, as though he understood.

Dave assured everyone that he was fine and the only abnormality noted in the CAT scan was the absence of a brain. He looked straight at me when he said, "From now on, I'll pay more attention to Holly's wacky theories. Even if she doesn't have evidence."

As I had suspected, the white denim jacket had bloodstains on it, probably Hank's.

Ben's phone rang and he excused himself for a moment to take the call. When he returned, he said, "That was Laura. She needs a lawyer."

Everyone stopped eating. There was no clanking of utensils, no chatter, not a sound except for birdcalls.

"I'm not representing her!" he protested.

"Dave," said Zelda, "I know why she killed Randall. But what about Hank? Why did she kill him?"

"Because he caught her," Dave said. "Hank was hanging around your house, and he saw her spying on John."

"I knew someone was watching me," John said.

Dave continued. "From what I gather, Hank blackmailed her. He threatened to tell John unless she paid him. So she gave him Randall's wallet. I guess, sort of like me, he didn't perceive her as a threat, and the second he turned his back, she brought that hoe down on his neck."

"What I don't understand," I said, "is why Laura clobbered you, Dave."

Dave's eyes met Ben's and a rosy flush flooded Ben's cheeks when he said, "I might have told Laura that Dave was about to make an arrest."

"You might have?" I said, seeking clarification.

"She wouldn't talk about anything else. She was obsessed with the murders—"

"You mean she was pumping you for information." Ben had been her source of news all along.

"I thought she would be satisfied if I said an arrest was imminent. I'm sorry, Dave."

"No problem. You didn't know she was the killer." Dave was exceedingly gracious about it. He turned his gaze to me. "You were next, Holly. If Aunt Birdy hadn't stopped her, she would have been on her way over here to eliminate you. She saw you as her rival for John's affections."

John excused himself and called Cooper.

When they returned, Cooper carried flowers in his mouth and brought them to me.

I took the bouquet and patted Cooper. "Thank you!"

"That's a little apology from the two of us. Well,

actually just from me. Cooper never doubted you for a moment."

Oma raised her orange juice in a toast. "Thank goodness this is over, and we have our peaceful Wagtail once again!"

"How about you, John?" asked Macon. "What will you do now?"

"I'm beginning to think I need to go deeper into the woods to concentrate on writing. Wagtail is a busy place."

"How's the thriller coming?" asked Ben.

"I have decided that I am a very unthrilling guy. But I'm thinking about a story in which a woman tracks down a guy she dated ten years before . . ."

Macon and I scooted over to make room for Nessie and Sky.

With a twinkle in his eye, Macon asked, "How are your daughters?"

"You knew all along who Maddie's artist was," Sky stated.

Macon beamed. "I gather you approve?"

"Who is he?" I asked.

"Such a delightful young man. Turns out I know his parents. He *is* an artist but he also started a charity to bring chickens and goats to impoverished families in developing nations."

I was itching to hear about the fellow Celeste met. "Nessie?"

She raised her chin and sighed. "I was wrong. Celeste's musician plays the piano beautifully, but he works as a talent agent for musicians. I gather he makes a rather good living."

To his credit, Macon merely smiled and didn't point out Nessie's folly.

After breakfast, I sat down on the terrace steps with Huey for a moment. "You're a very special boy."

He pawed me gently.

Oma walked over with Ben. "Holly, Ben, I have a confession to make. Huey's real name is Houdini. He has been quite a headache at WAG because he can open everything. He opens his cage, he opens other dog cages. He even opens doors. I'm sorry, Ben. We set you up with a difficult dog on purpose."

I thought it a shame that a smart dog like Huey would be considered difficult.

Ben took a deep breath. "That's okay. Huey—er, Houdini—taught me a lot about dogs. He's a great guy. But, as you know, I live in a tiny apartment in a building that doesn't allow pets. I thought I might appeal to Holly more if I seemed like a dog kind of guy. I never intended to adopt him."

"Is that why you rubbed catnip on your clothes?" I asked.

"Same principle, but to attract cats to me," Ben said.

Duchess ran toward us and immediately nuzzled Huey.

Sky followed her. "Ben! There you are. I wanted

to talk to you about Huey. It's pretty obvious to me that Huey and Duchess are a bonded pair. Paige said they split them up because no one wanted two big dogs, and Huey's escape artist antics were preventing them from being adopted. I know you had your eye on Huey, but I'd like to adopt him so he and Duchess can stay together."

I watched Huey and Duchess nuzzle each other out on the lawn. Some love stories didn't need a matchmaker to have a happy ending.

RECIPES

One of my dogs suffered from severe food allergies that did not allow him to eat commercial dog food. Consequently, I learned to cook for my dogs and have done so for many years. Consult your veterinarian if you want to switch your dog over to home-cooked food. It's not as difficult as one might think. Keep in mind that, like children, dogs need a balanced diet, not just a hamburger. Any changes to your dog's diet should be made gradually so your dog's stomach can adjust.

Chocolate, alcohol, caffeine, fatty foods, grapes, raisins, macadamia nuts, onions, garlic, salt, xylitol, and unbaked dough can be toxic to dogs. For more information about foods your dog should not eat, consult the Pet Poison Helpline at www.petpoisonhelpline.com/pet-owners/.

APPLE BARKSCOTTIES
Twice-baked cookies for dogs

½ cup applesauce
1 tablespoon sunflower oil (or canola oil)
2 tablespoons maple syrup
1 egg

⅛ teaspoon of baking soda
1 teaspoon cinnamon
2 cups whole wheat flour

Preheat oven to 350°F. Line a baking sheet with parchment paper. Using the sharp blade in a food processor, pulse to combine the applesauce, oil, maple syrup, egg, baking soda, and cinnamon. Add the flour and pulse again until the dough sticks together. It will not be in a perfect ball. Shape the dough into a log on a piece of waxed paper and flatten the top slightly. Bake 35 to 40 minutes. It should be firm to the touch.

Remove from oven and allow to cool on a rack for 30 minutes. Slice the log into ½-inch pieces. Lay on baking sheet and bake another 30 minutes until crunchy.

MANGO DAIQUIRIS
For people only

1 cup water
½ cup sugar
2 10-ounce packages frozen mango chunks
½ cup rum (or to taste)
¼ cup peach schnapps

Cook the water and the sugar until the sugar has completely dissolved. Cool. Reserve 6 chunks of mango and thaw. Place the sugar mixture, remaining frozen mango chunks, rum, and peach schnapps in a blender and frappé.

Pour into tall glasses and garnish with thawed mango chunks or fresh strawberries.

FRIED CHICKEN
For people

¾ cup flour
2 tablespoons garlic powder
1 tablespoon smoked paprika
1 tablespoon salt
½ teaspoon turmeric
½ teaspoon pepper
2½ to 3 pounds cut-up chicken
canola oil

Place flour, garlic powder, paprika, salt, turmeric, and pepper in a large plastic bag and shake well to mix. Add two or three pieces of chicken and shake. Place on a rack. Add more chicken and shake until all pieces are coated. Pour canola oil ¼-inch deep in a wide frying skillet and heat until a drop of water sizzles. Add the chicken pieces but do not crowd. (You may want to use two pans.) Brown the chicken and turn with tongs. Brown the second side 15 minutes or so. Reduce heat and cover with a tight lid. Cook 30–35 minutes. Remove lid and cook another 10 minutes to allow the skin to crisp.

EGG AND AVOCADO TOAST
For two people—double or triple for more

1 avocado
olive oil
2 eggs
2 slices of bread
salt and pepper
baby spinach leaves and cherry tomatoes
for garnish (optional)

Peel and pit the avocado. Heat the olive oil in a frying pan over medium-low heat. After a couple of minutes, turn the heat up to medium. Crack the eggs into the pan and cover with a lid. Reduce heat to medium-low. Toast the bread. Mash the avocado and spread half on each slice of toast. Sprinkle with salt and pepper. When the whites are set, remove eggs from heat, leaving the lid on until the yolks are done to your liking. Place one egg on each piece of toast. Add salt and pepper to taste. Make a little fan with a few baby spinach leaves and add a grape tomato as garnish. Serve immediately.

LEMON MERINGUE PIE
For people

1 9-inch pie crust, baked
Lemon Filling:
  4 egg yolks
  ½ cup lemon juice (3 to 4 lemons)
  1½ cups sugar
  ½ cup cornstarch
  ½ teaspoon salt
  1½ cups water
  3 tablespoons butter
Meringue:
  4 egg whites
  ⅔ cup sugar
  ¼ teaspoon salt

Lemon Filling:
Whisk together the egg yolks and the lemon juice in a mixing bowl and set aside. In a heavy-bottomed saucepan, combine the 1½ cup sugar with the cornstarch and ½ teaspoon salt and whisk together. Add 1½ cups water, mix well, and bring to a boil. Stir constantly and cook until thick and clear. Remove from heat. Add the lemon mixture and stir to combine. Heat, stirring the whole time, until it gently boils. Remove from heat and stir in butter. Allow to cool briefly.

Pour into baked pie crust.

Meringue:

Locate a pan in which your mixer's bowl fits. Add about an inch of water to the pan and bring to a simmer. In the mixing bowl, whisk together the egg whites, ⅔ cup sugar, and ¼ teaspoon salt. Place over the water in the pan and whisk until the meringues register 140 degrees. Then whisk for 2 more minutes.

Preheat oven to 400°F.

Take the mixing bowl to your mixer and beat the egg whites until they can hold a shape but are not dry. Add the meringue to the top of the pie, piping decoratively or smoothing to the edges and leaving some peaks.

Place in oven 5–10 minutes. Watch carefully for light browning on the meringue at this point, because 1 minute can make a big difference.

Refrigerate several hours to set before serving.

CHOCOLATE-COVERED STRAWBERRIES
For people only
Dogs can die from eating chocolate!
Do not feed to dogs.

6 ounces semisweet chocolate
4 ounces white chocolate
1 pound strawberries

Cover a baking sheet with parchment paper. Place the semisweet chocolate in a microwave safe bowl and microwave for 40 seconds. Stir. Microwave for 30 seconds. Stir. If not melted, microwave 10 more seconds until melted and smooth. Repeat with the white chocolate in another bowl.

Grasping the strawberry by the stem, dip into the semisweet chocolate. As it begins to set, use a fork to drizzle white chocolate over it. Allow the chocolate to set.

SUMMER SUPPER
For dogs

*Makes two Gingersnap-sized portions
and multiple Trixie-sized portions*

*1–2 tablespoons olive oil
1 pound chicken tenders
1 cup cooked summer (yellow) squash
1 cup cooked green beans
2 cups cooked barley*

Pour olive oil into a pan large enough to hold the chicken. Warm over medium heat. Add the chicken tenders, place the lid on top, and lower the heat slightly. When the bottoms are white, flip them and put the top back on a couple more minutes. Cut one to make sure they're white all the way through. Remove from pan and set aside.

While the chicken tenders rest, place the squash, green beans, and barley into the pan and turn in the chicken juices. Warm gently. Slice the chicken tenders in half lengthwise and cut into small pieces. Stir into the pan. Serve to happy dogs!

COUNTRY-STYLE SURF AND TURF
For dogs

Makes two Gingersnap-sized portions and multiple Trixie-sized portions

½ pound catfish
½ pound chicken tenders
1–2 zucchini
6–8 cherry tomatoes
2 tablespoons olive oil
cooked barley or white rice

Preheat oven to 400°F. Cut the catfish and chicken into ¾-inch pieces and place in a large baking pan. Slice the zucchini and add to the pan. Cut the cherry tomatoes in half and add to the pan. Sprinkle with olive oil and turn to coat everything. Give the pan a good shake and separate pieces in a single layer. Bake 10 minutes, stir, and bake another 10 minutes or until the fish and chicken are cooked through. Serve over cooked barley or white rice.

Books are produced in the United States using U.S.-based materials

Books are printed using a revolutionary new process called THINKtech™ that lowers energy usage by 70% and increases overall quality

Books are durable and flexible because of Smyth-sewing

Paper is sourced using environmentally responsible foresting methods and the paper is acid-free

Center Point Large Print
600 Brooks Road / PO Box 1
Thorndike, ME 04986-0001 USA

(207) 568-3717

US & Canada:
1 800 929-9108
www.centerpointlargeprint.com